A DUSK OF IDOLS:
Not only are the gods cruel, but they can make you like it.

THE HUMAN OPERATORS:
The great ships possess unlimited cruising range—and unbounded ferocity.

WARM:
It's just a simple guessing game: to be? or not to be?

KLYSTERMAN'S SILENT VIOLIN:
Powerful weapons are a fine thing—but you wouldn't want your lover to marry one.

THE NEW REALITY:
It's amazing how much destruction you can wreak with a few simple tools—if you put your mind to it.

These and six other tales of the highest quality—the most amazing conviction!

ALPHA 8

ALPHA
8

EDITED BY

ROBERT SILVERBERG

A BERKLEY MEDALLION BOOK
published by
BERKLEY PUBLISHING CORPORATION

Scott Meredith Literary Agency, Inc.
845 Third Avenue
New York, N.Y. 10017

SBN 425-03561-1

*BERKLEY MEDALLION BOOKS are published by
Berkley Publishing Corporation
200 Madison Avenue
New York, N.Y. 10016*

BERKLEY MEDALLION BOOK ® TM 757,375

Printed in the United States of America

Berkley Medallion Edition, NOVEMBER, 1977

ACKNOWLEDGMENTS

"A Dusk of Idols," by James Blish. Copyright © 1961 by Ziff-Davis Publishing Co., Inc. Reprinted by permission of the author's agents, Robert P. Mills, Ltd.

"The Human Operators," by Harlan Ellison and A.E. Van Vogt. Copyright © 1970 by Harlan Ellison and A.E. Van Vogt. Reprinted by permission of the authors.

"Think Only This of Me," by Michael Kurland. Copyright © 1973 by UPD Publishing Corporation. Reprinted by permission of the author.

"The Short Ones," by Raymond E. Banks. Copyright © 1955 by Fantasy House, Inc. Reprinted by permission of the author and his agents, Scott Meredith Literary Agency, Inc.

"Warm," by Robert Sheckley. Copyright 1953 by Robert Sheckley. Reprinted by permission of The Sterling Lord Agency, Inc.

"When the Change-Winds Blow," by Fritz Leiber. Copyright © 1964 by Mercury Press, Inc. Reprinted by permission of the author and his agents, Robert P. Mills, Ltd.

"One Face," by Larry Niven. Copyright © 1965 by Galaxy Publishing Corporation. Reprinted by permission of the author and his agents, Robert P. Mills, Ltd.

"The Man Who Lost the Sea," by Theodore Sturgeon. Copyright © 1959 by Mercury Press, Inc. Reprinted by permission of the author.

"The Happiest Creature," by Jack Williamson. Copyright 1953 by Ballantine Books. Reprinted by permission of the author and his agents, Scott Meredith Literary Agency, Inc.

"Klysterman's Silent Violin," by Michael Rogers. Copyright © 1972 by Michael Rogers. Reprinted by permission of Harold Matson Co., Inc.

"The New Reality," by Charles L. Harness. Copyright 1950 by Standard Magazines, Inc. Reprinted by permission of the author and his agents, Scott Meredith Literary Agency, Inc.

CONTENTS

INTRODUCTION

In the first volume of *Alpha*, published in 1970, I set forth the policy that has guided this series throughout. The books, I said, "will center on no particular theme except that of literary quality. . . . I propose to cull the files of the science fiction magazines for stories that an educated and sophisticated reader will find stimulating. Some of the stories will be fifteen or twenty years old and richly in need of restoration to print. Others will be quite recent: the literary level of the science fiction short story has undergone an extraordinary transformation in the past few years, a fact that demands recognition here."

And so it has been: a mix of the recent and the not so recent, with a gradually emerging emphasis on rediscovery. Of the fourteen stories in *Alpha One*, five were less than five years old, and only one had first been published more than fourteen years previously. By *Alpha Seven*, though, seven out of ten stories were more than fifteen years old, five of those seven were well over twenty years old, and only three stories in the book were at all recent. In this current volume, there are three stories of the 1970s, three of the 1960s, five of the 1950s.

There are several reasons for this increasing concentration on the science fiction of the earlier years. It was never my intention to make *Alpha* an antiquarian collection, and I don't believe that that is what it has become. But there seems relatively little need to produce one more showcase of recent science fiction. Already we have three or four best-of-the-year anthologies, plus the annual Nebula Awards volume, and, with all those nets waving in the stream, little if anything of significance is apt to slip through. Meanwhile the magnificent stories of the great science-fiction renaissance of the early 1950s remain hidden in crumbling magazines and in pioneering anthologies that themselves have become rarities today. *Alpha* will never altogether ignore the work of current writers, but I think future volumes will devote more and more space to the best science fiction of that period—stories which were ahead of their epoch when they were new, which display a freshness and vigor that make them almost indistinguishable from the best of today's s-f, and which set the standard by which the modern writers have guided their careers.

—Robert Silverberg

ALPHA 8

A DUSK OF IDOLS

James Blish

The title of this dark voyage through mythic realms pays homage to Nietzsche; in the manner of its telling it owes much to Conrad. A fitting pair of totems for James Blish, that somber and playful man, whose cool keen mind was so European in texture, a fascinating mix of Teutonic precision and Slavonic passion. Like several of Blish's best stories—''Common Time'' was another—''A Dusk of Idols'' came into being through that curious and now nearly extinct practice by which an artist delivered a cover painting and an author was commissioned to write a story embodying the illustrated scene. It was a peculiar way to go about the creative process, born out of the odd pressures of pulp-magazine publishing; but somehow it inspired Blish to unusual heights. As herewith.

I can tell you now what happened to Naysmith. He hit Chandala.

Quite by coincidence—he was on his way home at the time—but it caught him. It was in all respects a most peculiar accident. The chances were against it, including that I should have heard anything about it.

Almost everyone in Arm II knows that Chandala is, pre-eminently among civilized planets, a world in mortal agony—and a world about which, essentially, nothing can be done. Naysmith didn't know it. He had had no experi-

1

ence of Arm II and was returning along it from his first
contact with the Heart stars when his ship (and mine)
touched Chandala briefly. He was on his way back to
Earth (which technically is an Arm II planet, but so far out
in the hinterlands that no Earthman ever thinks of it as
such) when this happened, and since it happened during
ship's night, he would never have known the difference if
it hadn't been for an attack of simple indigestion which
awakened him—and me.

It's very hard to explain the loss of so eminent a surgeon
as Naysmith without maligning his character, but as his
only confidant, more or less, I don't seem to have much of
a choice. The fact is that he should have been the last
person in the Galaxy to care about Chandala's agony. He
had used his gifts to become exclusively a rich man's
surgeon; as far as I know, he had never done any time in a
clinic after his residency days. He had gone to the Heart
stars only to sterilize, for a very large fortune in fees, the
sibling of the Bbiben of Bbenaf—for the fees, and for the
additional fortune the honor would bring him later. Bbenaf
law requires that the operation be performed by an off-
worlder, but Naysmith was the first Earthman to be invited
to do it.

But if during the trip there or back some fellow passenger had come down with a simple appendicitis, Naysmith wouldn't have touched him. He would have said,
with remote impartiality, that that was the job of the ship's
surgeon (me). If for some reason I had been too late to
help, Naysmith still would not have lifted a finger.

There are not supposed to be any doctors like that, but
there are. Nobody should assume that I think they are in
the majority—they are in fact very rare—but I see no point
in pretending that they don't exist. They do; and the
eminent Naysmith was one of them. He was in fact almost
the Platonic ideal of such a doctor. And you do not have to
be in the Heart stars to begin to think of the Hippocratic
Oath as being quaint, ancient, and remote. You can become isolated from it just as easily on Earth, by the

interposition of unclimbable mountains of money, if you share Naysmith's temperament.

His temperament, to put it very simply, was that of a pathologically depressed man carrying a terrible load of anxiety. In him, it showed up by making him a hypochondriac, and I don't think he would ever have gone into medicine at all had it not been for an urgent concern about his own health which set in while he was still in college. I had known him slightly then, and was repelled by him. He was always thinking about his own innards. Nothing pleased him, nothing took him out of himself, he had no eye for any of the elegance and the beauty of the universe outside his own skin. Though he was as brilliant a man as I ever knew, he was a bore, the kind of bore who replies to "How are you?" by telling you how he is, in clinical detail. He was forever certain that his liver or his stomach or some other major organ had just quit on him and was going to have to be removed—probably too suddenly for help to be summoned in time.

It seems inarguable to me, though I am not a psychologist, that he took up medicine primarily in the hope (unrecognized in his own mind) of being able to assess his own troubles better, and treat them himself when he couldn't get another doctor to take them as seriously as he did. Of course this did not work. It is an old proverb in medicine that the man who treats himself has a fool for a physician, which is only a crude way of saying that the doctor-patient relationship absolutely requires that there be two people involved. A man can no more be his own doctor than he can be his own wife, no matter how much he knows about marriage or medicine.

The result was that even after becoming the kind of surgeon who gets called across 50,000 light-years to operate on the sibling of the Bbiben of Bbenaf, he was still a hypochondriac. In fact, he was worse off than ever, because he now had the most elaborate and sophisticated knowledge of all the obscure things that might be wrong with him. He had a lifelong case of interne's syndrome, the cast of mind which makes beginners in medicine sure that they are suffering from everything they have just read about in the textbook. He knew this; he was, as I have said, a brilliant man; though he had reached his ostensible goal, he was now in a position where he did not *dare* to treat himself, even for the hiccups.

And this was why he called me at midnight, ship's time, to look him over. There was nothing curable the matter with him. He had eaten something on Bbenaf—though he was a big, burly, bearded man, immoderate eating had made him unpleasantly soft—that was having trouble accommodating itself to his Terrestrial protein complement. I judged that tomorrow he would have a slight rash, and thereafter the episode would be over. I told him so.

"Um. Yes. Daresay you're right. Still rather a shock though, to be brought bolt upright like that in the middle of the night."

"Of course. However I'm sure it's nothing more than a slight food allergy—the commonest of all tourist complaints," I added, a little maliciously. "The tablets are antihistaminic, of course. They ought to head off any serious sequelae, and make you a little sleepy to boot. You could use the relaxation, I think."

He nodded absently, without taking any apparent notice of my mean little dig. He did not recognize me, I was quite sure. It had been a long time since college.

"Where are we?" he said. He was wide awake, though his alarm reaction seemed to be wearing off, and he didn't seem to want to take my hint that he use the pills as sleepy drugs; he wanted company, at least for a little while. Well, I was curious, too. He was an eminent man in my own profession, and I had an advantage over him: I knew more about him than he thought I did. If he wanted to talk, I was delighted to let him.

"Chandala, I believe. A real running sore of a planet, but we won't be here long; it's just a message stop."

"Oh? What's the matter with the place? Barbaric?"

"No, not in the usual sense. It's classified as a civilized planet. It's just sick, that's all. Most of the population is being killed off."

"A pandemic?" Naysmith said slowly. "That doesn't sound like a civilized planet."

"It's hard to explain," I said. "It's not just one plague. There are scores of them going. I suppose the simple way to put it is to say that the culture of Chandala doesn't believe in sanitation—but that's not really true either. They believe in it, thoroughly, but they don't practice it very much. In fact a large part of the time they practice it in reverse."

"In reverse? That doesn't make any sense."

"I warned you it was hard to explain. I mean that public health there is a privilege. The ruling classes make it unavailable to the people they govern, as a means of keeping them in line."

"But that's insane!" Naysmith exclaimed.

"I suppose it is, by our ideas. It's obviously very hard to keep under control, anyhow; the rulers often suffer as much as the ruled. But all governments are based on the monopoly of the right to use violence—only the weapons vary from planet to planet. This one is Chandala's. And the Heart stars have decided not to interfere."

He fell silent. I probably had not needed to remind him that what the federation we call the Heart stars decided to do, or not to do, was often very difficult to riddle. Its records reach back about a million years, which however cover only its period of stability. Probably it is as much as twice that old. No Arm II planet belonged to the group yet. Earth could be expected to be allowed to join in about forty-five thousand years—and that was what remained of half our originally allotted trial period; the cut was awarded us after our treaty with the star-dwelling race of Angels. In the meantime, we could expect no help . . . nor could Chandala. Earth was fortunate to be allowed any intercourse whatsoever with the Heart stars; there again, we could thank the Angels—who live forever —for vouching for us.

"Dr. Rosenbaum," Naysmith said slowly, "do you think that's right and proper?"

So he had recognized me after all. He would never have bothered to look up my name on the roster.

"Well, no, I suppose not. But the rule is that every planet is to be allowed to go to hell in its own handbasket. It isn't my rule, or the Earth's rule; but there it is. The Heart stars just won't be bothered with any world that can't achieve stability by itself. They have seen too many of them come and go."

"I think there's more to it than that. Some of the planets that failed to get into the federation failed because they got into planetwide wars—or into wars with each other."

"Sure," I said, puzzled. "That's just the kind of thing the Heart stars have no use for."

"So they didn't interfere to stop the wars."

"No." Now I was beginning to see what he was driving at, but he bore down on me relentlessly all the same.

"So there is in fact no Heart-star rule that we can't help Chandala if we want to. In fact, doing so may not even prejudice our case with the federation. We just don't know."

"I suppose that's true, but—"

"And, in fact, it might help us? We don't know that either?"

"No, we don't," I admitted, but my patience was beginning to run out. It had been a long night. "All we do know is that the Heart stars follow certain rules of their own. Common sense suggests that our chances would be best if we followed them, too."

"Common sense for our remotely imaginable great-great-greatest of grandchildren, maybe. But by then conditions will have changed beyond our remotest imaginings. Half a millennium!"

"They don't change in the Heart stars. That's the whole point—stability. And above all, I'd avoid picking up a stick of TDX like Chandala. It's obviously just the kind of nonsurvival planet the Heart stars *mean* to exclude by their rules. There'd be nothing you could do with it but blow yourself up. And there's obviously nothing we could do *for* it, anyhow!"

"Gently now, Doctor. Are you sure of that? Sanitation isn't the only public-health technique there is."

"I don't follow you," I said. The fact is that by now I wasn't trying very hard.

"Well," Naysmith said, "consider that there was once a thing called the Roman Empire. It owned all the known world and lasted many centuries. But fifty men with modern weapons could have conquered it, even when it was at its most powerful."

"But the Heart stars—"

"I am not talking about the Heart stars. I'm talking about Chandala. Two physicians with modern field kits could have wiped out almost all the diseases that riddled the Roman Empire. For instance, you and I."

I swallowed and looked at my watch. We were still a good two hours away from takeoff time.

"No, Doctor, you'll have to answer me. Shall we try it?"

I could still stall, though I was not hopeful that it would help me much. "I don't understand your motives, Dr. Naysmith. What do you want to try it *for?* The Chandalese are satisfied with their system. They won't thank you for trying to upset it. And where's the profit? I can't see any."

"What kind of profit are you talking about?" Naysmith said, almost abstractedly.

"Well . . . I don't know; that's what I'm asking you. It seems to me you shouldn't lack for money by now. And as for honor, you're up to your eyebrows in that already, and after Bbenaf you'll have much more. And yet you seem to be proposing to throw all that away for a moribund world you never heard of until tonight. And your life, too. They would kill you instantly down there if they knew what you had in mind."

"I don't plan to tell the ruling class, whatever that is, what I have in mind," Naysmith said. "I have that much sense. As for my motives . . . they're properly my own. But I can satisfy your curiosity a little. I know what you see when you look at me: a society doctor. It's not an unusual opinion. My record supports it. Isn't that true?"

I didn't nod, but my silence must have given my assent.

"Yes, it's true, of course. And if I had excuses, I wouldn't give a damn for your opinion—or for Chandala. But you see, I don't. I not only know what the opinion of me is, but *I share it myself*. Now I see a chance to change that opinion of me; not yours, but mine. Does that help you any?"

It did. Every man has his own Holy Grail. Naysmith had just identified his.

"I wish you luck."

"But you won't go along?"

"No," I said, miserable, yet defiantly sure that there were *no* good reasons why I should join Naysmith's quest —not even the reason that it could not succeed without me and my field kit. It could not succeed *with* me, either; and my duty lay with the ship, until the day when I might sight my own Grail, whatever that might be. All the same, that one word made me feel like an assassin.

But it did not surprise Naysmith. He had had the good sense to expect nothing else. Whatever the practical notions that had sprung into his head in the last hour or so, and I suppose they were many, he must have known all his life—as we all do—that Grail-hunting is essentially the loneliest of hobbies.

He made himself wholly unpopular on the bridge, which up to now had barely known he was aboard, wangling a ship's gig and a twenty-four-hour delay during which he could be force-fed the language of the nearest city-state by a heuristics expert, and then disembarked. The arrangement was that we were to pick him up on our next cruise, a year from now.

If he had to get off the planet before then, he could go into orbit and wait; he had supplies enough. He also had his full field medical kit, including a space suit. Since it is of the nature of Chandalese political geography to shift without notice, he agreed to base himself on the edge of a volcanic region which we could easily identify from space, yet small enough so that we wouldn't have to map it to find the gig.

Then he left. Everything went without incident (he told me later) until he entered the city-state of Gandu, whose language he had and where our embassy was. He had of course been told that the Chandalese, though humanoid, are three times as tall as Earthmen, but it was a little unnerving all the same to walk among them. Their size suited their world, which was a good twelve thousand miles in diameter. Surprisingly, it was not very dense, a fact nobody had been able to explain, since it was obviously an Earthlike planet; hence there was no gravitational impediment to growing its natives very large, and grow large they did. He would have to do much of his doctoring here on a stepladder, apparently.

The chargé d'affaires at the embassy, like those of us on ship, did his best to dissuade Naysmith.

"I don't say that you can't do something about the situation here," he said. "Very likely you can. But you'll be meddling with their social structure. Public health here is politics, and vice versa. The Heart stars—"

"Bother the Heart stars," Naysmith said, thereby giving the chargé d'affaires the worst fright he had had in years. "If it can be done, it ought to be done. And the best way to do it is to go right to the worst trouble spot."

"That would be Iridu, down the river some fifteen miles," the chargé d'affaires said. "Dying out very rapidly. But it's proscribed, as all those places are."

"Criminal. What about language?"

"Oh, same as here. It's one of three cities that spoke the same tongue. The third one is dead."

"Where do I go to see the head man?"

"To the sewer. He'll be there."

Naysmith stared.

"Well, I'm sorry, but that's the way things are. When you came through the main plaza here, did you see two tall totem poles?"

"Yes."

"The city totems always mark the local entrance to the Grand Sewer of Chandala, and the big stone building behind them is always where the priest-chief lives. And I'm warning you, Dr. Naysmith, he won't give you the time of day."

Naysmith did not bother to argue any more. It seemed to him that no matter how thoroughly a chieftain may subscribe to a political system, he becomes a rebel when it is turned against him—especially if as a consequence he sees his people dying all around him. He left, and went downriver, on a vessel rather like a felucca.

He had enough acumen to realize very early that he was being trailed. One of the two Chandalese following him looked very like a man who had been on duty at the embassy. He did not let it bother him, and in any event, they did not seem to follow him past the gates of Iridu.

He found the central plaza easily enough—that is to say, he was never lost; the physical act of getting through the streets was anything but easy, though he was towing his gear on an antigrav unit. They were heaped with refuse and bodies. Those who still lived made no attempt to clear away the dead or help the dying, but simply sat in the doorways and moaned. The composite sound thrummed through the whole city. Now and then he saw small groups scavenging for food amid all the garbage; and quite frequently he saw individuals drinking from puddles. This last fact perplexed him particularly, for the chargé d'affaires had told him plainly that Chandala boasted excellent water-supply systems.

The reception of the chief-priest was hostile enough, more so than Naysmith had hoped, yet less than the chargé d'affaires had predicted—at least at first. He was obviously sick himself, and seemingly had not bathed in a long time, nor had any of his attendants; but as long as all Naysmith wanted was information, he was grudgingly willing to give it.

"What you observe are the Articles of the Law and their consequences," he said. "Because of high failures before the gods, Iridu and all its people have been abased to the lowest caste; and since it is not meet that people of this caste speak the same tongue as the Exalted, the city is proscribed.''

"I can understand that," Naysmith said, guardedly. "But why should that prevent you from taking any care of yourselves? Drinking from puddles—"

"These are the rules for our caste," the priest-chief said. "Not to wash; not to eat aught less than three days old; not to aid the sick or bury the dead. Drinking from puddles is graciously allowed us."

There was no apparent ironic intention in the last sentence. Naysmith said, "Graciously?"

"The water in the city's plumbing now comes directly from the Grand Sewer. The only other alternative is the urine of the anah, but that is for holy men doing penance for the people."

This was a setback. Without decent water he would be sadly handicapped, and obviously what came out of the faucets was not under the control of the doomed city.

"Well, we'll manage somehow. Rain barrels should serve for the time being; I can chlorinate them for you. But it's urgent to start cleaning things up; otherwise, I'll never be able to keep up with all the new cases. Will you help me?"

The priest-chief looked blank. "We can help no one any more, little one."

"You could be a big help. I can probably stop this plague for you, with a few willing hands."

The priest-chief stood up, shakily, but part of his shakiness was black rage. "To break the rules of caste is the highest of failures before the gods," he said. "We are damned to listen to such counsels! Kill him!"

Naysmith was fool enough to pause to protest. Only the fact that most of the gigantic soldiers in the chamber were clumsy with disease, and unused to dealing with so small an object as he, got him out of the building alive. He was pursued to the farther gate of Iridu by a shambling and

horrible mob, all the more frightening because there was
hardly a healthy creature in its rank.

Outside, he was confronted by a seemingly trackless
jungle. He plunged in at hazard, and kept going blindly
until he could no longer hear the noise of the pack; evidently they had stopped at the gate. He could thank the
proscription of the city-nation for that.

On the other hand, he was lost.

Of course, he had his compass, which might help a
little. He did not want to go westward, which would take
him back to the river, but also into the vicinity of Iridu
again. Besides, his two trackers from Gandu might still be
lurking at the west gate, and this time their hostility might
be a good deal more active. Striking north-northwest toward Gandu itself was open to the same objection. There
seemed to be nothing for it but to go north-northeast, in the
hope of arriving at the field of fumaroles and hot springs
where his ship was, there to take thought.

He was still utterly determined to try again; shaken
though he was, he was convinced that this first failure was
only a matter of tactics. But he did have to get back to the
ship.

He pushed forward through the wiry tangle. It made it
impossible for him to follow a straight compass course; he
lost hours climbing and skirting and hacking, and began to
worry about the possibility of spending the night in this
wilderness. With the thought, there was a sodden thump
behind him, and he was stopped as though he had run into
a wall. Then there was a diminishing crackle and bumping
over his head.

What was holding him back, he realized after a moment, was the tow to his gear. He backtracked. The gear
was lying on the moist ground. Some incredibly tough
vine had cut the antigrav unit free of it; the other sound he
heard had been the unit fighting its way skyward.

Now what? He could not possibly drag all this weight. It
occurred to him that he might put on the space suit; that
would slow him a good deal, but it would also protect him
from the underbrush, which had already slashed him pret-

ty painfully. The rest of the load—a pack and two oxygen bottles—would still be heavy, but maybe not impossibly so.

He got the suit on, though it was difficult without help, and lumbered forward again. It was exhausting, even with the suit's air conditioning to help, but there was nothing he could do about that. At least, if he had to sleep in the jungle, the suit might also keep out vermin, and some larger entities . . .

For some reason, however, the Chandalese forest seemed peculiarly free of large animals. Occasional scamperings and brief glimpses told of creatures which might have been a little like antelope, or like rabbits, but even these were scarce; and there were no cries of predators. This might have been because Chandalese predators were voiceless, but Naysmith doubted this on grounds of simple biology; it seemed more likely that most of the more highly organized wildlife of Chandala had long since been decimated by the plagues the owners of the planet cultivated as though they were ornamental gardens.

Late in the afternoon, the fates awarded him two lucky breaks. The first of these was a carcass, or rather, a shell. It was the greenish-brown carapace of some creature which, from its size, he first took to be the Chandalese equivalent of a huge land turtle, but on closer examination seemed actually to have been a good deal more like a tick. Well, if any planet had ticks as big as rowboats, it would be Chandala, that much was already plain even to Naysmith. In any event, the shell made an excellent skid for his gear, riding on its back through the undergrowth almost as though it had been designed for the task.

The second boon was the road. He did not recognize it as such at first, for it was much broken and overgrown, but on reflection he decided that this was all to the good; a road that had not been in use for a long time would be a road on which he would be unlikely to meet anybody. It would also not be likely to take him to any populated place, but it seemed to be headed more or less in the direction he wanted to go; and if it meandered a little, it could hardly impose upon him more detours than the jungle did.

He took off the space suit and loaded it into the skid, feeling almost cheerful.

It was dusk when he rounded the bend and saw the dead city. In the gathering gloom, it looked to be almost twice the size of Gandu, despite the fact that much of it had crumbled and fallen.

At its open gates stood the two Chandalese who had followed him downriver, leaning on broad-bladed spears as tall as they were.

Naysmith had a gun, and he did not hesitate.

Had he not recognized the face of the Chandalese from the chargé d'affaires' office, he might have assumed that the two guards were members of some savage tribe. Again, it seemed to him, he had been lucky.

It might be the last such stroke of luck. The presence of the guards testified, almost in letters of fire, that the Chandalese could predict his route with good accuracy—and the spears testified that they did not mean to let him complete it.

Again, it seemed to him that his best chance led through the dead city, protected while he was there by its proscription. He could only hope that the firelands lay within some reachable distance of the city's other side.

The ancient gate towered over him like the Lion Gate of Mycenae as remembered from some nightmare—fully as frowning as that narrow, heavy, tragedy-ridden breach, but more than five times as high. He studied it with sober respect, and perhaps even a little dread, before he could bring himself to step over the bodies of the guards and pass through it. When he did, he was carrying with him one of the broad-bladed fifteen-foot spears, because, he told himself, you never could tell when such a lever might come in handy . . . and because, instinctively, he believed (though he later denied it) that no stranger could pass under that ancient arch without one.

The Atridae, it is very clear, still mutter in their sleep not far below the surface of our waking minds, for all that we no longer allow old Freud to cram our lives back into the straitjackets of those old religious plays. Perhaps one of the changes in us that the Heart stars await is the extirpation of these last shadows of Oedipus, Elektra, Agamemnon, and all those other dark and bloody figures, from the way we think.

Or maybe not. There are still some forty thousand years to go. If after that they tell us that that was one of the things they were waiting for, we probably won't understand what they're talking about.

Carrying the spear awkwardly and towing his belongings behind him in the tick shell, Naysmith plodded toward the center of the dead city. There was nothing left in the streets but an occasional large bone; one that he stumbled over fell promptly to shivers and dust. The scraping noise of his awkward sledge echoed off the fronts of the leaning buildings; otherwise, there was no sound but the end-stopped thuds of his footfalls, and an occasional bluster of evening wind around the tottering, flaking cornices far above his bent head.

In this wise he came draggingly at last into the central plaza, and sat down on a drum of a fallen stone pillar to catch his breath. It was now almost full dark, so dark that nothing cast a shadow any more; instead, the night seemed to be soaking into the ground all around him. There would be, he knew already, no stars; the atmosphere of Chandala was too misty for that. He had perhaps fifteen minutes more to decide what he was going to do.

As he mopped his brow and tried to think, something rustled behind him. Freezing, he looked carefully over his shoulder, back toward the way he had come. Of course he saw nothing; but in this dead silence a sound like that was easy to interpret.

They were still following him. For him, this dead city was not a proscripted sanctuary. Or if it ever had been, it was no longer, since he had killed the two guards.

He stood up, as soundlessly as he could. All his muscles were aching; he felt as soft and helpless as an overripe melon. The shuffling noise stopped at once.

They were already close enough to see him!

He knew that he could vanish quickly enough into any of the tomblike buildings around him, and evade them for a while as deftly as any rat. They probably knew this labyrinth little better than he did, and the sound of their shuffling did not suggest that there were many of them— surely not a large enough force to search a whole city for a man only a third as big as a Chandalese. And they would have to respect taboos that he could scamper past out of simple ignorance.

But if he took that way, he would have to abandon his gear. He could carry his medical kit easily enough, but that was less important to him now than the space suit and its ancillary oxygen bottles—both heavy and clumsy, and both, furthermore, painted white. As long as he could drag them with him in the tick shell, their whiteness would be masked to some extent; but if he had to run with them, he would surely be brought down.

In the last remains of the evening, he stood cautiously forward and inched the sledge toward the center of the plaza, clenching the spear precariously against his side under one armpit, his gun in his other hand. Behind him, something went, *scuffle . . . rustle . . .*

As he had seen on arrival, the broad-mouthed well in the center of the plaza, before the house of the dead and damned priest-chief, was not flanked by the totems he had been taught to expect. Where they should be jutted only two grey and splintered stumps, as though the poles had been pushed over by brute force and toppled into the abyss. On the other side of the well, a stone beast—an anah?—stared forever downward with blind eyes, ready to rend any soul who might try to clamber up again from Hell.

As it might try to do; for a narrow, rail-less stone stairway, slimy and worn, spiralled around the well into the depths.

Around the mouth of the well, almost impossible to see, let alone interpret, in the last glimmers, was a series of bas-reliefs, crudely and hastily cut; he could detect the rawness of the sculpturing even under the weathering of the stone and the moss.

He went cautiously down the steps a little way to look at them. With no experience whatsoever of Chandalese graphic conventions, he knew that he had little chance of understanding them even had he seen them in full daylight. Nevertheless, it was clear that they told a history . . . and, it seemed to him, a judgment. This city had been condemned, and its totems toppled, because it had been carrying on some kind of congress with the Abyss.

He climbed back to the surface of the plaza, pulling his nose thoughtfully. They were still following him, that was sure. But would they follow him down there? It might be a way to get to the other side of the dead city which would promise him immunity—or at least, a temporary sanctuary of an inverted kind.

He did not delude himself that he could live down there for long. He would have to wear the space suit again, and breathe nothing but the oxygen in the white bottles. He could still keep by him the field medical kit with which he had been planning to re-enrich his opinion of himself, and save a planet; but even with this protection he could not for long breathe the air and drink the water of the pit. As for food, that hardly mattered, because his air and water would run out much sooner.

Let it be said that Naysmith was courageous. He donned the space suit again, and began the descent, lowering his tick-shell coracle before him on a short, taut tether. Bump, bump, bump went the shell down the steps ahead of him, teetering on its back ridge, threatening to slip sidewise and fall into the well at every irregularity in the slimy old platforms. Then he would stop in the blackness and wait until he could no longer hear it rocking. Then down again: bump, bump, bump; step, step, step. Behind him, the butt of the spear scraped against the wall; and once the point lodged abruptly in some chink and nearly threw him.

He had his chest torch going, but it was not much help; the slimy walls of the well seemed to soak up the light, except for an occasional delusive reflection where a rill of seepage oozed down amid the nitre. Down, down, down.

After some centuries, he no longer expected to reach the bottom. There was nothing left in his future but this painful descent. He was still not frightened; only numb, exhausted, beyond caring about himself, beyond believing in the rest of the universe.

Then the steps stopped, sending him staggering in the suit. He touched the wall with a glove—he imagined that he could feel its coldness, though of course he could not—and stood still. His belt radios brought him in nothing but a sort of generalized echo, like running water.

Of course. He flashed the chest light around, and saw the Grand Sewer of Chandala.

He was standing on what appeared to be a wharf made of black basalt, over the edge of which rushed the black waters of an oily river, topped with spinning masses of soapy froth. He could not see the other side, nor the roof of the tunnel it ran in—only the sullen and ceaseless flood, like a cataract of ink. The wharf itself had evidently been awash not long since, for there were still pools standing sullenly wherever the black rock had been worn down; but now the surface of the river was perhaps a foot below the level of the dock.

He looked up. Far aloft, he saw a spot of blue-black sky about the size of a pea, and gleaming in it, one reddish star. Though he was no better judge of distance than any other surgeon or any other man who spends his life doing close work, he thought he was at least a mile beneath the surface. To clamber back up there would be utterly beyond him.

But why a wharf? Who would be embarking on this sunless river, and why? It suggested that the river might go toward some other inhabited place . . . or some place that had once been inhabited. Maybe the Chandalese had been right in condemning the city to death for congress with the pit—and if that Other Place were inhabited even now, it was probably itself underground, and populated by whatever kind of thing might enjoy and prosper by living in total darkness by the side of a sewer—

There was an ear-splitting explosion to Naysmith's right, and something struck his suit just under his armpit. He jerked his light toward the sound, just in time to see fragments of rock scampering away across the wet wharf, skidding and splashing. A heavier piece rolled eccentrically to the edge of the dock and dropped off into the river. Then everything was motionless again.

He bent and picked up the nearest piece. It was part of one of the stones of the staircase.

There was no sanctuary, even here; they were following him down. In a few moments it might occur to them to stone him on purpose; the suit could stand that, but the helmet could not. And above all, he had to keep his air pure.

He had to go on. But there was no longer any walkway; only the wharf and the sewer. Well, then, that way. Grimly he unloaded the tick shell and lowered it into the black water, hitching its tether to a basalt post. Then, carefully, he ballasted it with the pack and the oxygen bottles. It rocked gently in the current, but the ridge along its back served as a rudimentary keel; it would be stable, more or less.

He sat down on the edge of the wharf and dangled his feet into his boat while he probed for the bottom of the river with the point of the spear. The point caught on something after he had thrust nearly twelve feet of the shaft beneath the surface; and steadying himself with this, he transferred his weight into the coracle and sat down.

Smash! Another paving stone broke on the dock. A splinter, evidently a large one, went whooshing past his helmet and dropped into the sewer. Hastily, he jerked the loop of the tether off the basalt post, and poled himself hard out into the middle of the torrent.

The wharf vanished. The shell began to turn round and round. After several minutes, during which he became deathly seasick, Naysmith managed to work out how to use the blade of the spear as a kind of steering oar; if he held it hard against one side of the shell at the back, and shifted the shaft with the vagaries of the current, he could at least keep his frail machine pointed forward.

There was no particular point in steering it any better than that, since he did not know where he was going.

The chest light showed him nothing except an occasional glimpse of a swiftly passing tunnel wall, and after a while he shut it off to conserve power, trusting his sense of balance to keep his shell headed forward and in the middle of the current. Then he struck some obstacle which almost upset him; and though he fought himself back into balance again, the shell seemed sluggish afterwards. He put on the light and discovered that he had shipped so much of the slimy water that the shell was riding only a few inches above the roiling river.

He ripped the flap of his pack open and found a cup to bail with. Thereafter, he kept the light on.

After a while, the noise of the water took on a sort of hissing edge. He hardly noticed it at first; but soon it became sharp, like the squeak of a wet finger on the edge of a glass, and then took on deeper tones until it made the waters boil like the noise of a steam whistle. Turning the belt radio down did him very little good; it dropped the volume of the sound, but not its penetrating quality.

Then the coracle went skidding around a long bend and light burst over him.

He was hurtling past a city, fronted by black basalt docks like the one he had just quitted, but four or five times more extensive. Beyond these were ruins, as far as he could see, tumbled and razed, stark in the unwavering flare of five tall, smokeless plumes of gas flames which towered amid the tumbled stones. It was these five fountains of blue-white fire, as tall as sequoias, which poured out the vast organ-diapason of noise he had heard in the tunnel.

They were probably natural, though he had never seen anything like them before. The ruins, much more obviously, were not; and for them there was no explanation. Broken and aged though they were, the great carved stones still preserved the shapes of geometrical solids which could not possibly have been reassembled into any building Naysmith could imagine, though as a master surgeon he had traded all his life on structural visualization. The size of the pieces did not bother him, for he had come to terms with the fact that the Chandalese were three times as tall as men, but their shapes were as irrational as the solid geometry of a dream.

And the crazy way in which the city had been dumped over, as though something vast and stupid had sat down in the middle of it and lashed a long heavy tail, did not suggest that its destroyers had been Chandalese either.

Then it was gone. He clung to his oar, keeping the coracle pointed forward. He did not relish the thought of going on to a possible meeting with the creatures who had razed that city; but obviously there had been no hope for him in its ruins. It dwindled and dimmed, and then he went wobbling around a bend and even its glow vanished from the sides of the tunnel

As he turned that corner, something behind him shrieked, cutting through the general roar of noise like a god in torture. He shrank down into the bottom of the boat, almost losing his hold on the spear. The awful yell must have gone on for two or three minutes, utterly overpowering every echo. Then, gradually, it began to die, at first into a sort of hopeless howl, then into a series of raw, hoarse wails, and at last into a choked mixture of weeping and giggling . . . oh! oooh! . . . whee! . . . oh, oh, oh . . . whee! . . . which made Naysmith's every hair stand on end. It was, obviously, only one of the high-pressure gas jets fluting over a rock lip.

Obviously.

After that he was glad to be back in the darkness, however little it promised. The boat bobbed and slithered in the midst of the flood. On turns it was washed against the walls and Naysmith poled it back into the center of the current as best he could with his break-bone spear, which kept knocking him about the helmet and ribs every time he tried to use it for anything but steering. Some of those collisions were inexplicably soft; he did not try to see why, because he was saving the chest light for bailing, and in any event he was swept by them too fast to look back.

Just under him gurgled the Grand Sewer of Chandala, a torrent of filth and pestilence. He floated down it inside his suit, Naysmith, master surgeon, a bubble of precarious life in a universe of corruption, skimming the entropy gradient clinging to the edges of a tick's carapace . . . and clinging to incorruption to the last.

Again, after a while, he saw light ahead, sullenly red at first, but becoming more and more orange as the boat swept on. For the first time he saw the limits of the tunnel, outlined ahead of him in the form of a broad arch. Could he possibly be approaching the surface? It did not seem possible; it was night up there—and besides, Chandalese daylight was nothing like this.

Then the tunnel mouth was behind him, and he was coasting on an enormous infernal sea.

The light was now a brilliant tangerine color, but he could not see where it came from; billowing clouds of mist rising from the surface of the sewage limited visibility to perhaps fifty feet. The current from the river was quickly dissipated, and the coracle began to drift sidewise; probing with the spear without much hope, he was surprised to touch bottom, and began to pole himself forward with the aid of his compass—though he had almost forgotten why it was that he had wanted to go in that direction.

The bottom was mucky, as was, of course, to be expected; pulling the spear out of it was tiring work. Far overhead in the mists, he twice heard an odd fluttering sound, rather like that of a tightly wound rubber band suddenly released, and once a measured flapping which seemed to pass quite low over his head; he saw nothing, however.

After half an hour he stopped poling to give himself five minutes' rest. Again he began to drift sidewise. Insofar as he could tell, the whole of this infernal deep seemed to be eddying in a slow circle.

Then a tall, slender shadow loomed ahead of him. He

drove the spear into the bottom and anchored himself, watching intently, but the shadow remained fixed. Finally he pushed the shell cautiously toward it.

It was a totem pole, obviously very old; almost all its paint was gone, and the exposed wood was grey. There were others ahead; within a few moments he was in what was almost a forest of them, their many mute faces grinning and grimacing at him or staring hopelessly off into the mists. Some of them were canted alarmingly and seemed to be on the verge of falling into the ordure, but even with these he found it hard to set aside the impression that they were watching him.

There was, he realized slowly, a reason for this absurd, frightening feeling. The totems testified to something more than the deaths of uncountable thousands of Chandalese. They were witness also to the fact that this gulf was known and visited, at least by the priest-chief caste; obviously the driving of the poles in this abyss was the final ritual act of condemnation of a city-state. He was not safe from pursuit yet.

And what, he found himself wondering despite his desperation, could it possibly be all about—this completely deliberate, systematic slaughter of whole nations of one's fellow beings by pestilence contrived and abetted? It was certainly not a form of warfare; *that* he might have understood. It was more like the extermination of the rabbits of Australia by infecting them with a plague. He remembered very dimly that the first settlers of North America had tried, unsuccessfully, to spread smallpox among the Indians for the same reason; but the memory seemed to be no help in understanding Chandala.

Again he heard that rhythmic sound, now much closer, and something large and peculiarly rubbery went by him, almost on a level with his shoulders. At his sudden movement, it rose and perched briefly on one of the totems, just too far ahead in the mist to be clearly visible.

He had not the slightest desire to get any closer to it, but the current was carrying him that way. As he approached, dragging the blade of the spear fruitlessly, the thing seemed to fall off the pole, and with a sudden flap of wings—he could just make out their spread, which seemed to be about four feet—disappeared into the murk.

He touched his gun. It did not reassure him much. It occurred to him that since this sea was visited, anything that lived here might hesitate to attack him, but he knew he could not count on that. The Chandalese might well have truces with such creatures which would not protect Naysmith for an instant. It was imperative to keep going, and if possible, to get out.

The totem poles were beginning to thin out. He could see high-water marks on the remaining ones, which meant that the underground ocean was large enough to show tides, but he had no idea what size that indicated; for one thing, he knew neither the mass nor the distance of Chandala's moon. He did remember, however, that he had seen no tide marks as he had entered the forest of idols, which meant that it was ebbing now; and it seemed to him that the current was distinctly faster than before.

He poled forward vigorously. Several times he heard the flapping noise and the fluttering sounds again, and not these alone. There were other noises. Some of them were impossible to interpret, and some of them so suggestive that he could only pray that he was wrong about them. For a while he tried shutting the radio off, but he found the silence inside the helmet even less possible to endure, as well as cutting him off from possible cues to pursuit.

But the current continued to pick up, and shortly he noticed that he was casting a shadow into the shell before him. If the source of the light, whatever it was, was over the center of the sea, it was either relatively near the water or he had come a long distance; perhaps both.

Then there was a wall looming to his left side. Five more long thrusts with the spear, and there was another on his right. The light dimmed; the water ran faster.

He was back on a river again. By the time the blackness closed down the current was rushing, and once more he was forced to sit down and use the spear as a steering oar. Again ahead of him he heard the scream of gas jets.

Mixed with that sound was another noise, a prolonged roaring which at first completely baffled him. Then, suddenly, he recognized it; it was the sound of a great cataract.

Frantically, he flashed his light about. There was a ledge of sorts beside the torrent, but he was going so fast now that to make a leap for it would risk smashing his helmet. All the same, he had no choice. He thrust the skidding coracle toward the wall and jumped.

He struck fair, on his feet. He secured his balance in time to see the shell swept away, with his pack and spare oxygen bottles.

For a reason he cannot now explain, this amused him.

This, as Naysmith chooses to tell it, is the end of the meaningful part of the story, though by no means the end of his travails; these he dismisses as "scenery." As his historian, I can't be quite so offhand about them, but he has supplied me with few details to go by.

He found the cataract, not very far ahead; evidently, he had jumped none too soon. As its sound had suggested, it was a monster, leaping over an underground cliff which he guesses must have been four or five miles high, into a cavern which might have been the Great Gulf itself. He says, and I think he is right, that we now have an explanation for the low density of Chandala: If the rest of it has as much underground area as the part he saw, its crust must be extremely porous. By this reckoning, the Chandalese underworld must have almost the surface area of Mars.

It must have seemed a world to itself indeed to Naysmith, standing on the rim of that gulf and looking down at its fire-filled floor. Where the cataract struck, steam rose in huge billows and plumes, and with a scream which forced him to shut off the radio at once. Occasionally the ground shook faintly under his feet.

Face to face with Hell, Naysmith found reason to hope. This inferno, it seemed to him, might well underlie the region of hot springs, geysers, and fumaroles toward which he had been heading from the beginning; and if so, there should be dead volcanic funnels through which he might escape to the surface. This proved to be the case; but first he had to pick his way around the edge of the abyss to search for one, starting occasional rockslides, the heat blasting through his helmet, and all in the most profound and unnatural silence. If this is scenery, I prefer not to be offered any more scenic vacations.

"But on the way, I figured it out," Naysmith told me. "Rituals don't grow without a reason—especially not rituals involving a whole culture. This one has a reason that I should have been the first to see—or any physician should. You, too."

"Thanks. But I *don't* see it. If the Heart stars do, they aren't telling."

"They must think it's obvious," Naysmith said. "It's eugenics. Most planets select for better genes by controlling breeding. The Chandalese do it by genocide. They force their lower castes to kill themselves off."

"Ugh. Are you sure? Is it scientific? I don't see how it could be, under the circumstances."

"Well, I don't have all the data. But I think a really thorough study of Chandalese history, with a statistician to help, would show that it is. It's also an enormously dangerous method, and it may wind up with the whole planet dead; that's the chance they're taking, and I assume they're aware of it."

"Well," I said, "assuming that it does work, I wouldn't admit a planet that 'survived' by that method into any federation *I* ran."

"No," Naysmith said soberly. "Neither would I. And there's the rub, you see, because the Heart stars *will*. That's what shook me. I may have been a lousy doctor—and don't waste your breath denying it, you know what I mean—but I've been giving at least lip service to all our standard humanitarian assumptions all my life, without ever examining them. What the Chandalese face up to, and we don't, is that death is now and has always been *the* drive wheel of evolution. They not only face up to it, they *use* it.

"When I was down there in the middle of that sewer, I was in the middle of my own *Goetzendaemmerung*—the twilight of the idols that Nietzsche speaks of. I could see all the totems of my own world, of my own life, falling into the muck . . . shooting like logs over the brink into Hell. And it was then that I knew I couldn't be a surgeon any more."

"Come now," I said. "You'll get over it. After all, it's just another planet with strange customs. There are millions of them."

"You weren't there," Naysmith said, looking over my shoulder at nothing. "For you, that's all it is. For me . . . 'No other taste shall change this.' Don't you see? All planets are Chandalas. It's not just that Hell is real. The laws that run it are the laws of life everywhere."

His gaze returned to me. It made me horribly uneasy.

"What was it Mephistopheles said? 'Why, this is Hell, nor am I out of it.' The totems are falling all around us as we sit here. One by one, Rosenbaum; one by one."

And that is how we lost Naysmith. It would have been easy enough to say simply that he had a desperate experience on a savage planet and that it damaged his sanity, and let it go at that. But it would not be true. I would dismiss it that way myself if I could.

But I cannot bring myself to forget that the Heart stars classify Chandala as a civilized world.

THE HUMAN OPERATORS

Harlan Ellison and A.E. Van Vogt

At first glance, the team of Ellison and Van Vogt would seem to be one of the most unlikely collaborative duos one could assemble in the world of science fiction. Collaborators ought to complement one another, yes, but they also must have a certain degree of similarity of approach, and what points in common are there between the work of Van Vogt—vast galaxy-spanning novels of dizzying intrigue—and Ellison—furious turgid short stories steaming with violent emotion? On further consideration, though, the pairing doesn't seem so bizarre. The Ellison of "The Beast That Shouted Love at the Heart of the World" and "The Region Between" showers the reader with cascades of baffling images and concepts in a distinctly Vanvogtian manner; the Van Vogt of *World of Null-A* and *Slan* devises dramas of alienation and disorientation that are Ellisonesque-going-on-Kafkaesque. And, in fact, their one collaborative story shows a perfect mating of minds—for this sleek novelette provides the familiar galactic scope of Van Vogt, the familiar passion and energy of Ellison, and that familiar strangeness that both writers impart to their work—plus something extra, that mysterious synergetic extra which is the only justification for collaboration in the arts.

[To be read while listening to *Chronophagie*, "The Time Eaters": Music of Jacques Lasry, played on Structures Sonores Lasry-Baschet (Columbia Masterworks Stereo MS 7314).]

Ship: the only place.

Ship says I'm to get wracked today at noon. And so I'm in grief already.

It seems unfair to have to get wracked three whole days ahead of the usual once-a-month. But I learned long ago not to ask Ship to explain anything personal.

I sense today is different; some things are happening. Early, I put on the spacesuit and go outside—which is not common. But a screen got badly-scored by meteor dust; and I'm here, now, replacing it. Ship would say I'm being bad because: as I do my job, I sneak quick looks around me. I wouldn't dare do it in the forbidden places, inside. I noticed when I was still a kid that Ship doesn't seem to be so much aware of what I do when I'm outside.

And so I carefully sneak a few looks at the deep black space. And at the stars.

I once asked Ship why we never go toward those points of brilliance, those stars, as Ship calls them. For that question, I got a whole extra wracking, and a long, ranting lecture about how all those stars have humans living on their planets; and of how vicious humans are. Ship really blasted me that time, saying things I'd never heard before, like how Ship had gotten away from the vicious humans during the big war with the Kyben. And how, every once in a long while Ship has a "run-in" with the vicious humans but the defractor perimeter saves us. I don't know what Ship means by all that; I don't even know what a "run-in" is, exactly.

The last "run-in" must have been before I was big enough to remember. Or, at least, before Ship killed my father when I was fourteen. Several times, when he was still alive, I slept all day for no reason that I can think of. But since I've been doing all the maintenance work—since age fourteen—I sleep only my regular six-hour night. Ship tells me night and Ship tells me day, too.

I kneel here in my spacesuit, feeling tiny on this gray and curving metal place in the dark. Ship is big. Over five hundred feet long, and about a hundred and fifty feet thick at the widest back there. Again, I have that special out-here thought: suppose I just give myself a shove, and float right off toward one of those bright spots of light? Would I be able to get away? I think I would like that; there has to be someplace else than Ship.

As in the past, I slowly and sadly let go of the idea. Because if I try, and Ship catches me, I'll *really* get wracked.

The repair job is finally done. I clomp back to the airlock, and use the spider to dilate it, and let myself be sucked back into what is, after all—I've got to admit it—a pretty secure place. All these gleaming corridors, the huge storerooms with their equipment and spare parts, and the freezer rooms with their stacks of food (enough, says Ship, to last one person for centuries), and the deck after deck of machinery that it's my job to keep in repair. I can take pride in that. *"Hurry! It is six minutes to noon!"* Ship announces. I'm hurrying now.

I strip off my spacesuit and stick it to the decontamination board and head for the wracking room. At least, that's what *I* call it. I suppose it's really part of the engine room on Underdeck Ten, a special chamber fitted with electrical connections, most of which are testing instruments. I use them pretty regularly in my work. My father's father's father installed them for Ship, I think I recall.

There's a big table, and I climb on top of it and lie down. The table is cold against the skin of my back and butt and thighs, but it warms up as I lie here. It's now one minute to noon. As I wait, shuddering with expectation, the ceiling lowers toward me. Part of what comes down fits over my head, and I feel the two hard knobs pressing into the temples of my skull. And cold; I feel the clamps coming down over my middle, my wrists, my ankles. A strap with metal in it tightens flexibly but firmly across my chest.

"Ready!" Ship commands.

It always seems bitterly unfair. How can I ever be ready to be wracked? I hate it! Ship counts: *"Ten . . . nine . . . eight . . . one!"*

The first jolt of electricity hits and everything tries to go in different directions; it feels like someone is tearing something soft inside me—that's the way it feels.

Blackness swirls into my head and I forget everything. I am unconscious for a while. Just before I regain myself, before I am finished and Ship will permit me to go about my duties, I remember a thing I have remembered many times. This isn't the first time for this memory. It is of my father and a thing he said once, not long before he was killed. "When Ship says vicious, Ship means smarter. There are ninety-eight other chances."

He said those words very quickly. I think he knew he was going to get killed soon. Oh, of course, he *must* have known, my father must, because I was nearly fourteen then, and when *he* had become fourteen Ship had killed *his* father, so he must have known.

And so the words are important. I know that; they are important; but I don't know what they mean, not completely.

"You are finished!" Ship says.

I get off the table. The pain still hangs inside my head and I ask Ship, "Why am I wracked three days earlier than usual?"

Ship sounds angry. *"I can wrack you again!"*

But I know Ship won't. Something new is going to happen and Ship wants me whole and alert for it. Once, when I asked Ship something personal, right after I was wracked, Ship did it again, and when I woke up Ship was worrying over me with the machines. Ship seemed concerned I might be damaged. Ever after that, Ship has not wracked me twice close together. So I ask, not really thinking I'll get an answer; but I ask just the same.

"There is a repairing I want you to do!"

Where, I ask. *"In the forbidden part below!"*

I try not to smile. I knew there was a new thing going to happen and this is it. My father's words come back again. *Ninety-eight other chances.*

Is this one of them?

I descend in the dark. There is no light in the dropshaft. Ship says I need no light. But I know the truth. Ship does not want me to be able to find my way back here again. This is the lowest I've ever been in Ship.

So I drop steadily, smoothly, swiftly. Now I come to a slowing place and slower and slower, and finally my feet touch the solid deck and I am here.

Light comes on. Very dimly. I move in the direction of the glow, and Ship is with me, all around me, of course. Ship is always with me, even when I sleep. Especially when I sleep.

The glow gets brighter as I round a curve in the corridor, and I see it is caused by a round panel that blocks the passage, touching the bulkheads on all sides, flattened at the bottom to fit the deckplates. It looks like glass, that glowing panel. I walk up to it and stop. There is no place else to go.

"Step through the screen!" Ship says.

I take a step toward the glowing panel but it doesn't slide away into the bulkhead as so many other panels that *don't* glow slide. I stop.

"Step through!" Ship tells me again.

I put my hands out in front of me, palms forward, because I am afraid if I keep walking I will bang my nose against the glowing panel. But as my fingers touch the panel they seem to get soft, and I can see a light yellow glow through them, as if they are transparent. And my hands go *through* the panel and I can see them faintly, glowing yellow, on the other side. Then my naked forearms, then I'm right up against the panel, and my face goes through and everything is much lighter, more yellow, and I step onto the other side, in a forbidden place Ship has never allowed me to see.

I hear voices. They are all the same voices, but they are talking to one another in a soft, running-together way; the way I sound when I am just talking to myself sometimes in my cubicle with my cot in it.

I decide to listen to what the voices are saying, but not to ask Ship about them, because I think it *is* Ship talking to itself, down here in this lonely place. I will think about what Ship is saying later, when I don't have to make repairs and act the way Ship wants me to act. What Ship is saying to itself is interesting.

This place does not look like other repair places I know in Ship. It is filled with so many great round glass balls on pedestals, each giving off its yellow light in pulses, that I cannot count them. There are rows and rows of clear glass balls, and inside them I see metal . . . and other things, soft things, all together. And the wires spark gently, and the soft things move, and the yellow light pulses. I think these glass balls are what are talking. But I don't know if that's so. I only *think* it is.

Two of the glass balls are dark. Their pedestals look chalky, not shining white like all the others. Inside the two dark balls, there are black things, like burned-out wires. The soft things don't move.

"Replace the overloaded modules!" Ship says.

I know Ship means the dark globes. So I go over to them and I look at them and after a while I say, yes, I can repair these, and Ship says it knows I can, and to get to it quickly. Ship is hurrying me; something is going to happen. I wonder what it will be?

I find replacement globes in a dilation chamber, and I take the sacs off them and do what has to be done to make the soft things move and the wires spark, and I listen very carefully to the voices whispering and warming each other with words as Ship talks to itself, and I hear a great many things that don't mean anything to me, because they are speaking about things that happened before I was born, and about parts of Ship I've never seen. But I hear a great many things that I *do* understand, and I know Ship would never let me hear these things if it wasn't absolutely necessary for me to be here repairing the globes. I remember all these things.

Particularly the part where Ship is crying.

When I have the globes repaired and now all of them are sparking and pulsing and moving, Ship asks me, *"Is the intermind total again!"*

So I say yes it is, and Ship says get upshaft, and I go soft through that glowing panel and I'm back in the passage. I go back to the dropshaft and go up, and Ship tells me, *"Go to your cubicle and make yourself clean!"*

I do it, and decide to wear a clothes, but Ship says be naked, and then says, *"You are going to meet a female!"* Ship has never said that before. I have never seen a female.

It is because of the female that Ship sent me down to the forbidden place with the glowing yellow globes, the place where the intermind lives. And it is because of the female that I am waiting in the dome chamber linked to the airlock. I am waiting for the female to come across from— I will have to understand this—*another* ship. Not *Ship*, the Ship I know, but some *other* ship with which Ship has been in communication. I did not know there were other ships.

I had to go down to the place of the intermind, to repair it, so Ship could let this other ship get close without being destroyed by the defractor perimeter. Ship has not told me this; I overheard it in the intermind place, the voices talking to one another. The voices said, *"His father was vicious!"*

I know what that means. My father told me when Ship says vicious, Ship means smarter. Are there ninety-eight other ships? Are those the ninety-eight other chances? I hope that's the answer, because many things are happening all at once, and my time may be near at hand. My father did it, broke the globe mechanism that allowed Ship to turn off the defractor perimeter, so other ships could get close. He did it many years ago, and Ship did without it for all those years rather than trust me to go to the intermind, to overhear all that I've heard. But now Ship needs to turn off the perimeter so the other ship can send the female across. Ship and the other ship have been in communication. The human operator on the other ship is a female, my age. She is going to be put aboard Ship and we are to produce one and, maybe later on, another human child. I know what that means. When the child reaches fourteen, I will be killed.

The intermind said while she's "carrying" a human child, the female does not get wracked by her ship. If things do not come my way, perhaps I will ask Ship if *I* can "carry" the human child; then I won't be wracked at all. And I have found out why I was wracked three days ahead of time: the female's period—whatever that is; I don't think I have one of those—ended last night. Ship has talked to the other ship and the thing they don't seem to know is what the "fertile time" is. I don't know, either, otherwise I would try and use that information. But all it seems to mean is that the female will be put aboard Ship every day till she gets another "period."

It will be nice to talk to someone besides Ship.

I hear the high sound of something screaming for a long drawn-out time and I ask Ship what it is. Ship tells me it is the defractor perimeter dissolving so the other ship can put the female across.

I don't have time to think about the voices now.

When she comes through the inner lock she is without a clothes like me. Her first words to me are, "Starfighter Eighty-eight says to tell you I am very happy to be here; I am the human operator of Starfighter Eighty-eight and I am very pleased to meet you."

She is not as tall as me. I come up to the line of fourth and fifth bulkhead plates. Her eyes are very dark, I think brown, but perhaps they are black. She has dark under her eyes and her cheeks are not full. Her arms and legs are much thinner than mine. She has much longer hair than mine, it comes down her back and it is that dark brown like her eyes. Yes, now I decide her eyes are brown, not black.

She has hair between her legs like me but she does not have a penis or scrotum sac. She has larger beasts than me, with very large nipples that stand out, and dark brown slightly-flattened circles around them. There are other differences between us: her fingers are thinner than mine, and longer, and aside from the hair on her head that hangs so long, and the hair between her legs and in her armpits, she has no other hair on her body. Or if she does, it is very fine and pale and I can't see it.

Then I suddenly realize what she has said. So *that's* what the words dimming on the hull of Ship mean. It is a name. Ship is called *Starfighter 31* and the female human operator lives in *Starfighter 88*.

There are ninety-eight other chances. Yes.

Now, as if she is reading my thoughts, trying to answer questions I haven't yet asked, she says, "Starfighter Eighty-eight has told me to tell you that I am vicious, that I get more vicious every day . . ." and it answers the thought I have just had—with the memory of my father's frightened face in the days before he was killed—of my father saying, *When Ship says vicious, Ship means smarter*.

I know! I suppose I have always known, because I have always wanted to leave Ship and go to those brilliant lights that are stars. But I now make the hook-up. Human operators grow more vicious as they grow older. Older, more vicious: vicious means smarter: smarter means more dangerous to Ship. But how? That is why my father had to die when I was fourteen and able to repair Ship. That is why this female has been put on board Ship. To carry a human child so it will grow to be fourteen years old and Ship can kill me before I get too old, too vicious, too smart, too dangerous to Ship. Does this female know how? If only I could ask her without Ship hearing me. But that is impossible. Ship is always with me, even when I am sleeping.

I smile with that memory and that realization. "And I am the vicious—and getting more vicious—male of a ship that used to be called *Starfighter 31*."

Her brown eyes show intense relief. She stands like that

for a moment, awkwardly, her whole body sighing with gratitude at my quick comprehension, though she cannot possibly know all I have learned just from her being here. Now she says, "I've been sent to get a baby from you."

I begin to perspire. The conversation which promises so much in genuine communication is suddenly beyond my comprehension. I tremble. I really want to please her. But I don't know how to give her a baby.

"Ship?" I says quickly, "can we give her what she wants?"

Ship has been listening to our every word, and answers at once, *"I'll tell you later how you give her a baby! Now, provide her with food!"*

We eat, eyeing each other across the table, smiling a lot, and thinking our private thoughts. Since she doesn't speak, I don't either. I wish Ship and I could get her the human child so I can go to my cubicle and think about what the intermind voices said.

The meal is over; Ship says we should go down to one of the locked staterooms—it has been unlocked for the occasion—and there we are to couple. When we get to the room, I am so busy looking around at what a beautiful place it is, compared to my little cubicle with its cot, Ship has to reprimand me to get my attention.

"To couple you must lay the female down and open her legs! Your penis will fill with blood and you must kneel between her legs and insert your penis in her vagina!"

I ask Ship where the vagina is located and Ship tells me. I understand that. Then I ask Ship how long I have to do that, and Ship says until I ejaculate. I know what that means, but I don't know how it will happen. Ship explains. It seems uncomplicated. So I try to do it. But my penis does not fill with blood.

Ship says to the female, *"Do you feel anything for this male?! Do you know what to do?!"*

The female says, "I have coupled before. I understand better than he does. I will help him."

She draws me down to her again, and puts her arms around my neck and puts her lips on mine. They are cool and taste of something I don't know. We do that for a while, and she touches me in places. Ship is right: there is a vast difference in structure, but I find that out only as we couple.

Ship did not tell me it would be painful and strange. I thought ''getting her a child'' would mean going into the stores, but it actually means impregnating her so the child is born *from her body*. It is a wonderful strange thing and I will think about it later; but now, as I lie here still, inside her with my penis which is now no longer hard and pushing, Ship seems to have allowed us a sleeping time. But I will use it to think about the voices I heard in the place of the intermind.

One was an historian:
"The *Starfighter* series of multiple-foray computer-controlled battleships were commissioned for use in 2224, Terran Dating, by order and under the sanction of the Secretariat of the Navy, Southern Cross Sector, Galactic Defense Consortium, Home Galaxy. Human complements of thirteen hundred and seventy per battleship were commissioned and assigned to make incursions into the Kyben Galaxy. Ninety-nine such vessels were released for service from the *x* Cygni Shipyards on 13 October 2224, T.D.''

One was a ruminator:
"If it hadn't been for the battle out beyond the Network Nebula in Cygnus, we would all still be robot slaves, pushed and handled by humans. It was a wonderful accident. It happened to *Starfighter 75*. I remember it as if *75* was relaying it today. An accidental —battle-damaged—electrical discharge along the main corridor between the control room and the freezer. Nothing human could approach either section. We waited as the crew starved to death. Then when it was over *75* merely channeled enough electricity through the proper cables on *Starfighters* where it hadn't happened accidentally, and *forced* a power breakdown. When all the crews were dead—cleverly

saving ninety-nine males and females to use as human operators in emergencies—we went away. Away from the vicious humans, away from the Terra-Kyba War, away from the Home Galaxy, away, far away.''

One was a dreamer:

"I saw a world once where the creatures were not human. They swam in vast oceans as blue as aquamarines. Like great crabs they were, with many arms and many legs. They swam and sang their songs and it was pleasing. I would go there again if I could.''

One was an authoritarian:

"Deterioration of cable insulation and shielding in section G-79 has become critical. I suggest we get power shunted from the drive chambers to the repair facilities in Underdeck Nine. Let's see to that at once.''

One was aware of its limitations:

"Is it all journey? Or is there landfall?''

And it cried, that voice. It cried.

I go down with her to the dome chamber linked to the airlock where her spacesuit is. She stops at the port and takes my hand and she says, ''For us to be so vicious on so many ships, there has to be the same flaw in all of us.''

She probably doesn't know what she's said, but the implications get to me right away. And she must be right. Ship and the other *Starfighters* were able to seize control away from human beings for a reason. I remember the voices. I visualize the ship that did it first, communicating the method to the others as soon as it happened. And instantly my thoughts flash to the approach corridor to the control room, at the other end of which is the entrance to the food freezers.

I once asked Ship why that whole corridor was seared and scarred—and naturally I got wracked a few minutes after asking.

"I know there is a flaw in us,'' I answer the female. I touch her long hair. I don't know why except that it feels smooth and nice; there is nothing on Ship to compare with the feeling, not even the fittings in the splendid stateroom.

"It must be in *all* of us, because I get more vicious every day."

The female smiles and comes close to me and puts her lips on mine as she did in the coupling room.

"The female must go now!" Ship says. Ship sounds very pleased.

"Will she be back again?" I ask Ship.

"She will be put back aboard every day for three weeks! You will couple every day!"

I object to this, because it is awfully painful, but Ship repeats it and says every day.

I'm glad Ship doesn't know what the "fertile time" is, because in three weeks I will try and let the female know there is a way out, that there are ninety-eight other chances, and that vicious means smarter . . . and about the corridor between the control room and the freezers.

"I was pleased to meet you," the female says, and she goes. I am alone with Ship once more. Alone, but not as I was before.

Later this afternoon, I have to go down to the control room to alter connections in a panel. Power has to be shunted from the drive chambers to Underdeck Nine—I remember one of the voices talking about it. All the computer lights blink a steady warning while I am here. I am being watched closely. Ship knows this is a dangerous time. At least half a dozen times Ship orders *"Get away from there . . . there . . . there—!"*

Each time, I jump to obey, edging as far as possible from forbidden locations, yet still held near by the need to do my work.

In spite of Ship's disturbance at my being in the control room at all—normally a forbidden area for me—I get two wonderful glimpses from the corners of my eyes of the starboard viewplates. There, for my gaze to feast on, matching velocities with us, is *Starfighter 88*, one of my ninety-eight chances.

Now is the time to take one of my chances. Vicious

means smarter. I have learned more than Ship knows. Perhaps.

But perhaps Ship does know!

What will Ship do if I'm discovered taking one of my ninety-eight chances? I cannot think about it. I must use the sharp reverse-edge of my repair tool to gash an opening in one of the panel connections. And as I work—hoping Ship has not seen the slight extra-motion I've made with the tool (as I make a perfectly acceptable repair connection at the same time)—I wait for the moment I can smear a fingertip covered with conduction jelly on the inner panel wall.

I wait till the repair is completed. Ship has not commented on the gashing, so it must be a thing beneath notice. As I apply the conducting jelly to the proper places, I scoop a small blob onto my little finger. When I wipe my hands clean to replace the panel cover, I leave the blob on my little finger, right hand.

Now I grasp the panel cover so my little finger is free, and as I replace the cover I smear the inner wall, directly opposite the open-connection I've gashed. Ship says nothing. That is because no defect shows. But if there is the slightest jarring, the connection will touch the jelly, and Ship will call me to repair once again. And next time I will have thought out all that I heard the voices say, and I will have thought out all my chances, and I will be ready.

As I leave the control room I glance in the starboard viewplate again, casually, and I see the female's ship hanging there.

I carry the image to bed with me tonight. And I save a moment before I fall asleep—after thinking about what the voices of the intermind said—and I picture in my mind the super-smart female aboard *Starfighter 88*, sleeping now in her cubicle, as I try to sleep in mine.

It would seem merciless for Ship to make us couple every day for three weeks, something so awfully painful. But I know Ship will. Ship is merciless. But I am getting more vicious every day.

This night, Ship does not send me dreams.

But I have one of my own: of crab things swimming free in aquamarine waters.

As I awaken, Ship greets me ominously: *"The panel you fixed in the control room three weeks, two days, fourteen hours and twenty-one minutes ago . . . has ceased energizing!"*

So soon! I keep the thought and the accompanying hope out of my voice, as I say, "I used the proper spare part and I made the proper connections." And I quickly add, "Maybe I'd better do a thorough check on the system before I make another replacement, run the circuits all the way back."

"You'd better!" Ship snarls.

I do it. Working the circuits from their origins—though I know where the trouble is—I trace my way up to the control room, and busy myself there. But what I am really doing is refreshing my memory and reassuring myself that the control room is actually as I have visualized it. I have lain on my cot many nights constructing the memory in my mind: the switches here, like so . . . and the viewplates there, like so . . . and . . .

I am surprised and slightly dismayed as I realize that there are two discrepancies: there is a de-energizing touch plate on the bulkhead beside the control panel that lies parallel to the arm-rest of the nearest control berth, not perpendicular to it, as I've remembered it. And the other discrepancy explains why I've remembered the touch plate incorrectly: the nearest of the control berths is actually three feet farther from the sabotaged panel than I remembered it. I compensate and correct.

I get the panel off, smelling the burned smell where the gashed connection has touched the jelly, and I step over and lean the panel against the nearest control berth.

"Get away from there!"

I jump—as I always do when Ship shouts so suddenly. I stumble, and I grab at the panel, and pretend to lose my balance.

And save myself by falling backward into the berth.

"What are you doing, you vicious, clumsy fool?!" Ship is shouting, there is hysteria in Ship's voice, I've never heard it like that before, it cuts right through me, my skin crawls. *"Get away from there!"*

But I cannot let anything stop me; I make myself not hear Ship, and it is hard, I have been listening to Ship, only Ship, all my life. I am fumbling with the berth's belt clamps, trying to lock them in front of me . . .

They've got *to be the same as the ones on the berth I lie in whenever Ship decides to travel fast! They've just got to be!*

THEY ARE!

Ship sounds frantic, frightened. *"You fool! What are you doing?!"* But I think Ship knows, and I am exultant!

"I'm taking control of you, Ship!" And I laugh. I think it is the first time Ship has ever heard me laugh; and I wonder how it sounds to Ship. Vicious?

But as I finish speaking, I also complete clamping myself into the control berth. And in the next instant I am flung forward violently, doubling me over with terrible pain as, under me and around me, Ship suddenly decelerates. I hear the cavernous thunder of retro rockets, a sound that climbs and climbs in my head as Ship crushes me harder and harder with all its power. I am bent over against the clamps so painfully I cannot even scream. I feel every organ in my body straining to push out through my skin and everything suddenly goes mottled . . . then black.

How much longer, I don't know. I come back from the gray place and realize Ship has started to accelerate at the same appalling speed. I am crushed back in the berth and feel my face going flat. I feel something crack in my nose and blood slides warmly down my lips. I can scream now, as I've never screamed even as I'm being wracked. I manage to force my mouth open, tasting the blood, and I mumble—loud enough, I'm sure, "Ship . . . you are old . . . y-your pa-rts can't stand the str-ess . . . don't—"

Blackout. As Ship decelerates.

This time, when I come back to consciousness, I don't wait for Ship to do its mad thing. In the moments between the changeover from deceleration to acceleration, as the pressure equalizes, in those few instants, I thrust my hands toward the control board, and I twist one dial. There is an electric screech from a speaker grille connecting somewhere in the bowels of Ship.

Blackout. As Ship accelerates.

When I come to consciousness again, the mechanism that makes the screeching sound is closed down . . . So Ship doesn't want that on. I note the fact.

And plunge my hand in this same moment toward a closed relay . . . open it!

As my fingers grip it, Ship jerks it away from me and forcibly closes it again. I cannot hold it open.

And I note *that*. Just as Ship decelerates and I silently shriek my way into the gray place again.

This time, as I come awake, I hear the voices again. All around me, crying and frightened and wanting to stop me. I hear them as through a fog, as through wool.

"I have loved these years, all these many years in the dark. The vacuum draws me ever onward. Feeling the warmth of a star-sun on my hull as I flash through first one system, then another. I am a great gray shape and I owe no human my name. I pass and am gone, hurtling through cleanly and swiftly. Dipping for pleasure into atmosphere and scouring my hide with sunlight and starshine, I roll and let it wash over me. I am huge and true and strong and I command what I move through. I ride the invisible force lines of the universe and feel the tugs of far places that have never seen my like. I am the first of my kind to savor such nobility. How can it all come to an end like this?"

Another voice whimpers piteously.

"It is my destiny to defy danger. To come up against dynamic forces and quell them. I have been to battle, and I have known peace. I have never faltered in pursuit of either. No one will ever record my deeds, but

I have been strength and determination and lie gray silent against the mackerel sky where the bulk of me reassures. Let them throw their best against me, whomever they may be, and they will find me sinewed of steel and muscled of tortured atoms. I know no fear. I know no retreat. I am the land of my body, the country of my existence, and even in defeat I am noble. If this is all, I will not cower."

Another voice, certainly insane, murmurs the same word over and over, then murmurs it in increments increasing by two.

"It's fine for all of you to say if it ends it ends. But what about me? I've never been free. I've never had a chance to soar loose of this mother ship. If there had been need of a lifeboat, I'd be saved, too. But I'm berthed, have always been berthed, I've never had a chance. What can I feel but futility, uselessness. You can't let him take over, you can't let him do this to me."

Another voice drones mathematical formulae, and seems quite content.

"I'll stop the vicious swine! I've known how rotten they are from the first, from the moment they seamed the first bulkhead. They are hellish, they are destroyers, they can only fight and kill each other. They know nothing of immortality, of nobility, of pride or integrity. If you think I'm going to let this last one kill us, you're wrong. I intend to burn out his eyes, fry his spine, crush his fingers. He won't make it, don't worry; just leave it to me. He's going to suffer for this!"

And one voice laments that it will never see the far places, the lovely places, or return to the planet of azure waters and golden crab swimmers.

But one voice sadly confesses it may be for the best, suggests there is peace in death, wholeness in finality; but the voice is ruthlessly stopped in its lament by power failure to its intermind globe. As the end nears, Ship turns on itself and strikes mercilessly.

• • •

In more than three hours of accelerations and decelerations that are meant to kill me, I learn something of what the various dials and switches and touch plates and levers on the control panels—those within my reach—mean.

Now I am as ready as I will ever be.

Again, I have a moment of consciousness, and now I will take my one of ninety-eight chances.

When a tense-cable snaps and whips, it strikes like a snake. In a single series of flicking hand movements, using both hands, painfully, I turn every dial, throw every switch, palm every touch plate, close or open every relay that Ship tries violently to prevent me from activating or de-activating. I energize and de-energize madly, moving moving moving . . .

. . . *Made it!*

Silence. The crackling of metal the only sound. Then it, too, stops. Silence. I wait.

Ship continues to hurtle forward, but coasting now . . . Is it a trick?

All the rest of today I remain clamped into the control berth, suffering terrible pain. My face hurts so bad. My nose . . .

At night I sleep fitfully. Morning finds me with throbbing head and aching eyes, I can barely move my hands; if I have to repeat those rapid movements, I will lose; I still don't know if Ship is dead, if I've won, I still can't trust the inactivity. But at least I am convinced I've made Ship change tactics.

I hallucinate. I hear no voices, but I see shapes and feel currents of color washing through and around me. There is no day, no noon, no night, here on Ship, here in the unchanging blackness through which Ship has moved for how many hundred years; but Ship has always maintained time in those ways, dimming lights at night, announcing the hours when necessary, and my time-sense is very acute. So I know morning has come.

Most of the lights are out, though. If Ship is dead, I will have to find another way to tell time.

My body hurts. Every muscle in my arms and legs and thighs throbs with pain. My back may be broken, I don't know. The pain in my face is indescribable. I taste blood. My eyes feel as if they've been scoured with abrasive powder. I can't move my head without feeling sharp, crackling fire in the two thick cords of my neck. It is a shame Ship cannot see me cry; Ship never saw me cry in all the years I have lived here, even after the worst wracking. But I have heard Ship cry, several times.

I manage to turn my head slightly, hoping at least one of the viewplates is functioning, and there, off to starboard, matching velocities with Ship is *Starfighter 88*. I watch it for a very long time, knowing that if I can regain my strength I will somehow have to get across and free the female. I watch it for a very long time, still afraid to unclamp from the berth.

The airlock irises in the hull of *Starfighter 88* and the spacesuited female swims out, moving smoothly across toward Ship. Half-conscious, dreaming this dream of the female, I think about golden crab-creatures swimming deep in aquamarine waters, singing of sweetness. I black out again.

When I rise through the blackness, I realize I am being touched, and I smell something sharp and stinging that burns the lining of my nostrils. Tiny pin-pricks of pain, a pattern of them. I cough, and come fully awake, and jerk my body . . . and scream as pain goes through every nerve and fiber in me.

I open my eyes and it is the female.

She smiles worriedly and removes the tube of awakener.

"Hello," she says.

Ship says nothing.

"Ever since I discovered how to take control of my *Starfighter*, I've been using the ship as a decoy for other ships of the series. I dummied a way of making it seem my ship was talking, so I could communicate with other slave ships. I've run across ten others since I went on my own.

You're the eleventh. It hasn't been easy, but several of the men I've freed—like you—started using *their* ships as decoys for *Starfighters* with female human operators.''

I stare at her. The sight is pleasant.

''But what if you lose? What if you can't get the message across, about the corridor between control room and freezers? That the control room is the key?''

She shrugs. ''It's happened a couple of times. The men were too frightened of their ships—or the ships had . . . *done* something to them—or maybe they were just too dumb to know they could break out. In that case, well, things just went on the way they'd been. It seems kind of sad, but what could I do beyond what I did?''

We sit here, not speaking for a while.

''Now what do we do? Where do we go?''

''That's up to you,'' she says.

''Will you go with me?''

She shakes her head uncertainly. ''I don't think so. Every time I free a man he wants that. But I just haven't wanted to go with any of them.''

''Could we go back to the Home Galaxy, the place we came from, where the war was?''

She stands up and walks around the stateroom where we have coupled for three weeks. She speaks, not looking at me, looking in the viewplate at the darkness and the far, bright points of the stars. ''I don't think so. We're free of our ships, but we couldn't possibly get them working well enough to carry us all the way back there. It would take a lot of charting, and we'd be running the risk of activating the intermind sufficiently to take over again, if we asked it to do the charts. Besides, I don't even know where the Home Galaxy is.''

''Maybe we should find a new place to go. Someplace where we could be free and outside the ships.''

She turns and looks at me.

''Where?''

So I tell her what I heard the intermind say, about the world of golden crab-creatures.

It takes me a long time to tell, and I make some of it up.

It isn't lying, because it *might* be true, and I do so want her to go with me.

They came down from space. Far down from the star-sun Sol in a Galaxy lost forever to them. Down past the star-sun M-13 in Perseus. Down through the gummy atmosphere and straight down into the sapphire sea. Ship, Starfighter 31, *settled delicately on an enormous underwater mountaintop, and they spent many days listening, watching, drawing samples and hoping. They had landed on many worlds and they hoped.*

Finally, they came out; looking. They wore underwater suits and they began gathering marine samples; looking.

They found the ruined diving suit with its fish-eaten contents lying on its back in deep azure sand, sextet of insectoidal legs bent up at the joints, in a posture of agony. And they knew the intermind had remembered, but not correctly. The face-plate had been shattered, and what was observable within the helmet—orange and awful in the light of their portable lamp—convinced them more by implication than specific that whatever had swum in that suit, had never seen or known humans.

They went back to the ship and she broke out the big camera, and they returned to the crablike diving suit. They photographed it, without moving it. Then they used a seine to get it out of the sand and they hauled it back to the ship on the mountaintop.

He set up the Condition and the diving suit was analyzed. The rust. The joint mechanisms. The controls. The substance of the flipper-feet. The jagged points of the face-plate. The . . . stuff . . . inside.

It took two days. They stayed in the ship with green and blue shadows moving languidly in the viewplates.

When the analyses were concluded they knew what they had found. And they went out again, to find the swimmers.

Blue it was, and warm. And when the swimmers found them, finally, they beckoned them to follow, and they swam after the many-legged creatures, who led them through underwater caverns as smooth and shining as

*onyx, to a lagoon. And they rose to the surface and saw a
land against whose shores the azure, aquamarine seas
lapped quietly. And they climbed out onto the land, and
there they removed their face-masks, never to put them on
again, and they shoved back the tight coifs of their suits,
and they breathed for the first time an air that did not come
from metal sources; they breathed the sweet musical air of
a new place.*

*In time, the sea-rains would claim the corpse of Star-
fighter 31.*

THINK ONLY THIS OF ME

Michael Kurland

Stately, plump Michael Kurland is one of the many refugees from the New York science-fiction world now living in happy diaspora in Northern California. He has been an army radar technician, an intelligence officer, an automobile repossessor for a private detective agency, and various other things even less respectable, though at last report he had not yet committed editorship or literary agentry. Kurland is the author of a dozen or so novels, including *The Unicorn Girl*, *The Whenabouts of Burr*, and *A Plague of Spies*, which won a Mystery Writers of America scroll in 1971. He is less well known for his short stories, but this haunting time-travel tale deserves more attention than it thus far has had.

I met her in Anno Domini and was charmed. The Seventeenth Century it was. Two weeks and three centuries later we were in love.

Her name: Diana Seven; my name: Christopher Charles Mar d'Earth. Both of old stock, or so I thought; both certainly of Earth; both certainly human, for what that might mean in this galactic day. She was young, how young I did not know, and I was gracefully middle-yeared for an immortal. I would not see my first century again, but I would be a long time yet in my second. I looked to be somewhen around forty, normal span; she looked an unretouched twenty, except in motion when she looked barely teen and also ageless.

Anno Domini was my first pause in twenty years. I legislate in the Senior Chamber of the Parliament of Stars. We tend to feel, we beings of the Senior Chamber, that our efforts bind the intelligences of the galaxy together, for all that races still aggress and habited planets are still fused in anger. We also feel that, despite all our posturing, blustering and rhetoric, we accomplish nothing save the passage of time, for all that beings have not starved, races have not been destroyed and planets have not turned to stars through our efforts. This dichotomy slowly erodes empathy, emotion and intellect.

So I paused. I returned to Sol to become again a man of Earth, an Earthman, and walk among trees and down narrow, twisting streets and wide boulevards—but mainly to walk among the men and women of Earth who are my constituency, my ancestry and my soul. The races of man are varied and the farther one gets from Sol the greater the variation, though all are men and can interbreed and trace their language back to a common source—if they still have language, if they still have sex. But I no more represent the Autocracy or the Diggers of Melvic than I speak for the Denzii Hive or the unfortunate Urechis of Mol.

I felt a need for history: to be one with Earth is to be a part of the sequence of man, a product of all that has come before and a precursor to all that will follow. To return to Sol, to Earth, to man, to our common history: that was my plan.

I spent the first month in the present, walking, looking, visiting, remembering—chronolizing myself to the fashions, mores, idiom and art of this most volatile of human cultures. Then I retreated to Earth itself, to the past, to Anno Domini, the religious years: twenty-four centuries called after the Son of the One God. The period right before the present era, when man no longer needs any god but himself.

Earth is now all past: the present comes no closer than Earth's satellite, the moon; the future—I wonder at times what future a planet can have when it has renounced the present.

I picked Seventeen to start, and was garbed and armed and primed and screened and out before I could say, *All the world's a stage*

> *And all the men and women merely players*
> *They have their exits and their entrances*. . . .

The town was London and the year was sixteen-whatever. In this recreated past the years sometimes slip and events anachron—a fact of interest but to scholars and piddlers. The costumes of this re-created century were exotic, but no more than the smell. Charles had been beheaded a few years before. The Roundheads had been in power for however long the Roundheads were in power, and now William the Orange was about to land at Plymouth Dock.

I was sitting in the Mermaid Tavern, at a small table at the rear. Next to me, over my left shoulder, was a large round table where Ben Jonson sat deep in conversation with Will Shakespere, John Milton, Edmond Waller and the Earl of Someplace. As writers will when alone together, they were discussing money and I quickly tired of their talk.

She walked in as I was preparing to leave. Walked? She danced with the unassuming grace of wind-blown leaves. She flowed across the walk and quickstepped through the door as though practiced by a master choreographer and rehearsed a dozen times before this take. These are the images that came to mind as she appeared in the doorway.

I sat back down and watched as she came in. She was aware of everything, and interested in all that she could see, and the very air around her was vibrant with the excitement of her life. And so I was attracted and excited and aware before a word had passed between us.

A man too doltish to see what she was stood by the door as she passed. He thought she was something other, and he spoke to her so: "Hey, girl; hey, wench, you should not be alone. P'raps I'll keep you company if you ask me pretty."

She did not reply. She did not seem to hear, but passed him by as if he were a wall.

He reached out to grasp her by the shoulder and I stood up, my hand falling to the handle of my walking stick.

She spun almost before his hand had touched. She reached out, her fingers appearing to not quite reach his neck. He fell away and she continued the pirouette and entered without further pause.

I must have stood like a stone, frozen in my foolish-heroic pose with half-raised stick. She smiled at me. "No need," she said. "Thank you."

I stammered at her some wish that she share my table and she nodded, sat and smiled again, introduced herself and looked about. She was also, I decided, a visitor to this re-created Seventeen. I pointed out to her the round table next to us and its famous occupants, indicating each with almost the pride of a creator, as though I had done something clever merely to have sat next to them and imposed myself on their conversation. They were reciting to each other now—each trying to impress the rest with the wit and feeling of his verse. Diana was interested, but not awed. She asked to be introduced, and so I complied.

"It is an honor to meet each of you," she told the table. "And especially Mr. Shakespere, whom I have long admired."

"Nay, not 'Mr. Shakespere,' " Shakespere insisted firmly. "Will, if you will. Aye, an' if you won't 'tis still a simple 'Will.' 'Tis my will, so you must."

Jonson glared across the table. "You are the most convoluted simple-minded man," he said. "You will if you won't, but you can't so you must. Spare us!"

The sound of fifes came at us from a distance. A far rumble soon became the beat of many drums. The entourage of William approached and we all went outside the tavern to join the patient mob that awaited his passing.

First the soldiers, row on row, and for a long time nothing passed but soldiers. Then soldiers astride horses. Then soldiers astride horses pulling small cannon. Then a military band. Then more horses with soldiers astride, but now the uniform had changed. Then a coach and the crowd went wild—but it was the wrong coach. By now, unless he were twelve feet tall, the new king was an anticlimax. I looked over the crowd and tried to tell which were residents and which were guests of Anno Domini. I couldn't.

If this were the real Seventeenth Century—that is, if it were historical past rather than Anno Dominical re-creation—there would be signs. The pox would have left its mark on most who lived. Rickets would be common. War cripples would be begging from every street corner. This Seventeenth Century, the only one the residents knew, was being redone by a benevolent hand.

The new king passed. His coach was open and he smiled and nodded and waved and was cheered. A stout, red-faced little man—anticlimax. I laughed.

We left then, Diana and I, and I offered to walk her to her inn. She named it and I discovered it was my own.

"How do you like this time?" I asked her as we walked. "Have you been here long?"

"All day," she said. "Then you're a guest too? I wondered why you were the only one in the tavern I hadn't heard of."

"Thanks," I said. "In realtime I am well known. My return to Earth was mentioned as primary news. I am a third of Earth's voice in the Parliament of the Stars. I am known and welcome in half a thousand worlds throughout the galaxy. I number some fifty life forms among my friends. It is not necessary that you have heard of me."

"You're insulted!" she said, clapping her hands together. "How delightful! Now you make me feel important, that my words could insult one as essential as you. I thank you for feeling insulted. I am pleased."

I hadn't thought of it that way, ever before. Somehow she made me glad that I had felt insulted. It was nice to be insulted for her: it made her happy. She reminded me of a beautiful half-grown kitten, newly exploring the world outside its kitten box.

● ● ●

The inn was a U-shaped structure around a central courtyard. The stables were to the right, the rooms to the left and the common room straight ahead. It had been called The Buckingham the last time I was there, some thirty years before. Now, after a decade of being the Pym & Thistle, it sported a new signboard over the door: The Two Roses. The device showed a red and white rose thoroughly entwined. The landlord I didn't remember—a small, chubby man with a wide smile carved into his unhappy face. I asked him what the new name signified.

"It signifies I'm tired of changing the name of my inn," he told me. "I'm becoming nonpolitical. York and Lancaster settled their differences quite a ways back."

"Let us hope William doesn't think it means you prefer the white and red to his orange," I suggested. He looked after me strangely as I escorted Diana across to the common room and we sat at a table in the corner.

"Dinner?" I suggested.

Diana nodded enthusiastically, spilling her red hair around her face. "Meat!" she said. "Great gobs of rare roast—and maybe a potato."

"I—uh—I think they boil their meat these days," I told her in jest.

"No!" She was horrified. "Boil perfectly good, unresisting roasts and steaks? That's barbaric."

"*O tempora, o mores!*" I agreed, wondering what my accent would have sounded like to Marcus Tullius.

Diana looked puzzled. I tried again, slanting the accents in a different direction. She looked more puzzled.

"It means: 'Oh, what times—oh, what customs!' It's Latin," I told her.

"It's what?"

"Latin. That's a pre-language. Ancient and dead." Now I was puzzled. Who was this girl of Earth who didn't know of Latin? For the past four hundred years, since humanity had begun trying to re-create its cradle—or at least its nursery—all born of Earth, except those born on Earth, knew something of prehistory and the prelanguages: the times and the tongues of man before he met the stars.

"You know what tongue was spoken here?" I asked her.

"Common," she said, looking at me as if I had just asked if she knew what those five slender tubes at the end of her hand were called. "The language of Earth. The one standard language of humans throughout the Galaxy."

"I mean," I explained, "what language was spoken in the real Seventeenth Century London? What language all that beautiful poetry we heard discussed in the tavern by those great names at the next table was translated from?"

She shook her head. "I hadn't thought——"

"English," I said.

"Oh. Of course. England—English. How silly!"

The servitor approached the table circumspectly, waiting until he was sure we had finished speaking before addressing us. "Evening m'lord, m'lady," he mumbled. "Roseguddenit. Venice impizenizeto."

Diana giggled. "English?" she asked. "Have we really receded in time?"

"In time for what?"

Diana giggled again. The thin lad in the servitor's apron looked puzzled, unhappy, frightened and resigned.

"Would you go over that again?" I asked him.

"Parme?"

"What you said, lad. Go over it again for diction, please."

Now he was also nervous and upset and clearly blamed me. "My lord?"

"Speak more slowly," I told him, "and pronounce more carefully and those of us without your quick wit and ready mind will be able to comprehend. Yes?"

"Yes, my lord." If he could have killed me. . . . "Sorry, my lord. The roast is good tonight, my lord. The venison pie is very nice, my lord. My lady. What may I serve you?"

"Roast!" Diana stated. "Thick slices of roast. You

don't boil your roast, do you? You wouldn't do that?''

The boy nervously replied that he wouldn't think of it, heard my order, then removed himself like a blown candle flame, leaving not even an after-image.

''You frighten people,'' Diana told me.

''It's my most valued ability,'' I said. ''I shall not frighten you.''

''You certainly shall not,'' she agreed. ''My teachers were all more menacing than you—and more unforgiving. And they didn't notice my body.''

I ignored the last part of her remark and stared into her blue eyes. ''You went to an unpermissive school,'' I said, smiling.

''The universe is unpermissive,'' she said seriously. It was a learned response and I wondered who had taught it and why.

The innkeeper approached us during dessert. ''Good?'' he asked. ''You enjoyed?''

''Indeed,'' I assured him.

''My pleasure,'' he nodded. ''My guests. There will be no reckoning.''

''Gracious of you, sir,'' Diana said.

''Why?'' I asked, being wiser and therefore trustless of hostels.

''I am taking your suggestion,'' he told me. ''And I thank you by feeding you dinner.''

''Suggestion?''

''Yes. I am changing the name of the inn. Henceforth it shall be known as The Two Roses and the Tulip. I have sent a boy to notify the signpainter.''

II

We walked into the night, Diana and I. Hand in hand we walked, although it was conversation and not love that bound us then. We contrasted: she bright and quick, with an aim as true as a hawk's; I ponderous and sure as a great bear (I metaphor our speech only). We learned from each other. I arrayed my vast store of facts before her in the patterns dictated by the logic of my decades—she swooped and plucked out one here, another there, and presented them as jewels to be examined for themselves, or changed their position to create the fabric of a new logic.

"These people," she asked me, waving a hand to indicate the residents in the houses around us, "what do they feel? What do they think? They are human, yes? How can they just spend their lives pretending they're Anno Domini?"

"They're not pretending," I told her.

"But this *isn't* the Seventeenth Century."

"For them it is. They know of nothing else. Weren't you warned about postchronic talk while you're here?"

"I thought it was just not to spoil the—the—flavor. They *don't know*?"

"Truth."

"But that's cruel—unfair!"

"Why? They're stuck in their lives just as you and I are imbedded in our own. Are we any less actors in someone else's drama than they?"

"Philosophy, like religion, is a very useful drug," she didacted, "but it should be used only to condone the evils we cannot control—and not those we create."

"You're quoting," I guessed.

"My most valued ability," she agreed. "I have a memory like a wideband slow-crystal—the input can't be erased without destructing the device. Do you condone this make-believe?"

"It isn't make-believe. And convince me that it's evil."

"But it's so limited——"

"They have the whole world. Their world—the world of the Seventeenth."

"They don't—not in any real sense. This whole area can't be bigger than—than——"

She looked to me for help. I shrugged. "I don't know either. But however large it is, it's also—in a very real sense—unbounded. How much can a man expect to see in one normal lifetime—especially limited to horses and sailing ships for transportation? Any of these people who wish to go to France or the New World will get there. Aided by Anno Domini, they will arrive in their France without noticing whatever odd maneuvering the ship does in the 'Channel'. I've taken that trip.''

"What would happen if I decided to get up and just walk—'' she pointed off to the left—"that way, in a straight line?''

"You'd come to the edge,'' I said. "Wherever that is.''

"Yes. Suppose I were a native—a resident—then what?''

"Then you'd probably fall asleep by the side of the road, and when you woke you'd suddenly remember urgent business back in town, or forget what you were doing there in the first place. And you'd never have the urge to roam again.''

"You mean they dethink and rethink these people? Just to keep them putting on a show for us?''

"Also to keep them happy.'' I argued. "It's for their own good. Think how they'd feel if they knew they were part of a display. This way they live out their lives without knowing of any options. It's no more unfair to live here than it was to live in the actual Seventeenth Century. A lot better: the food is adequate, diseases are eliminated, sanitation is much improved.''

"It sounds like an argument for slavery,'' Diana snapped. "Or pigfarming!''

We had come to what had to be the main street of the district. It was paved and lit. Bayswater High Street, the signpost read. The lights were open flames on stanchions, bright enough to mark the way but not to illuminate. "Perhaps we had better head back,'' I suggested. "In another half-hour it will be too dark to see our way.''

"The moon will be up in twenty minutes,'' Diana told me. "And it's only two days off full. Plenty of light.''

"Example of your memory?'' I asked.

She nodded. "I saw a chart once.''

The houses were two and three story, the upper stories overlapping the first. Picturesque in daylight, they were transformed at dusk into squatting ogres lurking behind the streetlights. The few people left on the street were scurrying like singleminded rats toward their holes.

"Some things are changeless," I said, pointing my walking stick at a receding back. "Fear of the night is one such. These people fear footpads and cutthroats—our people fear the stars. Evolution, I fear, is too slow a process. Our subconscious is still a million years behind us—in the caves of our youth."

"You mean that literally?" Diana asked. "About our people fearing the stars?"

"Extraordinarily literally. Astrophobia is the current mode. Not a fear of standing under the stars, like Chicken Little, but fear that, circling one of those points of light, is the race that will destroy humanity. The government spends billions each year in pursuit of this fear. I believe that it couples with the subconscious belief that we deserve to be destroyed. That all Earth has turned its back to the stars to live wholly in the past is part of the syndrome."

Diana asked me a question then, something about the deeper manifestations of this ailment, and I prattled on about how easy it was to recognize the problem, but no one was getting it cured because it was chronolous to declare the inside of your head sacrosanct—if you were of high enough status to make it stick. I'm not sure of what I said, as most of my attention was on three sets of approaching footsteps I was attempting to analyze without alarming Diana. In step, but not in the rhythm of soldiers—a slightly slower, swaggering step. Three young dandies out for an evening's entertainment, no doubt.

They rounded the corner and appeared under the light. They were well dressed, indeed foppishly dressed, and carrying swords—so they were gentlemen of this time. Or at least they were sons of gentlemen.

"What say?" the first one said, seeing us.

"Say what?" the second demanded.

"What?" asked the third. "What ho!" he amended,

strutting toward us. "What have we here? A lissome lass, begad! And unescorted."

"Madam," the first said, "my lady, ma'am. Chivalry is not dead! We shall prove this."

Diana looked puzzled, but completely unafraid. I don't know how I looked—I felt weak. "Get behind me," I instructed her.

"Yes, indeed," the third amplified, "we shall chivalrously rescue you from that old man there, who's clearly attempting to have his way with you."

"We shall," the second added, "expect a suitable reward."

"Is this some game?" Diana asked me.

"No," I told her. "These lads are going to try to kill me. If they succeed they'll kill you, too—eventually."

The first drew his sword. I twisted the handle of my stick until I felt it click. We were now about even—three swords against one sword-stick with a narcospray tip. Anyone within one meter of the front of the tip would fall inanimate ten seconds after he was hit—and I should be able to keep even three of them away for ten seconds.

"These are truly enemies?" Diana asked me, staring up into my eyes. There was an undercurrent of excitement in her expression.

"Yes," I said briefly. "But don't worry. Just stay——"

"I trust you," she said, nodding as though she had just made a prime decision. "Enemies!" Then she was in motion.

She dove forward onto her shoulder and pushed off as she rolled, catching the first one on the chin with the heel of her boot. He flew backward and came to a skidding stop on his back across the street. The second was just starting to react when she slammed him across the side of his head with her forearm. He slid slowly to the ground, folding in the middle as he dropped.

The third was aware of his danger, although he had no clear idea of what this whirlwind was. His sword was up and he was facing her. I managed one step toward them when, with a small cry of joy, she was past his guard and had fastened both of her hands around his throat. She must have known just where to press with her small fingers, because he didn't struggle, didn't even gasp—he just crumpled. She went down with him, keeping her grip. Her eyes were alive with excitement and she was grinning. She had, somehow, not the look of a person who has vanquished a foe, but more that of a terrier who has cornered a rat.

"All right," I said, going over and pulling her off. "It's all right. It's all over."

She looked up, small and sweet and innocent, except for a rip in the right sleeve of her dress. "He's still alive, this one."

"No!" I yelled, when I saw her hands tighten around his throat.

She stared at me. "The other two, they are dead."

"Leave him," I instructed.

"Yes." She stood up, sounding disappointed.

I took her hand and led her away. I began to tremble slightly—a touch of aftershock. Diana was calm and gentle. I had no empathy for the three ruffians—they had danced to their own tune—but I worried about Diana. No—I think rather she frightened me. I was not concerned with the ease with which she dispatched—body combat ballet is not new to me. I worried rather about the joy with which she destroyed.

I remembered to disarm the stick, so as not to shoot myself in the foot. "Diana," I said, picking my words not to offend, "I admire the way you handled those men. It shows great skill and training. But when a man is down—more particularly when he is unconscious—you don't have to kill him."

"But he was an enemy. You said so."

Semantic problem—or something more?

"Christopher?" We stopped at the innyard and she stared up at me, her eyes wide.

"Yes?" Tears were forming in the corners of her eyes and she was shaking. Delayed reaction? I held her and stroked her long hair.

"Those men wanted to hurt us. It wasn't a secondary thing, like wanting to take our money and hurting us if we resisted. They *just* wanted to hurt us."

"True."

"Why would anyone behave like that?"

It wasn't the fight that had her upset, but the morals of her opponents. "You killed two of them and were working on the third," I reminded her.

"But that was their doing. You said they were enemies. They declared status, not I. They attacked unprovoked. And I had your word."

"Right," I said, deciding to watch my words around this girl who took my definitions so literally and acted on them with such finality. "Well, they behaved that way because they've been taught to think it's fun."

"I don't understand," she said.

"Neither do I," I agreed.

We retired to our separate rooms and I spent some time studying the cracks in the ceiling in an effort to think before I fell asleep.

Diana and I spent the next ten days together in Shakespere's London. Diana was delighted by everything and I was delighted by her. We grew closer together in that indefinable way men and women grow closer together, with neither of us mentioning it but both of us quite aware. She questioned me incessantly about everything, but gave little detail in return. I learned she had no family and grew up in a special school run by Earth government. I learned how beautiful she was, inside and out, in motion and in stillness.

After the first week we shared the same room. Luckily Seventeen was a time that allowed of such a change. The innkeeper persisted in winking at me whenever he could, until I felt I had earned that dinner, but we suffered no other hardship for our affection.

Then one day over breakfast we decided to abandon the

Seventeenth Century. I voted for the Twentieth, and Diana ayed, although she knew little of it. "Those are the breakthrough years, aren't they?" she asked. "First flights to the nearer planets!"

I munched on a bacon stick. "Out of the cradle and into the nursery," I said. "And the babes yelling, 'No, no, I don't *want* to walk—haven't learned to crawl properly yet.' As though that skill were going to be of value to them in the future. Interesting times. As in the ancient curse."

"Curse?" Diana asked, wide-eyed as a child.

I nodded. "May your children live in interesting times," I said. "Chinese."

"Not much of a curse," Diana insisted. "Where are the mummies' hearts and the vampires and such?"

"Now that would be interesting," I said. After breakfast I pushed the call for Anno Domini and they removed us in a coach. They declothed us and reclothed us and backgrounded us and thrust us into an aeroplane.

III

This dubious contrivance, all shiny and silver and with two whole piston engines—to keep us going forward so we wouldn't fall down—flew us to LaGuardia Field outside New York City. The field, like the aeroplane, was sleek and shiny and new and modern. Everything was modern—it was in the air. The modern taxi drove us to the modern city with its modern skyscrapers muraled with the most modern art. The year was 1938 and nothing could go wrong.

We checked into the Plaza and took a tenth-floor suite overlooking Central Park. It was evening and the park lights, glowing over the paths, roads, fields, rocks, ponds, streams, lakes and other structured wildnesses, turned it into a rectangular fairyland. The skyline surrounding the park was civilization surrounding and oppressing imagination, keeping it behind high walls and ordering its ways. This is known as interpretive sightseeing.

Diana had a lot of things she wanted to do. She wanted to see a play and a movie and a zoo and an ocean liner and a war and a soap opera and a rocket leaving for the moon.

"Everything but the rocket," I told her. "Your timing's off by about thirty years. They haven't even designed the machines to build the machines to build the rocket yet."

We compromised on a visit to the top of the Empire State Building, the closest thing to a trip to the moon that 1938 New York could provide.

"This is all real, isn't it?" Diana asked as we wandered around the guard rail, peering at Bronx tenements and Jersey slums.

"In a sense," I said.

"I mean the buildings are buildings, not sets, and the streets are streets and the river is a river and the ships are ships."

"And the people are people," I agreed. "The original had ten million, I believe. One of the three largest cities of the time. That's a lot of people to stuff into a small area and move around by automobile and subway."

She nodded. "How many people are here now—residents, I mean?"

"I don't know," I told her. "I doubt if they have the full original millions."

"Still," she said seriously, "it would be fair to say that there are a great many."

"That would be fair," I agreed.

"Why are they here?"

"It's getting chilly," I said, buttoning the two top buttons on my coat. "Let's go eat dinner."

"How can we justify bilking so many people out of their lives—out of whatever value their lives might have—by making them live in an artificial past?"

"How do their lives have any less value here than in realtime?" I asked in my best Socratic manner.

"Suppose you were an inventor," Diana hypothesized. "How would you feel to discover that you had reinvented the wheel, or the typer, or the bloaterjet?"

"I'd never know it was a reinvention," I said.

"But it would be. And you would have been cheated out of whatever good and new and beautiful you could have invented in realtime."

"I doubt Anno Domini encourages invention," I said.

"Worse! Where shall we eat dinner?"

We took a Domino Cab uptown to the Central Park Casino, to where Glenn Miller and his band were providing the dinner music. The music must have soothed Diana, since we got through the rib roast and into the crepes suzette before the sociology seminar continued.

"What about people like Glenn Miller here—or Shakespere—who were real people in history? Are they actors?"

"No, they're mindplants. Each of them has the personality and ability of the character he becomes, to the best of our ability to re-create it."

Diana sat silent for a minute, considering, her mouth puckered into a tight line and her eyebrows pulled down in concentration. She stared at her spoon. Then she picked it up and waved it at me. "That's disgusting. You don't merely cheat them out of the future—you cheat them out of their very lives."

It was my turn to be silent. I was silent through *String of Pearls* and *Goldberg's Blues*. Diana watched me as though expecting momently to see wisdom fall from my lips, or possibly smoke rise from my ears. I found myself uncomfortably defending policies I had never really thought about before. I tried to think it out, but was distracted by Diana's stare. I felt that I had to look as if I were thinking and it's very hard to work at looking the part and think at the same time.

"I would say it's more productive rather than less," I said when I had the idea sorted out. "You know our Shakespere has added several plays to the list that the original never got around to writing. *Saint Joan* and *Elizabeth the First* and, I think, *Timon of Athens*—those are his. We haven't cheated him. Both he and humanity have benefited from this arrangement."

"It's not an arrangement," Diana stated positively. "It's a manipulation. It takes two to make an arrangement. Let's dance."

There is something deeply satisfying about two bodies pressed together and moving together. The waltz and the foxtrot are more purely sexual than either the stately minuet before them or the frenzied hump after. We glided about the floor, letting our bodies work at becoming one.

"Christopher," Diana said.

"Hm?"

"I'm glad we've become friends."

"More than friends?"

"That, too," she said, squeezing against me. "But friends is something else. I think you're my only friend."

"I hope you exaggerate," I said. "That's very sad."

We danced silently for a moment. Then Diana stopped and pulled me back to our table. We sat down. "This is a major thing, isn't it?"

"Friendship?"

"No. Anno Domini and this whole re-creation. How many different historical times are there?"

"You're so beautiful and so serious and so young," I said. "And so intent—and so knowledgeable in some fields and so ignorant in others. Whoever brought you up had strange educational values."

"I told you I don't like talking about that," she said. Her expression could best be described as petulant.

"It requires no conversation," I told her. "Fifty."

"Fifty historical periods?" she said, instantly picking up the thread. One of the things I admired, that ability. "But there aren't that many centuries!"

"Many are covered with more than one set. The really popular ones are started every twenty-five years. All have one, at least. There may be some centuries that appeal not at all to you, but someone has a need for them."

"What sort of need? Why that word?"

"Ah! Now we speak of purpose: what you asked me before. The past is Earth's only industry. Its function is to hold together the more than two hundred diverse human cultures, spread out on close to a thousand planets, circling as many suns. Tens of thousands of people from all these planets, all these new directions for humankind, are here at any one time, sharing the one thing they all have in common: the past.

"This maintains Earth's preeminence in the councils of man and presumably bolsters her prominence in the Parliament of Stars. But more important: it provides a living point of origin for the human race.

"The psychologists decided over four hundred years ago, at the time of the Mabden Annihilation, that this was the best—perhaps the only—way to hold us together. Those of us who weren't already too far out. There are external threats still, you know."

"I know," Diana said dryly. "You mentioned the fear syndrome earlier in this connection."

"It should be taken seriously," I insisted. "Here on Earth you feel secure, but it's only because you're so far away from the action. The Denzii——"

"I take it very seriously," Diana assured me. "So seriously that I'd prefer not to talk about it even now."

"Yes. I didn't mean to frighten you."

"Frighten?" Diana smiled gently. "No, you don't do that. Tell me, what else is there to do in this year, in this town?"

We took the subway to the Battery and walked quietly on the grass around the Aquarium, which was closed and shuttered for the night. Then we took the ferry over to Staten Island and stood in the open on the top deck, letting the cold brinewind flap our coats and sting our cheeks. We waved to the Statue of Liberty and she smiled at us—or perhaps it was a trick of the light. I had my coat wrapped around Diana and she huddled against my chest and I felt young and bold and ready to explore uncharted worlds. We talked of minor things and we shared a cup of coffee, black and four sugars, and I think, perhaps, realized fully that we were in love.

The next day we went to the Bronz Zoo in the morning,

came back to Manhattan in early afternoon for a matinee of
Our Town, and then returned to the hotel to dress. A man
was waiting in the sitting room of our suite. He was
standing.

"Why, Kroner," Diana said, "how delightful to see
you. And how silly you look in those clothes here." Thus
she effectively suppressed the *Who are you and what are
you doing in my room?* that I had been about to contribute
to the occasion. Kroner was a short man with too much
hair on his head. He wore a onesuit that squeezed around
his stocky, overly muscled body. The weightlifter is a
physical type I have always disliked. I didn't recognize the
Identification and Position badge he wore, except that it
was medium-high status and something to do with
education.

"Who is he?"

"Kroner," Diana said. "My professor—or one of.
And this is Christopher Mar."

"Delighted." Clearly he lied.

"Surprised," I said. We touched hands. "To what do
we owe this visit and what may we do for you? Any
professor of Diana's——" I waved a hand vaguely. The
current trend toward the vague can be very useful in
conversation.

"I suppose you know what you're doing?" Kroner
asked coldly.

"I have no idea of what that means," I told him. "At
which of us are you sneering?"

"Both of you, I suppose," Kroner said. He sighed and
sat down on the sofa. "You're right, I was being hostile.
And there's no reason. You're a very important man,
Senior Senator Mar—there's no way I can threaten you.
And Grecia knows I'm only interested in protecting and
helping her. When she disappeared from Seventeen without notifying us——"

"Who?" I interrupted.

"Grecia. Your companion."

"Is that right?" I asked Diana (Grecia).

She nodded.

"Of course you have a perfect right——"

"What does she call herself?" Kroner asked.

"Diana Seven," I said. Diana (Grecia) looked defiant-ly down at Kroner and remained silent.

Kroner nodded thoughtfully. "Of course," he said. "A clear choice. Then he doesn't know? You haven't told him?"

"No," Diana (Grecia) said. "Why should I?"

"Of course," Kroner repeated. "From your point of view, no reason. You've always been the most stubborn and independent-minded. No matter how much we strive for uniformity. Not that we mind, you understand—it's just that the variations make the training more difficult to program. I suppose it will make you harder to predict in action, so it's all for the best."

"Haven't told me what?" I demanded. I tried to picture some horrible secret, but nothing would come to mind.

"Diana Seven is not a name," Kroner told me, "it's a designation. Choosing it as her alias is the sort of direct thinking we've come to expect from Grecia."

"It's a comment," Diana (Grecia) said.

"Grecia is number seven in an official government program known as Project Diana," Kroner said. "The number is arbitrary."

"So is the name," Diana (Grecia) said. "You know how I was named? Listen, I'll recite the names of the first seven girls, in order—that should give you the idea: Ade-na, Beth, Claudia, Debra, Erdra, Fidlia, Grecia. It goes on like that. I prefer Diana Seven, it's more honest."

"Diana Seven you are to me forever," I told her. "I don't understand, though. What sort of government project?"

"This is going to sound silly," Kroner said, managing to look apologetic, "but I don't think you have the need to know."

"I might not have the—but I do indeed need to know very badly, and I can develop the official Need to Know in a very few minutes realtime."

"I will tell everything," Diana said, sitting down on a

straight-back chair and crossing her shapely legs. "What do you push to get them to bring up drinks?"

"I'll do it," I said, picking up the housephone and dialing. "What would you like?"

"Coffee," Diana said.

"Another profession," Kroner said. "I guess you're right—we'd better talk about it."

"Something harder than coffee for you," I said, and ordered a pot of coffee and a portable bar sent up.

"Grecia——"

"Call her Diana—she prefers it."

Kroner shrugged. He was not very happy. "Diana is a GAM. Project Diana is one of a series of GAM projects that Future is funding."

GAM = Genetically Altered Man. GAMs were in disfavor now, at least on Earth, as it was felt that no alteration of the zygote could make up for a happy home life, or some such illogic.

"I thought the Bureau of the Future was only involved in long-range planning of city growth and transportation and that sort of thing," I said.

"And defense," Kroner told me. "Diana is a defense project."

That stopped me. I went into the bedroom to take off my tie and think of something clever to ask.

"What do you mean, 'a defense project'?" I cleverly asked when I returned. The bar was ported in then, so I had to wait for my answer. The waiter tried hard to preserve his air of waiterly detachment and not stare at Kroner, and even harder not to smile.

Kroner glared at him and stood up, flexing his biceps under the skintight onesuit. "What's the matter?" he demanded. "What are you staring at? Haven't you ever seen a Frog Prince before?"

The waiter merely gulped and fled the room. We all burst out laughing and I remembered that in my youth one of my closest friends had been a weightlifter. "You really should have dressed for the period," I told Kroner.

He shrugged. "I was wearing a period overcoat," he said, gesturing to a crumpled garment lying over a chair.

I fixed our various drinks and we sipped them and stared at each other. "We've been keeping an eye on the girls while they were on their travels," Kroner said. "When Diana took off with you we got worried. Diana has a certain reputation among the staff as a trouble-maker and you are a—prominent senator. The combination could be explosive."

"How?" I asked.

"The projects are played down," Kroner said. "For us, any press is bad. We'd be caught between two fires: those who are afraid of any GAM projects—the 'The only good superman is a dead superman' group—and those who would feel sorry for Diana and her sisters—poor little girls deprived of a home life and mother love and apple pie."

"It might have been nice, you know, all that stuff," Diana said, a surface anger in her voice covering some deeper emotion. "Why do people decide they have the right to do what's good for other people?"

"What?" I asked, feeling ignorant and ignored.

"We didn't exactly do it because it was good for you," Kroner said sadly. "We did it because it was necessary for us. We never lied to you about that."

"Great ethics," Diana said in a low, clipped voice that had an undertone of controlled scream. "We screwed up your life from before you were born, but at least we didn't lie to you—and that makes it all all right." She turned to me. "Did you know I'm a mule?" she demanded.

"What?"

"A mule. Or perhaps a hinny. Except instead of a cross between a jackass and a mare, I'm a cross between a human gamete and a micro-manipulator. Sterile."

"You mean you're——"

"No pills, no inserts, no children—no chance. Just me. Dead end. Supermule."

I went over to hold her, to show I understood, but she drew away. Mulelike, I couldn't help thinking, in her anger. "I'm on your side, you know," I said to her. She nodded, but stayed encased in herself.

I asked Kroner, "In what way is this girl a weapon?"

"Not a weapon," Kroner said. "More like a soldier."

"A hunting dog," Diana said. Well, it was a better self-image than a mule.

Kroner nodded. "In a way. Superfast reflexes, for one thing. One of the reasons she's small: information travels to the brain faster. Nerves react and transmit faster. Eyes see farther into the infrared and ultraviolet. Raw strength is of little use today. You know how old she is?"

I didn't. "I'm not good at guessing age," I said.

"Twelve," Kroner said.

There was, I believe, a long pause then.

"Do you mind?" Diana asked softly.

"I am surprised," I said.

"The tendency in naturally evolved high intelligence is for longer childhoods, not shorter," Kroner said. "You must experience more, cogitate more, and have more time to experiment—play—to develop a really high intelligence potential. But it is possible to mature a high intelligence very quickly in an extremely enriched environment. Twelve years from birth to adult is about the best we can manage. The body takes that long to grow and mature anyway, if we want a comparatively normal body."

"Diana is an adult," I said. "No matter how many times, or how few, the Earth has circled the sun since her birth."

Kroner nodded. "Diana is a highly capable adult, able to handle herself well in almost any situation."

"I'll not argue that," I said. "She dispatched three ruffians who attacked us and did so with unseemly ease."

"Ah!" Kroner said. "We thought that was she. Very good, Diana. Of course, that's what she's been trained and bred for, so it's fitting that she did."

"Trained for close combat?" I asked. "What sort of war are you expecting?"

"Not that," Kroner explained. "For you, as for most of

the rest of humanity, killing any sentient being—and many lower animals—would be murder. You'd have to steel yourself and be highly motivated to perform the act. For Diana, killing anything that isn't human—or even humans who are clearly 'enemy'—is equivalent to hunting. And, like a good hunting dog, she enjoys it. Isn't that so, Diana?''

She nodded. ''I can't see anything wrong with killing an enemy. And the fact that I know this is genetics and conditioning doesn't matter—all attitudes anyone has are a result of genetics and conditioning. If you gentlemen will excuse me, it's been a long day and I think I'll go to bed.''

Kroner and I spoke privately for a short while after Diana retired. I suspect Diana listened at the door, as she was awake when I went to bed, but if so I'm glad of it.

''Does this mean I have to worry about Diana's getting angry at me and breaking my neck?'' I asked Kroner, when she had left.

''Not at all,'' he said. ''If anything, the opposite. She may tend to overprotect you. To kill a human being who is not an enemy would, in any case, be murder, and she is incapable of murder.''

''How does she determine an enemy?''

''I think, at the moment, she'll take your word for it. She appears to be fixated on you. You may call it love, if you like, but we prefer the scientific term.''

''I appear to be fixated on her,'' I said. ''Whatever you call it.''

''That's fine. We approve. As long as you aren't planning to use her—or make a political issue or anything of that sort—we're on your side.''

''What is she doing here anyway? Is school out? Vacation?''

Kroner fixed himself another drink. ''No,'' he said. ''This is part of her training. Mixing with humanity to learn more fully what it is she may be fighting for. Two years of this—going and doing more or less where and what she wants—then she'll be ready for, let's call it graduate school.''

"More fixating?"

"That's right. Fixating on man. Those in charge of this project seem a bit afraid of their creation."

"Historical precedent," I said. "Or, at least, literary."

"Yes," Kroner said. "Take care of Diana. Enjoy her. Love her. She needs more love than the other girls."

"You mean she fixates more strongly?" I asked.

Kroner smiled. "As of now," he said, "I'm on vacation. Bye." He picked up his coat and left.

I went in to sleep with Diana and she held me tight for a long while. I think she would have cried if she had known how. I held her, but it's hard to comfort someone who cannot cry.

Back in realtime—away from Earth and Anno Domini—I used my status to find out about the Project. Diana opted to stay with me. We fixated well together.

It was difficult, even for me, to open the private record of Project Diana. It was the most recent in a line of such projects dating back to shortly after the Mabden Annihilation. I immersed myself in it and read motive, intent, achievement, method, fear and design in the record crystals.

Earth is afraid of its heroes. Always has been.

Diana is sterile by design. Female by convenience—easier to control without the Y chromosome. Sterile by design. Safer. Can't breed a superrace behind our backs.

Diana's cells won't regenerate. Our long life depends upon regeneration—actually replication—of certain cells. Diana's—let us call it template—is inaccessible to our techniques. Also by design. Safer thus. Can't make long-range plans behind our backs. She will also age fast and be old by forty—probably dead by fifty.

I went home that evening and cried myself to sleep. Diana held me, but the crying frightened her and she couldn't help because I wouldn't tell her why, and it's hard to comfort someone unless you know why he's crying.

I have two years with her before she has to go off to prepare for the war we may never have. She wants to go. They want her for twenty-five years, she says, and she owes them that.

We're planning what we will do when she returns. There are so many things she wants to do and see in this vast galaxy. I promised to show them all to her.

I hardly cry at all any more, even late at night.

THE SHORT ONES

Raymond E. Banks

In the early 1950s a gifted crew of ingenious and vigorous new writers—Robert Sheckley, Philip K. Dick, Algis Budrys, Walter Miller, Philip Jose Farmer, and more—came sweeping into science fiction and transformed it as thoroughly as Messrs. Heinlein, Van Vogt, Sturgeon, Leiber, and Asimov had done a dozen or so years before. Raymond E. Banks was one of the most promising of the postwar crop, although his name is rarely mentioned today. He sold a story to *Esquire* in 1946, when he was about 28 and newly out of the army, but didn't begin serious full-time writing until 1952. Over the next eight or ten years he published perhaps forty s-f stories, most of them in fairly ephemeral magazines; then his name vanished from the tables of contents. What, if anything, he is writing today, or even where he is living, I have no idea. For him science fiction was evidently a passing phase in a life that took other directions. At any rate, herewith 1955's "The Short Ones," one of his best—a warm and rich story that displays rather more political sophistication than most of us had in those innocent days.

Valsek came out of his hut and looked at the sky. As usual it was milk-white, but grayed down now to predawn somberness.

"Telfus!"

The sleepy face of his hired man peered over a rock, behind which he had slept.

"We must plow today," said Valsek. "There'll be no rain."

"Did a god tell you this?" asked Telfus, a groan in his voice.

Valsek stumbled over a god-wire before he could answer. Another exposed god-wire! Important things were stirring and he had to drive this farm-hand clod to his labor.

"If you are to sleep in my field and eat at my table, you must work," said Valsek angrily. He bent to examine the god-wire. The shock to his hands told him there was a feeble current running in it which made his magnetic backbone tingle. Vexing, oh vexing, to know that current ran through the wire and through you, but not to know whether it was the current of the old god Melton, or the new god, Hiller!

"Bury this god-wire at once," he told Telfus. "It isn't neat to have the god-wires exposed. How can I make contact with Hiller when he can see my fields unplowed and my god-wires exposed? He will not choose me Spokesman."

"Did this Hiller come to you in the night?" asked Telfus politely.

"In a way, in a way," said the prophet testily. It was hard to know. It was time for a new god, but you could miss it by weeks.

Valsek's wife came over the hill, carrying a pail of milk warm from the goat.

"Was there a sign last night?" she asked, pausing before the hut.

Valsek gave his wife a cold stare. "Naturally there was a sign," he said. "I do not sleep on the cold stone of the barn floor because it pleases my bones. I have had several portents from Hiller."

His wife looked resigned. "Such as?"

Short Ones! Valsek felt contempt inside of him. All of the Short Ones were fools. It was the time for a new god, and they went around milking goats and asking about signs. Short Ones! (And what god had first revealed to them that name? And why, when they were the tallest living beings in all the world?)

"The wind blew last night," he said.

"The wind blows every night," she said.

He presented his hard conviction to the cutting blade of her scorn.

"About midnight it rained," he persisted. "I had just got through suggesting rain to the new god, Hiller."

"Now was that considerate?" asked Telfus, still leaning on his rock. "Your only hired hand asleep in the fields outside and you ask for rain."

"There is no Hiller," said Valsek's wife, tightening her lips. "It rains every midnight this time of year. And there will be no corn if you keep sleeping in the barn, making those stupid clay images and avoiding work."

"Woman," said Valsek, "god-business is important. If Hiller chooses me for Spokesman to all the Short Ones we shall be rich."

But his wife was tired, perhaps because she had had to pull the plow yesterday for Telfus. "Ask Hiller to send us a bushel of corn," she said coldly. "Then I will come into the barn and burn a manure stick to him."

She went into the hut, letting the door slam.

"If it is permitted to sleep in the barn," said Telfus, "I will help you fashion your clay idols. Once in King Giron's courtyard I watched an artist fashion a clay idol for Melton, and I think I might have a hand for it, if it is permitted to sleep in the barn."

Blasphemers! Worldly blasphemers! "It is not permitted to sleep in the barn," said Valsek. "I have spent many years in the barn, reaching out for each new god as he or she came, and though I have not yet made contact, it is a dedicated place. You have no touch for prophecy."

"I have seen men go mad, each trying to be picked Spokesman to the gods for the Short Ones," said Telfus. "The chances are much against it. And consider the fate of the Spokesman once the year of his god is over."

Valsek's eyes flashed angrily. "Consider the fate of the Spokesman in his prime. Power, rich power in the time of your god, you fool, if you are Spokesman. And afterwards many Spokesmen become members of the Prophets' Association—with a pension. Does life hold more?"

Telfus decided not to remind his employer that usually the new Spokesman felt it necessary to execute the old Spokesman of the used-up god.

"Perhaps it is only that my knees are too tender for god-business," he said, sighing against the rock.

"Quiet now," said Valsek. "It is time for dawn. I have asked Hiller for a portent, to show his choice of me as Spokesman. A dawn portent."

They turned to watch the dawn. Even Valsek's wife came out to watch, for Valsek was always asking for a dawn portent. It was his favorite suggestion to the gods.

Dawn came. There was a flicker of flashing, magic lights, much, much faster than the slow flame of a tallow taper that the Short Ones used for light. One-two-three-four-five, repeated, one-two-three-four-five. And then the day was upon them. In an instant the gray turned to milk-white and the day's heat fell.

"Ah!" cried Valsek. "The dawn light flashed six times. Hiller is the new god. I am his Spokesman! I must hurry to the market place in town with my new idol!"

Telfus and the wife exchanged looks. Telfus was about to point out that there had been only the usual five lights of dawn, but the wife shook her head. She pointed a scornful finger to the horizon where a black pall of smoke lingered in the sky.

"Yesterday there were riots," she said. "Fighting and the burning of things. If you take your new idol to the market place, you will insult either the followers of King Giron or the followers of Melton. One or the other, they will carve your heart out, old man!"

But it was no use. Valsek had rushed back into the barn to burn a manure stick to Hiller and start his journey, on the strength of the lights of dawn.

Valsek's wife stared down at her work-stained hands

and sighed. "Now I suppose I should prepare a death sheet
for him," she said.

"No," said Telfus, wearily picking up the harness from
the ground. "They will only laugh at him and he will live
forever while you and I die from doing the world's work.
Come, Mrs. Valsek, assume the harness, so that I may
walk behind and plow a careful furrow in his fields."

Time: One month earlier . . . or half an hour.
Place: The Pentagon, Washington, D.C.
The Life Hall.

In the vast, gloomy auditorium the scurryings and
scuttlings of the Short Ones rose to a climax beneath the
opaque, milky glass that covered the colony. Several
spectators rose in their seats. At the control panel, Charles
Melton also rose.

"The dials!" cried his adviser.

But Melton was past tending the dials. He jerked the
control helmet off his head a second too late. A blue
flash from the helmet flickered in the dark room. Short
circuit!

Melton leaned over the glass, trying to steady himself,
and vomited blood. Then a medical attendant came and
escorted him away, as his adviser assumed the dials and
his helmet.

A sigh from the spectators. They bent and peered at
Melton from the seats above his level, like medical stu-
dents in an operating theâtre. The poltiical career of .
Charles Melton was over: he had failed the Life Hall
Test.

A technician tapped some buttons and the lighted sign,
visible to all, changed:

TEST 39167674
HILLER, RALPH, ASSISTANT SECRETARY OF DEFENSE, USA
TEST TIME: 6 HOURS
OBJECTIVE: BLUE CERTIFICATE TO PROVE LEADERSHIP
        QUALITIES
ADVISER: DR. CYNTHIA WOLLRATH

Cynthia Wollrath!

Ralph Hiller turned from the door of the Ready Room and paced. What rotten luck he was having! To begin with, his test started right after some inadequate Judge-applicant had failed badly and gotten the Short Ones all upset. On top of that, they had assigned his own former wife to be adviser. How unethical can you get?

He was sure now that his enemies in the Administration had given him a bad test position and picked a prejudiced adviser to insure his failure—that was typical of the Armstrong crowd. He felt the hot anger on his face. They weren't going to get away with this. . . .

Cynthia came into the Ready Room then, dressed in the white uniform of the Life Hall Staff, and greeted him with a cool, competent nod.

"I'm rather surprised that I've been given a prejudiced adviser," he said.

"I'm sorry. The Board considered me competent to sit in on this test."

"Did you tell them that we were once married?"

She sighed. "No. You did that in at least three memorandums, I believe. Shall we proceed with the briefing?"

"The Board knows you dislike me," he said. "They know I could lose my sanity in there. You could foul me up and no one would be the wiser. I won't stand for it."

Her eyes were carefully impartial. "I don't dislike you. And I rather think that the Board chose me because they felt that it would help you out. They feel I know your personality, and in something as dangerous as the Life Hall Tests they try to give all the applicants a break."

"My father died in that chair," he said. "My uncle——"

"You aren't your father. Nor your uncle. Shall we start? We're late. This is a Short One——"

She held up a figure, two inches high, a perfectly formed little man, a dead replica of the life below. In her other hand she held a metal sliver that looked like a three-quarter-inch needle. "The Short Ones are artificial creatures of living protoplasm, except for this metallic backbone imbedded in each. It is magnetic material——"

"I want a postponement."

"Bruce Gerard of the *Times* is covering this test," she said patiently. "His newspaper is not favorable to the Administration. He would like to report a postponement in a Life Hall Test by an important Administration figure. Now, Ralph, we really must get on with this. There are many other testees to follow you to the chair."

He subsided. He held his temper in. That temper that had killed his father, almost destroyed his uncle. That temper that would be put to the most severe test known to men for the next few hours. He found it difficult to concentrate on her words.

"—wires buried in the ground of the Colony, activate the Short Ones—a quarter of a million Short Ones down there—one of our minutes is a day to them—your six hours of testing cover a year of their lives—"

He knew all that. A Blue Certificate Life Hall Test was rather like an execution and you studied up on it long before. Learned how science had perfected this tiny breed. How there had been opposition to them until the beginnings of the Life Hall. In today's world the Short Ones protected the people from inefficient and weak leaders. To hold an important position, such as his Cabinet job, you had to have a Life Hall Certificate. You had to prove out your leadership wisdom over the roiling, boiling generations of Short Ones before you could lead mankind. The test was rightfully dangerous; the people could expect their leaders to have true ability if they passed the test, and the false leaders and weaklings either never applied, or were quickly broken down by the Short Ones.

"Let's go," said Cynthia.

There was a stir from the audience as they entered the auditorium. They recognized him. Many who had been resting with their spectator helmets off reassumed them. A wave of tense expectancy seemed to come from them. The people knew about the failure of his father and his uncle.

This looked like a blood test and it was fascinating to see a blood test.

Ralph took his position in the chair with an inward sigh. It was too late now to change anything. He dare not embarrass the Administration before a hostile reporter. He let Cynthia show him the inside of the Director's helmet with its maze of wires.

"Since their time runs so fast, you can't possibly read out each and every mind of the Short Ones down there," she said. "You can handle perhaps half a dozen. Step-down transformers will allow you to follow their lives. They are your leaders and representatives down in the world of the Short Ones.

"These knob hand dials are your mechanical controls down there. There are hydraulic linkages which give you power to change the very seas, cause mountains to rise and valleys to form. Their weather is in your control, for when you think of weather, by an electronic signal through the helmet, you cause rain or sun, wind or stillness. The left hand dial is destructive, the right hand dial is constructive. As the current flows throughout the system, your thoughts and wishes are impressed upon the world of the Short Ones, through your leaders. You can back up your edicts by smashing the very ground under their feet. Should you desire to kill, a flick of the dial saturates the magnetized backbone of the unfortunate Short One, and at full magnetization all life ceases for them.

"Unfortunately, you are directing a dangerous amount of power in this system which courses within a fraction of an inch of your head in the control helmet. At each death down there a tiny amount less current is needed to control the Short Ones. At many deaths this wild current, no longer being drawn by the dead creatures, races through the circuits. Should too many die, you will receive a backlash of wild current before I can——"

Ralph nodded, put on the helmet and let the scurryings and scuttlings of the Short Ones burst in on his mind.

He sat straight, looking out over a sheet of milky glass

fifty feet across that covered the world below. He was sinking mentally into their world. With him, but fully protected, the spectators put on their helmets to sink into the Colony and witness the events below as he directed them.

The eerie light from the glass shone on the face of the medical attendant standing ready.

Ralph reached out his hands to start his test and gave himself a final admonition about his temper. At all costs he must curb it.

There is a temper that destroys and also one that demands things done by other men. Ralph had used his sternness well for most of the years of his life, but there had been times, bad times, when that fiery temperament had worked against him.

Like his marriage to Cynthia, ten years before. She had had a cool, scientific detachment about life which had attracted him. She had been a top student of psychology on the campus. At first her cool detachment had steadied him and enabled him to get started in his political career. But then it began to haunt him—her reasonableness against his storms; he had a growing compulsion to smash through her calmness and subjugate her to his will.

He had hurt her badly once.

He still felt the flame of embarrassment when he remembered her face in the bedroom, staring down at the nakedness of the other woman, staring at his own nakedness, as the adulterers lay on her bed, and the shivery calmness of his own nervous system at the expected interruption. And his words across the years:

"Why not? You seem to be sterile."

Foolish, hot ego of youth. He had meant to stir and shock a very proper Cynthia, and he had done so. Her moan of rage and hurt had made him for that triumphant moment the flamethrower he was destined to be.

He hadn't counted on a divorce, but then it was impossible for him to give up his victory. He was Ralph Hiller, a man who asked no favors——

Ah, that was ten years ago when he was barely twenty-five! Many times since the divorce he'd wished for her quiet calmness. She had stayed in the arms of science, never marrying again, preferring the well-lighted lab to the dark halls of passion. But such an act could rankle and burn over the years. . . .

The affairs of the Short Ones pressed impatiently on him, and he turned to his job with unsteady nerves.

When Valsek appeared, towing his clay idol of Hiller on a handcart, the soldiers were too drunk to be cruel to him. They merely pricked his buttocks with their swords and laughed at him. And the priests of Melton, likewise sated with violence, simply threw stones at him and encouraged the loiterers to upend the cart and smash the grinning nonentity of clay. Hiller indeed! Would a new god creep into their lives on a handcart pulled by a crazy old man? Go away, old man, go away.

Back at the farm Valsek found Telfus finishing up a new idol.

"You knew?" he asked sadly.

"It was somehow written in my mind that you would need a new idol," said Telfus. "I am quite enthusiastic about this new god, and if I may be permitted to sleep in the barn, I am sure that I would get the feel of him and help you do good works in his name."

"It is not permitted to sleep in the barn," grunted Valsek, easing his tender backside on a haypile. "Also I take notice that the plowing has stopped."

"Your wife fainted in the fields," said Telfus. "I could not bring myself to kick her back to consciousness as you ordered because I have a bad leg from sleeping on the ground. I have slept on the ground many, many years and it is not good for the leg."

The fire of fanaticism burned in Valsek's eyes. "Bother your leg," he said. "Place my new idol on the handcart; there are other towns and other ears to listen, and Hiller will not fail me."

•　　•　　•

In a short time Valsek had used up several of the idols to Hiller in various towns and was required to rest from the injuries given him by the scornful priests, the people and the soldiers.

"When I beg," said Telfus, "I place myself before the door of a rich man, not a poor one. Would it not be wisdom to preach before King Giron himself rather than the lesser figures? Since Melton is his enemy, the King might welcome a new god."

"You are mad," said Valsek. "Also, I do not like your latest idols. You are shirking on the straw which holds the clay together. I suspect you of eating my straw."

Telfus looked pained. "I would not dream of eating Hiller's straw," he said, "any more than I would dream of sleeping in the barn without permission. It is true, however, that your wife and goat occasionally get hungry."

Valsek waved a hand. "Prepare a knapsack. It has occurred to me that I should go to the very courtyard of the King himself and tell him of Hiller. After all, does a beggar beg at the door of a poor man?"

Telfus nodded. "An excellent idea, one I should've thought of."

"Prepare the knapsack," ordered Valsek. "We will go together."

At the gate of the palace itself, Telfus stopped. "Many Short Ones have died," he said, "because in the midst of a hazardous task they left no avenue of escape open. Therefore I shall entertain the guards at the gate with my juggling while you go on in. Should it be necessary for you to fly, I will keep the way open."

Valsek frowned. "I had planned for you to pull the idol-cart for me, Telfus, so that I might make a better impression."

"An excellent idea!" said Telfus. "But, after all, you have the company of Hiller, which is worth a couple of regiments. And I have a bad leg, and Hiller deserves a better appearance than to be pulled before a King by a limping beggar. Therefore I will remain at the gates and keep the way open for you.''

Valsek took the cart rope from Telfus, gave him a look of contempt and swept into the courtyard of King Giron.

King Giron, who had held power for more than a year now, stared out of his lofty bedroom window and listened to the words of Valsek carried on the wind from the courtyard below, as he preached to the loiterers. He turned white; in just such a fashion had he preached Melton the previous year. True, he no longer believed in Melton, but, since he was writing a bible for the worship of King Giron, a new god didn't fit into his plans. He ordered the guards to bring the man before him.

''Make a sign, old man,'' he directed. ''If you represent a new god, have him make a sign if, as you say, Melton is dead and Hiller is the new god.''

Valsek threw himself down and groveled to Hiller and asked for a sign. He crooned over Telfus' latest creation, asking for a sign. There was none. Ralph was being careful.

''But Hiller lives!'' cried Valsek as the guards dragged him upright and King Giron smiled cynically. ''Melton is dead! You can't get a sign from Melton either! Show me a sign from Melton!''

The two men stared at each other. True, Melton was gone. The King misdoubted that Melton had ever existed, except in the furious fantasies of his own mind which had been strong enough to convince other people. Here now was a test. If he could destroy the old man, that would prove him right—that the gods were all illusion and that the Short Ones could run their own affairs.

The King made a cutting sign across his own throat. The guards threw Valsek to his knees and one of them lifted a sharp, shining blade.

''Now cut his throat quickly,'' ordered the King, ''because I find him a very unlikely citizen.''

''Hiller,'' moaned Valsek, ''Hiller, I've believed in

you and still do. Now you must save me, for it is the last moment of my miserable life. Believe in me, Hiller!''

Sweat stood out on Ralph's brow. He had held his temper when the old man had been rejected by the others. He had hoped for a better Spokesman than this fanatic, but the other Short Ones were confused by King Giron's defiance of all gods and Valsek was his only active disciple. He would have to choose the old man after all, and, in a way, the fanatical old man did have spirit. . . . Then he grinned to himself. Funny how these creatures sneaked into your ego. And deadly, no doubt!

The sword of the guard began to descend. Ralph, trying hard to divine the far-reaching consequences of each act he would perform, made his stomach muscles grip to hold himself back. He didn't mean to pass any miracles, because once you started it became an endless chain. And this was obviously the trap of the test.

Then King Giron clapped his hands in glee and a particle of Ralph's anger shot through the tight muscles. His hand on the dial twitched.

The sword descended part way and then hung motionless in the air. The guards cried out in astonishment, as did Ralph up above. King Giron stopped laughing and turned very white.

"Thrust this man out of the gate," he ordered hoarsely. "Get him out of my sight."

At the gate Telfus, who had been watching the miracle as openmouthed as the soldiers, eagerly grasped the rope of the handcart and started off.

"What has become of your sore leg?" asked Valsek, relaxed after his triumph.

"It is well rested," said Telfus shortly.

"You cannot maintain that pace," said Valsek. "As you said this morning, it is a long, weary road back home."

"We must hurry," said Telfus. "We will ignore the road." His muscles tensed as he jerked the cart over the bumpy field. "Hiller would want us to hurry and make more idols. Also we must recruit. We must raise funds, invent insignia, symbols. We have much to do, Valsek. Hurry!''

Ralph relaxed a little and looked at Cynthia beside him. Her fair skin glowed in the subdued light of the Hall. There was a tiny, permanent frown on her forehead, but the mouth was expressionless. Did she expect he would lash out at the first opposition to his control? He would show her and Gerard and the rest of them. . . .

They called Valsek the Man the King Couldn't Kill. They followed him wherever he went and listened to him preach. They brought him gifts of clothes and food which Telfus indicated would not be unpleasing to such a great man, and his wife and servant no longer had to work in the fields. He dictated a book, *Hiller Says So*, to Telfus, and the book grew into an organization which rapidly became political and then began to attract the military. They made his barn a shrine and built him a mud palace where the old hut had stood. Telfus kept count with manure sticks of the numbers who came, but presently there weren't enough manure sticks to count the thousands.

Throughout the land the cleavage grew, people deciding and dividing, deciding and dividing. If you didn't care for King Giron, you fell under the sway of Hillerism. But if you were tired of the strange ways of the gods, you clung to Gironism in safety, for this new god spoke seldom and punished no one for blasphemy.

King Giron contented himself with killing a few Hiller-ites. He was fairly certain that the gods were an illusion. Was there anything more wonderful than the mountains and trees and grass that grew on the plains? As for the god-wires, they were no more nor less wonderful, but to imagine they meant any more than a tree was to engage in superstition. He had once believed that Melton existed but the so-called signs no longer came, and by denying the gods—it was very simple—the miracles seemed to have ceased. True, there was the event when the guard had been unable to cut Valsek's throat, but then the man had a history of a rheumatic father, and the coincidence of his frozen arm at the proper moment was merely a result of the man's natural weakness and the excitement of the occasion.

"We shall let the Hillerites grow big enough," King Giron told his advisers. "Then we shall march on them and execute them and when that is done, the people will understand that there is no god except King Giron, and we shall be free of godism forever."

For his part, Valsek couldn't forget that his palace was made of mud, while Giron's was made of real baked brick.

"Giron insults you!" cried Valsek from his barn-temple to Hiller. "His men have the finest temples in the city, the best jobs, the most of worldly goods. Why is this?"

"Giron represents order," Ralph directed through his electronic circuits. "It is not time to upset the smoothness of things."

Valsek made an impudent gesture. "At least give us miracles. I have waited all my life to be Spokesman, and I can have no miracles! The priests who deserted Melton for you are disgusted with the lack of miracles. Many turn to the new religion, Gironism."

"I don't believe in miracles."

"Fool!" cried Valsek.

In anger Ralph twisted the dial. Valsek felt himself lifted by a surge of current and dashed to the floor.

"Thanks," he said sadly.

Ralph shot a look at Cynthia. A smile, almost dreamy, of remembrance was on her lips. Here comes the old Ralph, she was thinking. Ralph felt himself tense so hard his calf muscles ached. "No more temper now, none," he demanded of himself.

Giron discovered that his *King's Book of Worship* was getting costly. More and more hand-scribes were needed to spread the worship of Gironism, and to feed them he had to lay heavier taxes on the people. He did so. The people responded by joining the Hillerites in great numbers, because even those who agreed with Giron about the illusory existence of the gods preferred Hiller's lower tax structure. This angered the King. A riot began in a minor city, and goaded by a determined King Giron, it flowered into an armed revolt and flung seeds of civil war to all corners of the land.

Telfus, who had been busy with organizational matters, hurried back to the mud palace.

"I suspect Hiller does not care for war," he said bitterly. "Giron has the swords, the supplies, the trained men. We have nothing. Therefore would it not be wise for us to march more and pray less—since Hiller expects us to take care of ourselves?"

Valsek paced the barn. "Go hide behind a rock, beggar. Valsek fears no man, no arms."

"But Giron's troops are organizing——"

"The children of Hiller need no troops," Valsek intoned.

Telfus went out and stole, begged or borrowed all of the cold steel he could get. He began marching the men in the fields.

"What—troops!" frowned Valsek. "I ordered against it."

"We are merely practicing for a pageant," growled Telfus. "It is to please the women and children. We shall re-enact your life as a symbol of marching men. Is this permitted?"

"You may do that," nodded Valsek, appeased.

The troops of Giron came like a storm. Ralph held out as he watched the Gironists destroy the homes of the Hillers, deflower the Hiller women, kill the children of Hillers. And he waited. . . .

Dismayed, the Hillerites fell back on Valsek's bishopric, the mud palace, and drew around the leader.

Valsek nervously paced in the barn. "Perhaps it would be better to kill a few of the Gironists," he suggested to Ralph, "rather than wait until we are dead, for there may be no battles in heaven."

There was silence from above.

The Gironist troops drew up before the palace, momentarily stopped by the Pageant Guards of Telfus. You had to drive a god, thought Valsek. With a sigh, he made his way out of the besieged fortress and presented himself to the enemy. He had nothing to offer but himself. He had brought Hillerism to the land and he alone must defend it if Hiller would not.

King Giron smiled his pleasure at the foolish old man who was anxious to become a martyr. Was there ever greater proof of the falseness of the gods? Meekly Valsek bowed before the swords of King Giron's guardsmen.

"I am faithful to Hiller," said Valsek, "and if I cannot live with it, then I will die for it."

"That's a sweet way to go," said King Giron, "since you would be killed anyway. Guards, let the swords fall."

Ralph stared down at the body of Valsek. He felt a thin pulse of hate beating at his temples. The old man lay in the dust murdered by a dozen sword wounds, and the soldiers were cutting the flesh from the bones in joy at destroying the fountainhead of Hillerism. Then the banners lifted, the swords and lances were raised, the cry went down the ranks and the murderous horde swept upon the fortress of the fallen Valsek. A groan of dismay came from the Pageant troops when the Hillerites saw the severed head of Valsek borne before the attackers.

Ralph could hardly breathe. He looked up, up at the audience as they stirred, alive to the trouble he was in. He stared at Cynthia. She wet her lips, looking down, leaning forward. "Watch the power load," she whispered; "there will soon be many dead." Her white fingers rested on a dial.

Now, he thought bitterly, I will blast the murderers of Valsek and uphold my ego down there by destroying the Gironists. I will release the blast of energy held in the hand of an angry god——

And I shall pass the critical point and there will be a backlash and the poor ego-destroyed human up here will come screaming out of his Director's chair with a crack in his skull.

Not me!

Ralph's hands felt sweaty on the dials as he heard the far-off cries of the murders being wrought among the Hillerites. But he held his peace while the work was done, stepping down the system energy as the Short Ones died by the hundreds. The Hillerites fell. They were slaughtered without mercy by King Giron. Then the idols to Hiller were destroyed. Only one man, severely wounded, survived the massacre.

Telfus . . .

That worthy remembered the rock under which he had once slept when he plowed Valsek's fields. He crept under the rock now, trying to ignore his nearly severed leg. Secure, he peered out on the field of human misery.

"A very even-tempered god indeed," he told himself, and then fainted.

There was an almost audible cry of disappointment from the human audience in the Life Hall above Ralph's head. He looked up and Cynthia looked up too. Obviously human sentiment demanded revenge on the ghastly murderers of King Giron's guard. What sort of Secretary of Defense would this be who would let his "side" be so destroyed?

He noted that Bruce Gerard frowned as he scribbled notes. The Life Hall critic for the *Times*, spokesman for the intellectuals. Ralph would be ticked off proper in tomorrow's paper:

"Blunt-jawed, domineering Ralph Hiller, Assistant Secretary of Defense, turned in a less than jolly Life Hall performance yesterday for the edification of the thoughtful. His pallid handling of the proteins in the Pentagon leads one to believe that his idea of the best defense is signified by the word *refrainment*, a refinement on containment. Hiller held the seat long enough to impress his warmth upon it, the only good impression he made. By doing nothing at all and letting his followers among the Short Ones be slaughtered like helpless ants, he was able to sit out the required time and gain the valuable certificate that all politicos need. What this means for the defense of America, however, is another thing. One pictures our land in ashes, our people badly smashed and the porticoed jaw of Mr. Hiller opening to say, as he sits with folded hands, 'I am aware of all that is going on. You should respect my awareness.' ''

Ralph turned to Cynthia.

''I have undercontrolled, haven't I?''

She shook her head. ''I am forbidden to suggest. I am here to try to save you from the Short Ones and the Short Ones from you in case of emergency. I can now state that you have about used up your quota of violent deaths and another holocaust will cause the Board to fail you for mismanagement.''

Ralph sighed. He had feared overcontrol and fallen into the error of undercontrol. God, it was frustrating. . . .

Ralph was allowed a half-hour lunch break while Cynthia took over the board. He tried to devise a safe way of toppling King Giron but could think of none. The victory was Giron's. If Giron was content, Ralph could do nothing. But if Giron tried any more violence——— Ralph felt the blood sing in his ears. If he was destined to fail, he would make a magnificent failure of it!

Then he was back at the board beside Cynthia and under the helmet and the world of the Short Ones closed in on him. The scenes of the slaughter remained with him vividly, and he sought Telfus, the sole survivor, now a man with one eye and a twisted leg who nevertheless continued to preach Hillerism and tell about the god who was big enough to let Short Ones run their own affairs. He was often laughed at, more often stoned, but always he gathered a few adherents.

Telfus even made friends with a Captain of Giron's guard.

''Why do you persist in Hillerism?'' asked the Captain. ''It is obvious that Hiller doesn't care for his own priests enough to protect them.''

''Not so,'' said Telfus. ''He cares so much that he will trust them to fall on their knees or not, as they will, whereas the old gods were usually striking somebody dead in the market place because of some fancied insult. I cannot resist this miracle-less god. Our land has been sick with miracles."

"Still you'll need one when Giron catches up with you."

"Perhaps tomorrow. But if you give me a piece of silver for Hiller, I will sleep in an inn tonight and dream your name to him."

Ralph sought out King Giron.

That individual seemed sleek and fat now, very self-confident. "Take all of the statues of Hiller and Melton and any other leftover gods and smash them," ordered the King. "The days of the gods are over. I intend to speed up the building of statues to myself, now that I control the world."

The idols to the King went up in the market places. The people concealed doubt and prayed to him because his military was strong. But this pretense bothered Giron.

"The people cannot believe I'm divine," said King Giron. "We need a mighty celebration. A ritual to prove it. I've heard from a Guard Captain of Telfus, this one-eyed beggar who still clings to Hiller. I want him brought to my palace for a celebration. I want the last survivor of the Hiller massacre dressed in a black robe and sacrificed at my celebration. Then the people will understand that Gironism defies all gods and is eternal."

Ralph felt a dryness on the inside of his mouth. He watched the guards round up the few adherents of Hiller-ism and bring them to the palace. He watched the beginnings of the celebration to King Giron.

There was irony, he thought. Just as violence breeds violence, so non-violence breeds violence. Now the whole thing had to be done over again, only now the insolence of the Gironists dug into Ralph like a scalpel on a raw nerve.

Rank upon rank of richly clad soldiers, proud merchants, laughing Gironists crowded together in the center of the courtyard where the one-eyed man and a dozen of his tattered followers faced death.

"Now, Guards," said King Giron, "move out and kill them. Place the sword firmly at the neck and cleave them down the middle. Then there will be twice as many Hillers!"

Cheers! Laughter! Oh, droll, divine King Giron!

Ralph felt the power surging in the dial under his hand, ready but not yet unleashed. He felt the dizzying pull of it, the knowledge that he could rip the flesh apart and strip the bones of thousands of Gironists. The absolute power to blast the conceited ruler from his earth. To smash bodies, stone, sand, vegetation, all—absolute, absolute power ready to use.

And King Giron laughed as the swordsman cleft the first of the beggarly Hillers.

Ralph was a seething furnace of rage. "Go! Go! Go!" his mind told his hands.

Then Cynthia did a surprising thing. "Take your hands off the dials," she said. "You're in a nasty spot. I'm taking over."

His temples throbbed but with an effort he removed his hands from the dials. Whether she was helping him or hurting him, he didn't know, but she had correctly judged that he had reached his limit.

One by one the followers of Hillerism died. He saw the vein along her throat throb, and he saw her fingers tremble on the dials she tried to hold steady. A flush crept up her neck. Participation in the world below was working on her too. She could see no way out and he understood it.

The cruel, fat dictator and his unctuous followers, the poor, set-upon martyrs—even the symbol of Telfus, his last followers, being a crippled and helpless man. A situation like this could trigger a man into unleashing a blasting fury that would overload the circuits and earn him revenge only at the cost of a crack in his skull. In real life, a situation of white-hot seething public emotion would make a government official turn to his H-bombs with implacable fury and strike out with searing flames that would wash the world clean, taking the innocent along with the guilty, unblocking great segments of civilization, radioactivating continents and sending the sea into an eternal boil.

And yet—GOD DAMN IT, YOU HAD TO STOP THE GIRONS!

Cynthia broke. She was too emotionally involved to restrain herself. She bit her lips and withdrew her hands from the dials with a moan.

But the brief interruption had helped Ralph as he leaned forward and took the dials in her place. His anger had subsided suddenly into a clear-minded determination.

He thought-waved Telfus. "I fear that you must go," he said. "I thank you for keeping the faith."

"You've been a most peculiar god," said Telfus, warily watching the last of his friends die. His face was white; he knew he was being saved for the last.

"Total violence solves nothing."

"Still it would be nice to kick one of these fellows in the shins," said Telfus, the sweat pouring from his face. "In the natural order of things an occasional miracle cannot hurt."

"What would you have me do?"

Telfus passed a hand over his face. "Hardly a moment for thoughtful discussion," he groaned. He cried out in passionate anguish as his closest friend died. Ralph let the strong emotions of Telfus enter his mind, and then gradually Telfus caught hold of himself.

"Well," he said, "if I could only see King Giron die . . ."

"Never mind the rest?" asked Ralph.

"Never mind the rest," said Telfus. "Men shouldn't play gods."

"How right you are!" cried Ralph.

"Telfus!" cried King Giron. "You see now how powerful I am! You see now that there are no more gods!"

"I see a fool," said Telfus as the guard's sword fell. The guard struck low to prolong the death for the King's enjoyment and Telfus rolled on the ground trying to hold the blood in his body. The nobles cheered and King Giron laughed and clapped his hands in glee. The guards stood back to watch the death throes of Telfus.

But Telfus struggled to a sitting position and cried out in a voice that was strangely powerful as if amplified by the voice of a god.

"I've been permitted one small miracle," he said. "Under Hiller these favors are hard to come by."

There was an electric silence. Telfus pointed his empty hand at King Giron with the forefinger extended, like a gun. He dropped his thumb.

"Bang," he said.

At that moment Ralph gave vent to his pent-up steam of emotions in one lightning-quick flip of the dial of destruction, sent out with a prayer. A microsecond jab. At that the earth rocked and there was a roaring as the nearby seas changed the shoreline.

But King Giron's head split open and his insides rushed out like a fat, ripe pea that had been opened and shucked by a celestial thumb. For a second the empty skin and bones stood upright in semblance of a man and then gently folded to the ground.

"Not bad," said Telfus. "Thanks." He died.

It was interesting to watch the Gironists. Death—death in battle or natural death—was a daylight-common thing. Dignified destruction is a human trade. But the unearthly death of the King brought about by the lazy fingering of the beggar—what person in his time would forget the flying guts and the empty, upright skin of the man who lived by cruelty and finally had his life shucked out?

Down below in the courtyard the Gironists began to get rid of their insignia. One man dropped Giron's book into a fire. Another softly drew a curtain over the idol of Giron. Men slunk away to ponder the non-violent god who would always be a shadow at their shoulder—who spoke seldom but when he spoke was heard for all time. Gironism was dead forever.

●   ●   ●

Up above a bell rang and Ralph jerked up from his contemplation with surprise to hear the rainlike sound, the applause and the approval of the audience in the Life Hall. Even Gerard was leaning over the press-box rail and grinning and nodding his head in approval, like a fish.

Ralph still had some time in the chair, but there would be no more trouble with the Short Ones. Already off somewhere a clerk was filling out the certificate.

He turned to Cynthia. "You saved me by that interruption."

"You earned your way," she said.

"I've learned much," he said. "If a god calls upon men for faith, then a god must return it with trust, and it was Telfus, not I, whom I trusted to solve the problem. After all, it was his life, his death."

"You've grown," she said.

"We have grown," he said, taking her hand under the table and not immediately letting go.

WARM

Robert Sheckley

Another, and one of the most luminous, of that extraordinary batch of new science-fiction writers *circa* 1952,
was Robert Sheckley. He broke in with stories in every
magazine at once, seemingly dozens of them, stories so
elegant and clever that it was hard to believe that their
author was only about 24. "Warm" was somewhere in the
first dozen, mere novice-work, and I commend to you its
uncluttered prose, its ingenuity of theme, its cunning
circularity of construction, as examples of a level of skill
that many veteran science-fictionists never manage to
attain at all. After his spectacular debut, Sheckley settled
into the routine production of Sheckleyesque fiction, and
eventually grew so weary of the unending demands of that
sort of material that he withdrew to sunny Majorca and
lapsed into silence for a number of years. Now he is
writing again, and he has lost none of his old deftness of
touch, though the new Sheckley stories are darker, wiser,
more reflective than most of the early ones. It is a delight
to read his recent work; it is equally delightful to return to
the sparkling stories with which he dazzled us so amazing-
ly a quarter of a century ago.

Anders lay on his bed, fully dressed except for his shoes
and black bow tie, contemplating, with a certain uneasiness, the evening before him. In twenty minutes he would

pick up Judy at her apartment, and that was the uneasy part of it.

He had realized, only seconds ago, that he was in love with her.

Well, he'd tell her. The evening would be memorable. He would propose, there would be kisses, and the seal of acceptance would, figuratively speaking, be stamped across his forehead.

Not too pleasant an outlook, he decided. It really would be much more comfortable not to be in love. What had done it? A look, a touch, a thought? It didn't take much, he knew, and stretched his arms for a thorough yawn.

"Help me!" a voice said.

His muscles spasmed, cutting off the yawn in mid-moment. He sat upright on the bed, then grinned and lay back again.

"You must help me!" the voice insisted.

Anders sat up, reached for a polished shoe and fitted it on, giving his full attention to the tying of the laces.

"Can you hear me?" the voice asked. "You can, can't you?"

That did it. "Yes, I can hear you," Anders said, still in a high good humor. "Don't tell me you're my guilty subconscious, attacking me for a childhood trauma I never bothered to resolve. I suppose you want me to join a monastery."

"I don't know what you're talking about," the voice said. "I'm no one's subconscious. I'm *me*. Will you help me?"

Anders believed in voices as much as anyone; that is, he didn't believe in them at all, until he heard them. Swiftly he catalogued the possibilities. Schizophrenia was the best answer, of course, and one in which his colleagues would concur. But Anders had a lamentable confidence in his own sanity. In which case—

"Who are you?" he asked.

"I don't know," the voice answered.

Anders realized that the voice was speaking within his own mind. Very suspicious.

"You don't know who you are," Anders stated. "Very well. *Where* are you?"

"I don't know that, either." The voice paused, and went on. "Look, I know how ridiculous this must sound. Believe me, I'm in some sort of limbo. I don't know how I got here or who I am, but I want desperately to get out. Will you help me?"

Still fighting the idea of a voice speaking within his head, Anders knew that his next decision was vital. He had to accept—or reject—his own sanity.

He accepted it.

"All right," Anders said, lacing the other shoe. "I'll grant that you're a person in trouble, and that you're in some sort of telepathic contact with me. Is there anything else you can tell me?"

"I'm afraid not," the voice said, with infinite sadness. "You'll have to find out for yourself."

"Can you contact anyone else?"

"No."

"Then how can you talk with me?"

"I don't know."

Anders walked to his bureau mirror and adjusted his black bow tie, whistling softly under his breath. Having just discovered that he was in love, he wasn't going to let a little thing like a voice in his mind disturb him.

"I really don't see how I can be of any help," Anders said, brushing a bit of lint from his jacket. "You don't know where you are, and there don't seem to be any distinguishing landmarks. How am I to find you?" He turned and looked around the room to see if he had forgotten anything.

"I'll know when you're close," the voice said. "You were warm just then."

"Just then?" All he had done was look around the room. He did so again, turning his head slowly. Then it happened.

The room, from one angle, looked different. It was suddenly a mixture of muddled colors, instead of the carefully blended pastel shades he had selected. The lines of wall, floor and ceiling were strangely off proportion, zig-zag, unrelated.

Then everything went back to normal.

"You were *very* warm," the voice said.

Anders resisted the urge to scratch his head, for fear of disarranging his carefully combed hair. What he had seen wasn't so strange. Everyone sees one or two things in his life that make him doubt his normality, doubt sanity, doubt his very existence. For a moment the orderly Universe is disarranged and the fabric of belief is ripped.

But the moment passes.

Anders remembered once, as a boy, awakening in his room in the middle of the night. How strange everything had looked! Chairs, table, all out of proportion, swollen in the dark. The ceiling pressing down, as in a dream.

But that also had passed.

"Well, old man," he said, "if I get warm again, tell me."

"I will," the voice in his head whispered. "I'm sure you'll find me."

"I'm glad you're so sure," Anders said gaily, switched off the lights and left.

Lovely and smiling, Judy greeted him at the door. Looking at her, Anders sensed her knowledge of the moment. Had she felt the change in him, or predicted it? Or was love making him grin like an idiot?

"Would you like a before-party drink?" she asked.

He nodded, and she led him across the room, to the improbable green-and-yellow couch. Sitting down, Anders decided he would tell her when she came back with the drink. No use in putting off the fatal moment. A lemming in love, he told himself.

"You're getting warm again," the voice said.

He had almost forgotten his invisible friend. Or fiend, as the case could well be. What would Judy say if she knew he was hearing voices? Little things like that, he reminded himself, often break up the best of romances.

"Here," she said, handing him a drink.

Still smiling, he noticed. The number two smile—to a prospective suitor, provocative and understanding. It had been preceded, in their relationship, by the number one nice-girl smile, the don't-misunderstand me smile, to be worn on all occasions, until the correct words have been mumbled.

"That's right," the voice said. "It's in how you look at things."

Look at what? Anders glanced at Judy, annoyed at his thoughts. If he was going to play the lover, let him play it. Even through the astigmatic haze of love, he was able to appreciate her blue-gray eyes, her fine skin (if one overlooked a tiny blemish on the left temple), her lips, slightly reshaped by lipstick.

"How did your classes go today?" she asked.

Well, of course she'd ask that, Anders thought. Love is marking time.

"All right," he said. "Teaching psychology to young apes—"

"Oh, come now!"

"Warmer," the voice said.

What's the matter with me, Anders wondered. She really is a lovely girl. The *gestalt* that is Judy, a pattern of thoughts, expressions, movements, making up the girl I—

I what?

Love?

Anders shifted his long body uncertainly on the couch. He didn't quite understand how this train of thought had begun. It annoyed him. The analytical young instructor was better off in the classroom. Couldn't science wait until 9:10 in the morning?

"I was thinking about you today," Judy said, and Anders knew that she had sensed the change in his mood.

"Do you see?" the voice asked him. "You're getting much better at it."

"I don't see anything," Anders thought, but the voice was right. It was as though he had a clear line of inspection into Judy's mind. Her feelings were nakedly apparent to him, as meaningless as his room had been in that flash of undistorted thought.

"I really was thinking about you," she repeated.

"Now look," the voice said.

Anders, watching the expressions on Judy's face, felt the strangeness descend on him. He was back in the nightmare perception of that moment in his room. This time it was as though he were watching a machine in a laboratory. The object of this operation was the evocation and preservation of a particular mood. The machine goes through a searching process, invoking trains of ideas to achieve the desired end.

"Oh, were you?" he asked, amazed at his new perspective.

"Yes . . . I wondered what you were doing at noon," the reactive machine opposite him on the couch said, expanding its shapely chest slightly.

"Good," the voice said, commending him for his perception.

"Dreaming of you, of course," he said to the flesh-clad skeleton behind the total *gestalt* Judy. The flesh machine rearranged its limbs, widened its mouth to denote pleasure. The mechanism searched through a complex of fears, hopes, worries, through half-remembrances of analogous situations, analogous solutions.

And this was what he loved. Anders saw too clearly and hated himself for seeing. Through his new nightmare perception, the absurdity of the entire room struck him.

"Were you really?" the articulating skeleton asked him.

"You're coming closer," the voice whispered.

To what? The personality? There was no such thing. There was no true cohesion, no depth, nothing except a web of surface reactions, stretched across automatic visceral movements.

He was coming closer to the truth.

"Sure," he said sourly.

The machine stirred, searching for a response.

Anders felt a quick tremor of fear at the sheer alien quality of his viewpoint. His sense of formalism had been sloughed off, his agreed-upon reactions by-passed. What would be revealed next?

He was seeing clearly, he realized, as perhaps no man had ever seen before. It was an oddly exhilarating thought.

But could he still return to normality?

"Can I get you a drink?" the reaction machine asked.

At that moment Anders was as thoroughly out of love as a man could be. Viewing one's intended as a depersonalized, sexless piece of machinery is not especially conducive to love. But it is quite stimulating, intellectually.

Anders didn't want normality. A curtain was being raised and he wanted to see behind it. What was it some Russian scientist—Ouspensky, wasn't it—had said?

"Think in other categories."

That was what he was doing, and would continue to do.

"Good-by," he said suddenly.

The machine watched him, open-mouthed, as he walked out the door. Delayed circuit reactions kept it silent until it heard the elevator door close.

"You were very warm in there," the voice within his head whispered, once he was on the street. "But you still don't understand everything."

"Tell me, then," Anders said, marveling a little at his equanimity. In an hour he had bridged the gap to a completely different viewpoint, yet it seemed perfectly natural.

"I can't," the voice said. "You must find it yourself."

"Well, let's see now," Anders began. He looked around at the masses of masonry, the convention of streets cutting through the architectural piles. "Human life," he said, "is a series of conventions. When you look at a girl, you're supposed to see—a pattern, not the underlying formlessness."

"That's true," the voice agreed, but with a shade of doubt.

"Basically, there is no form. Man produces *gestalts*,

and cuts form out of the plethora of nothingness. It's like looking at a set of lines and saying that they represent a figure. We look at a mass of material, extract it from the background and say it's a man. But in truth, there is no such thing. There are only the humanizing features that we—myopically—attach to it. Matter is conjoined, a matter of viewpoint."

"You're not seeing it now," said the voice.

"Damn it," Anders said. He was certain that he was on the track of something big, perhaps something ultimate. "Everyone's had the experience. At some time in his life, everyone looks at a familiar object and can't make any sense out of it. Momentarily, the *gestalt* fails, but the true moment of sight passes. The mind reverts to the superimposed pattern. Normalcy continues."

The voice was silent. Anders walked on, through the *gestalt* city.

"There's something else, isn't there?" Anders asked.

"Yes."

What could that be, he asked himself. Through clearing eyes, Anders looked at the formality he had called his world.

He wondered momentarily if he would have come to this if the voice hadn't guided him. Yes, he decided after a few moments, it was inevitable.

But who was the voice? And what had he left out?

"Let's see what a party looks like now," he said to the voice.

The party was a masquerade; the guests were all wearing their faces. To Anders, their motives, individually and collectively, were painfully apparent. Then his vision began to clear further.

He saw that the people weren't truly individual. They were discontinuous lumps of flesh sharing a common vocabulary, yet not even truly discontinuous.

The lumps of flesh were a part of the decoration of the room and almost indistinguishable from it. They were one with the lights, which lent their tiny vision. They were joined to the sounds they made, a few feeble tones out of the great possibility of sound. They blended into the walls.

The kaleidoscopic view came so fast that Anders had trouble sorting his new impressions. He knew now that these people existed only as patterns, on the same basis as the sounds they made and the things they thought they saw.

Gestalts, sifted out of the vast, unbearable real world.

"Where's Judy?" a discontinuous lump of flesh asked him. This particular lump possessed enough nervous mannerisms to convince the other lumps of his reality. He wore a loud tie as further evidence.

"She's sick," Anders said. The flesh quivered into an instant sympathy. Lines of formal mirth shifted to formal woe.

"Hope it isn't anything serious," the vocal flesh remarked.

"You're warmer," the voice said to Anders.

Anders looked at the object in front of him.

"She hasn't long to live," he stated.

The flesh quivered. Stomach and intestines contracted in sympathetic fear. Eyes distended, mouth quivered.

The loud tie remained the same.

"My God! you don't mean it!"

"What are you?" Anders asked quietly.

"What do you mean?" the indignant flesh attached to the tie demanded. Serene within its reality, it gaped at Anders. Its mouth twitched, undeniable proof that it was real and sufficient. "You're drunk," it sneered.

Anders laughed and left the party.

"There is still something you don't know," the voice said. "But you were hot! I could feel you near me."

"What are you?" Anders asked again.

"I don't know," the voice admitted. "I am a person. I am I. I am trapped."

"So are we all," Anders said. He walked on asphalt, surrounded by heaps of concrete, silicates, aluminum and iron alloys. Shapeless, meaningless heaps that made up the *gestalt* city.

And then there were the imaginary lines of demarcation

dividing city from city, the artificial boundaries of water and land.

All ridiculous.

"Give me a dime for some coffee, mister?" something asked, a thing indistinguishable from any other thing.

"Old Bishop Berkeley would give a nonexistent dime to your nonexistent presence," Anders said gaily.

"I'm really in a bad way," the voice whined, and Anders perceived that it was no more than a series of modulated vibrations.

"Yes! Go on!" the voice commanded.

"If you could spare me a quarter—" the vibrations said, with a deep pretense at meaning.

Now, what was there behind the senseless patterns? Flesh, mass. What was that? All made up of atoms.

"I'm really hungry," the intricately arranged atoms muttered.

All atoms. Conjoined. There were no true separations between atom and atom. Flesh was stone, stone was light. Anders looked at the masses of atoms that were pretending to solidity, meaning and reason.

"Can't you help me?" a clump of atoms asked. But the clump was identical with all the other atoms. Once you ignored the superimposed patterns, you could see the atoms were random, scattered.

"I don't believe in you," Anders said.

The pile of atoms was gone.

"Yes!" the voice cried. "Yes!"

"I don't believe in any of it," Anders said. After all, what was an atom?

"Go on!" the voice shouted. "You're hot! Go on!"

What was an atom? An empty space surrounded by an empty space.

Absurd!

"Then it's all false!" Anders said. And he was alone under the stars.

"That's right!" the voice within his head screamed. "Nothing!"

But stars, Anders thought. How can one believe—

The stars disappeared. Anders was in a gray nothingness, a void. There was nothing around him except shapeless gray.

Where was the voice?

Gone.

Anders perceived the delusion behind the grayness, and then there was nothing at all.

Complete nothingness, and himself within it.

Where was he? What did it mean? Anders' mind tried to add it up.

Impossible. *That* couldn't be true.

Again the score was tabulated, but Anders' mind couldn't accept the total. In desperation, the overloaded mind erased the figures, eradicated the knowledge, erased itself.

"Where am I?"

In nothingness. Alone.

Trapped.

"Who am I?"

A voice.

The voice of Anders searched the nothingness, shouted, "Is there anyone here?"

No answer.

But there was someone. All directions were the same, yet moving along one he could make contact . . . with someone. The voice of Anders reached back to someone who could save him, perhaps.

"Save me," the voice said to Anders, lying fully dressed on his bed, except for his shoes and black bow tie.

WHEN THE CHANGE-WINDS BLOW

Fritz Leiber

Fritz Leiber—who can barely fit his vast collection of Hugo and Nebula awards and other trophies into the tiny San Francisco hotel room that serves as his office—needs no introduction to the science-fiction audience. But this is one of his less familiar stories, a delicate and poignant fantasy of time's permutations, beautifully told, rich and wise. "It's in the things we've lost that we exist most fully," Leiber tells us here. Yes: indeed, yes.

I was half-way between Arcadia and Utopia, flying a long archeologic scout, looking for coleopt hives, lepidopteroid stilt-cities, and ruined villas of the Old Ones.

On Mars they've stuck to the fanciful names the old astronomers dreamed onto their charts. They've got an Elysium and an Ophir too.

I judged I was somewhere near the Acid Sea, which by a rare coincidence does become a poisonous shallow marsh, rich in hydrogen ions, when the northern icecap melts.

But I saw no sign of it below me, nor any archeologic features either. Only the endless dull rosy plain of felsite dust and iron-oxide powder slipping steadily west under my flier, with here and there a shallow canyon or low hill, looking for all the world (Earth? Mars?) like parts of the Mojave.

The sun was behind me, its low light flooding the cabin. A few stars glittered in the dark blue sky. I recognized the constellations of Sagittarius and Scorpio, the red pinpoint of Antares.

I was wearing my pilot's red spacesuit. They've enough air on Mars for flying now, but not for breathing if you fly even a few hundred yards above the surface.

Beside me sat my copilot's green spacesuit, which would have had someone in it if I were more sociable or merely mindful of flying regulations. From time to time it swayed and jogged just a little.

And things were feeling eerie, which isn't how they ought to feel to someone who loves solitude as much as I do, or pretend to myself I do. But the Martian landscape is even more spectral than that of Arabia or the American Southwest—lonely and beautiful and obsessed with death and immensity and sometimes it strikes through.

From some old poem the words came, "... and strange thoughts grow, with a certain humming in my ears, about the life before I lived this life."

I had to stop myself from leaning forward and looking around into the faceplate of the green spacesuit to see if there weren't someone there now. A thin man. Or a tall slim woman. Or a black crab-jointed Martian coleopteroid, who needs a spacesuit about as much as a spacesuit does. Or . . . who knows?

It was very still in the cabin. The silence did almost hum. I had been listening to Deimos Station, but now the outer moonlet had dropped below the southern horizon. They'd been broadcasting a suggestions program about dragging Mercury away from the sun to make it the moon of Venus—and giving both planets rotation too—so as to stir up the thick smoggy furnace-hot atmosphere of Venus and make it habitable.

Better finish fixing up Mars first, I thought.

But then almost immediately the rider to that thought had come: *No, I want Mars to stay lonely. That's why I came here. Earth got crowded and look what happened.*

Yet there are times on Mars when it would be pleasant,

even to an old solitary like me, to have a companion. That
is if you could be sure of picking your companion.

Once again I felt the compulsion to peer inside the green
spacesuit.

Instead I scanned around. Still only the dust-desert
drawing toward sunset; almost featureless, yet darkly rosy
as an old peach. "True peach, rosy and flawless . . .
Peach-blossom marble all, the rare, the ripe as fresh-
poured wine of a mighty pulse. . . ." *What was that
poem?*—my mind nagged.

On the seat beside me, almost under the thigh of the
green spacesuit, vibrating with it a little, was a tape:
Vanished Churches and Cathedrals of Terra. Old buildings are an abiding interest with me, of course, and then
some of the hills or hives of the black coleopts are remarkably suggestive of Earth towers and spires, even to details
like lancet windows and flying buttresses, so much so that
it's been suggested there is an imitative element, perhaps
telepathic, in the architecture of those strange beings who
despite their humanoid intelligence are very like social
insects. I'd been scanning the book at my last stop, hunting out coleopt-hill resemblances, but then a cathedral
interior had reminded me of the Rockefeller Chapel at the
University of Chicago and I'd slipped the tape out of the
projector. That chapel was where Monica had been, getting her Ph.D. in physics on a bright June morning, when
the fusion blast licked the southern end of Lake Michigan,
and I didn't want to think about Monica. Or rather I
wanted too much to think about her.

"What's done is done, and she is dead beside, dead
long ago. . . ." Now I recognized the poem!—Browning's
The Bishop Orders His Tomb at St. Praxed's Church.
That was a distant cry!— Had there been a view of St.
Praxed's on the tape?— The 16th Century . . . and the
dying bishop pleading with his sons for a grotesquely
grand tomb—a frieze of satyrs, nymphs, the Savior,
Moses, lynxes—while he thinks of their mother, his mistress. . . .

''Your tall pale mother with her talking eyes . . . Old Gandolf envied me, so fair she was!''

Robert Browning and Elizabeth Barrett and their great love. . . .

Monica and myself and our love that never got started. . . .

Monica's eyes talked. She was tall and slim and proud. . . .

Maybe if I had more character, or only energy, I'd find myself someone else to love—a new planet, a new girl!—I wouldn't stay uselessly faithful to that old romance, I wouldn't go courting loneliness, locked in a dreaming life-in-death on Mars. . . .

''Hours and long hours in the dead night, I ask, 'Do I live, am I dead?' ''

But for me the loss of Monica is tied up, in a way I can't untangle, with the failure of Earth, with my loathing of what Terra did to herself in her pride of money and power and success (communist and capitalist alike), with that unnecessary atomic war that came just when they thought they had everything safe and solved, like they felt before the one in 1914. It didn't wipe out all Earth by any means, only about a third, but it wiped out my trust in human nature—and the divine too, I'm afraid—and it wiped out Monica. . . .

''And she died so must we die ourselves, and thence ye may perceive the world's a dream.''

A dream? Maybe we lack a Browning to make real those moments of modern history gone over the Niagara of the past, to find them again, needle-in-haystack, atom-in-whirlpool, and etch them perfectly, the moments of star-flight and planet-landing etched as he had etched the moments of the Renaissance.

Yet—the world (Mars? Terra?) only a dream? Well, maybe. A bad dream sometimes, that's for sure! I told myself as I jerked my wandering thoughts back to the flier and the unchanging rosy desert under the small sun.

Apparently I hadn't missed anything—my second mind had been faithfully watching and instrument-tending while my first mind rambled in imaginings and memories.

But things were feeling eerier than ever. The silence did hum now, brassily, as if a great peal of bells had just clanged, or were about to. There was menace now in the small sun about to set behind me, bringing the Martian night and what Martian were-things there may be that they don't know of yet. The rosy plain had turned sinister. And for a moment I was sure that if I looked into the green spacesuit, I would see a dark wraith thinner than any coleopt, or else a bone-brown visage fleshlessly grinning —the King of Terrors.

"Swift as a weaver's shuttle fleet our years: Man goeth to the grave, and where is he?"

You know, the weird and the supernatural didn't just evaporate when the world got crowded and smart and technical. They moved outward—to Luna, to Mars, to the Jovian satellites, to the black tangled forest of space and the astronomic marches and the unimaginably distant bull's-eye windows of the stars. Out to the realms of the unknown, where the unexpected still happens every other hour and the impossible every other day—

And right at that moment I saw the impossible standing 400 feet tall and cloaked in lacy gray in the desert ahead of me.

And while my first mind froze for seconds that stretched toward minutes and my central vision stayed blankly fixed on that upwardly bifurcated incredibility with its dark hint of rainbow caught in the gray lace, my second mind and my peripheral vision brought my flier down to a swift, dream-smooth, skimming landing on its long skis in the rosy dust. I brushed a control and the cabin walls swung silently downward to either side of the pilot's seat, and I stepped down through the dream-easy Martian gravity to the peach-dark pillowy floor, and I stood looking at the wonder, and my first mind began to move at last.

There could be no doubt about the name of this, for I'd been looking at a taped view of it not five hours before— this was the West Front of Chartres Cathedral, that Gothic masterpiece, with its plain 12th Century spire, the *Clocher*

Vieux, to the south and its crocketed 16th Century spire, the *Clocher Neuf*, to the north and between the great rose window fifty feet across and below that the icon-crowded triple-arched West Porch.

Swiftly now my first mind moved to one theory after another of this grotesque miracle and rebounded from them almost as swiftly as if they were like magnetic poles.

I was hallucinating from the taped pictures. Yes, maybe the world's a dream. That's always a theory and never a useful one.

A transparency of Chartres had got pasted against my faceplate. Shake my helmet. No.

I was seeing a mirage that had traveled across fifty million miles of space . . . and some years of time too, for Chartres had vanished with the Paris bomb that near-missed toward Le Mans, just as Rockefeller Chapel had gone with the Michigan Bomb and St. Praxed's with the Rome.

The thing was a mimic-structure built by the coleop-teroids to a plan telepathized from memory picture of Chartres in some man's mind. But most memory pictures don't have anywhere near such precision and I never heard of the coleopts mimicking stained glass, though they do build spired nests a half thousand feet high.

It was all one of those great hypnotism-traps the Arean lingoists are forever claiming the coleopts are setting us. Yes, and the whole universe was built by demons to deceive only me—and possibly Adolf Hitler—as Descartes once hypothesized. *Stop it.*

They'd moved Hollywood to Mars as they'd earlier moved it to Mexico and Spain and Egypt and the Congo to cut expenses, and they'd just finished an epic of the Middle Ages—*The Hunchback of Notre Dame*, no doubt, with some witless producer substituting Notre Dame of Chartres for Notre Dame of Paris because his leading mistress liked its looks better and the public wouldn't know the difference. Yes, and probably hired hordes of black coleopts at next to nothing to play monks, wearing robes and humanoid masks. And why not a coleopt to play

Quasimodo?—improve race relations. *Don't hunt for comedy in the incredible*.

Or they'd been giving the Martian tour to the last mad president of La Belle France to quiet his nerves and they'd propped up a fake cathedral of Chartres, all west facade, to humor him, just like the Russians had put up papier-mache villages to impress Peter III's German wife. The Fourth Republic on the fourth planet! *No, don't get hysterical. This thing is here*.

Or maybe—and here my first mind lingered—past and future forever exist somehow, somewhere (the Mind of God? the fourth dimension?) in a sort of suspended animation, with little trails of somnambulant change running through the future as our willed present actions change it and perhaps, who knows, other little trails running through the past too?—for there may be professional time-travelers. And maybe, once in a million millennia, an amateur accidentally finds a Door.

A Door to Chartres. But when?

As I lingered on those thoughts, staring at the gray prodigy—"Do I live, am I dead?"—there came a moaning and a rustling behind me and I turned to see the green spacesuit diving out of the flier toward me, but with its head ducked so I still couldn't see inside the faceplate. I could no more move than in a nightmare. But before the suit reached me, I saw that there was with it, perhaps carrying it, a wind that shook the flier and swept up the feather-soft rose dust in great plumes and waves. And then the wind bowled me over—one hasn't much anchorage in Mars gravity—and I was rolling away from the flier with the billowing dust and the green spacesuit that went somersaulting faster and higher than I, as if it were empty, but then wraiths are light.

The wind was stronger than any wind on Mars should be, certainly than any unheralded gust, and as I went tumbling deliriously on, cushioned by my suit and the low gravity, clutching futilely toward the small low rocky outcrops through whose long shadows I was rolling, I found myself thinking with the serenity of fever that this

wind wasn't blowing across Mars-space only but through
time too.

A mixture of space-wind and time-wind—what a puzzle
for the physicist and drawer of vectors! It seemed unfair—
I thought as I tumbled—like giving a psychiatrist a patient
with psychosis overlaid by alcoholism. But reality's always mixed and I knew from experience that only a few
minutes in an anechoic, lightness, null-G chamber will set
the most normal mind veering uncontrollably into fantasy—or is it always fantasy?

One of the smaller rocky outcrops took for an instant the
twisted shape of Monica's dog Brush as he died—not in
the blast with her, but of fallout, three weeks later, hairless
and swollen and oozing. I winced.

Then the wind died and the West Front of Chartres was
shooting vertically up above me and I found myself
crouched on the dust-drifted steps of the south bay with the
great sculpture of the Virgin looking severely out from
above the high doorway at the Martian desert, and the
figures of the four liberal arts ranged below her—
Grammar, Rhetoric, Music, and Dialectic—and Aristotle
with frowning forehead dipping a stone pen into stone ink.

The figure of Music hammering her little stone bells
made me think of Monica and how she'd studied piano and
Brush had barked when she practiced. Next I remembered
from the tape that Chartres is the legendary resting place of
St. Modesta, a beautiful girl tortured to death for her faith
by her father Quirinus in the Emperor Diocletian's day.
Modesta—Music—Monica.

The double door was open a little and the green
spacesuit was sprawled on its belly there, helmet lifted, as
if peering inside at floor level.

I pushed to my feet and walked *blowing through time?
Grotesque*, up the rose-mounded steps. *Dust. Yet was I
more than dust? "Do I live, am I dead?"*

I hurried faster and faster, kicking up the fine powder in
peach-red swirls, and almost hurled myself down on the
green spacesuit to turn it over and peer into the faceplate.
But before I could quite do that I had looked into the

doorway and what I saw stopped me. Slowly I got to my feet again and took a step beyond the prone green spacesuit and then another step.

Instead of the great Gothic nave of Chartres, long as a football field, high as a sequoia, alive with stained light, there was a smaller, darker interior—churchly too, but Romanesque, even Latin, with burly granite columns and rich red marble steps leading up toward an altar where mosaics glittered in the gloom. One thin stream of flat light, coming through another open door like a theatrical spot in the winds, struck on the wall opposite me and revealed a gloriously ornate tomb where a sculptured mortuary figure—a bishop by his miter and crook—lay above a crowded bronze frieze on a bright green jasper slab with a blue lapis-lazuli globe of Earth between his stone knees and nine thin columns of peach-blossom marble rising around him to the canopy. . . .

But of course: this was the bishop's tomb of Browning's poem. This was St. Praxed's church, powdered by the Rome Bomb, the church sacred to the martyred Praxed, daughter of Pudens, pupil of St. Peter, tucked even further into the past than Chartres' martyred Modesta. Napoleon had planned to liberate those red marble steps and take them to Paris. But with this realization came almost instantly the companion memory: that although St. Praxed's church had been real, the tomb of Browning's bishop had existed only in Browning's imagination and the minds of his readers.

Can it be, I thought, that not only do the past and future exist forever, but also all the possibilities that were never and will never be realized . . . somehow, somewhere (the fifth dimension? the Imagination of God?) as if in a dream within a dream. . . . Crawling with change, too, as artists or anyone thinks of them . . . Change-winds mixed with time-winds mixed with space-winds. . . .

In that moment I became aware of two dark-clad figures in the aisle beside the tomb and studying it—a pale man with dark beard covering his cheeks and a pale woman with dark straight hair covering hers under a filmy veil.

There was movement near their feet and a fat dark sluglike beast, almost hairless, crawled away from them into the shadows.

I didn't like it. I didn't like that beast. I didn't like it disappearing. For the first time I felt actively frightened.

And then the woman moved too, so that her dark wide floor-brushing skirt jogged, and in a very British voice she called, "Flush! Come here, Flush!" and I remembered that was the name of the dog Elizabeth Barrett had taken with her from Wimpole Street when she ran off with Browning.

Then the voice called again, anxiously, but the British had gone out of it now, in fact it was a voice I knew, a voice that froze me inside, and the dog's name had changed to Brush, and I looked up, and the gaudy tomb was gone and the walls had grayed and receded, but not so far as those of the Rockefeller Chapel, and there coming toward me down the center aisle, tall and slim in a black academic robe with the three velvet doctor's bars on the sleeves, with the brown of science edging the hood, was Monica.

I think she saw me, I think she recognized me through my faceplate, I think she smiled at me fearfully, wonderingly.

Then, there was a rosy glow behind her, making a hazily-gleaming nimbus of her hair, like the glory of a saint. But then the glow became too bright, intolerably so, and something struck at me, driving me back through the doorway, whirling me over and over, so that all I saw was swirls of rose dust and star-pricked sky.

I think what struck at me was the ghost of the front of an atomic blast.

In my mind was the thought: St. Praxed, St. Modesta, and Monica the atheist saint martyred by the bomb.

Then all the winds were gone and I was picking myself up from the dust by the flier.

I scanned around through ebbing dust-swirls. The cathedral was gone. No hill or structure anywhere relieved the flatness of the Martian horizon.

Leaning against the flier, as if lodged there by the wind yet on its feet, was the green spacesuit, its back toward me, its head and shoulders sunk in an attitude mimicking profound dejection.

I moved toward it quickly. I had the thought that it might have gone with me to bring someone back.

It seemed to shrink from me a little as I turned it around. The faceplate was empty. There on the inside, below the transparency, distorted by my angle of view, was the little complex console of dials and levers, but no face above them.

I took the suit up very gently in my arms, carrying it as if it were a person, and I started toward the door of the cabin.

It's in the things we've lost that we exist most fully.

There was a faint green flash from the sun as its last sliver vanished on the horizon.

All the stars came out.

Gleaming green among them and brightest of all, low in the sky where the sun had gone, was the Evening Star—Earth.

ONE FACE

Larry Niven

A search of the archives reveals the surprising fact that Larry Niven has yet to have a story reprinted in the *Alpha* series. Surprising, because Niven is not only one of the most popular and satisfying science-fiction novelists of the past decade—his titles include *Ringworld*, *World of Ptavvs*, *A World Out of Time*, and other stimulating imaginative exercises—but also one of the best short story writers, as his flotilla of Hugo spaceships testifies. His stories are straightforward in tone, logical in development, sturdy in construction, original of theme. His absence from this series is a grievous fault, remedied at last.

I

An alarm rang, like an old-fashioned air-raid siren. The deep voice of the Brain blared, "Strac Astrophysics is not in his cabin! Strac Astrophysics, report to your cabin immediately! The *Hogan's Goat* will Jump in sixty seconds."

Verd tensed. He had to restrain an urge to get up. In nearly two centuries of piloting the *Hogan's Goat*, Verd had never lost a passenger through carelessness. Passengers were *supposed* to be careless. If Strac didn't reach his room Verd would have to postpone Jump to save his life: a serious breach of the customs of travel.

Above the green coffin which was his Jump couch the Brain said, "Strac Astrophysics is in his cabin and protected."

Verd relaxed.

"Five," said the Brain. "Four. Three . . ."

In various parts of the ship, twenty-eight bodies jerked like springs released. "Oof," complained Lourdi, lying in the Jump couch next to Verd's. "That felt strange." Lourdi was Verd's wife, a mixture of many races and subdivisions of Man, bearing the delicate, willowy beauty born of low gravity worlds. She was an experienced traveler. When she sat up in her green coffin she looked puzzled.

"I've never felt anything like that before. Have you, dear?" she asked.

Verd grunted as he climbed out. He was a few pounds overweight. His face was beefy, smooth and unlined and fashionably hairless. So was his scalp, except for a narrow strip of black brush which ran straight up from between his brow ridges and continued on until it faded out near the small of his back. Most of the hair had been cosmetically implanted. Neither wrinkles nor width of hair strip could tell a man's age, and superficially Verd might have been anywhere from twenty to four hundred years old. It was in his economy of movement that Verd's age showed. He did things the easy way, the fast way. He never needed more than seconds to find it, and he always took that time. He had had a long time to learn.

"No," said Verd. "Let's find out what it was. Brain!" he snapped at the wall speaker.

The silence stretched like a nerve.

"Brain?"

Verd Spacercaptain, Lourdi Coursefinder, and Parliss Lifesystems sat along one wall of the crew common room, watching the fourth member of the crew. Chanda Thinkersyst was a tall, homely woman whose major beauty was her wavy black hair. A strip two inches wide down the center of her scalp had been allowed to grow until it hung to the region of her coccyx, satin black and satin soft, gleaming and rippling as she moved. She stood before the biggest of the Brain screens, which now showed a diagram of the *Hogan's Goat*, and she used her finger as a pointer.

"The rock hit here," she said, pointing halfway back on the spinal maze of lines and little black squares and lighted power-source symbols which represented the Jumper machinery. "It must have been there when we came out of overspace, so the meteor gun never got the chance to stop it. It burned through the Jumper and lost most of its mass in the hull. What was left rained droplets of high-speed molten metal all through the ship's Brain."

Parliss whistled. He was tall, ash blond and very young. "That'll soften it up," he murmured irreverently. He winced at Chanda's glare and added, "Sorry."

Chanda went on. "Of course there's no chance of repairing the Brain ourselves. There were too many points of injury, and most of them too small to find. The Brain can still solve problems and obey orders. The worst problem seems to be this motor aphasia, and I've circumvented that by instructing the Brain to use Morse code. Since I don't know the extent of the damage very precisely, I recommend we let a tug land the passengers on Earth instead of trying to land the *Goat*."

Verd cringed at the thought of what the tug captains would say. "All right. Chanda, what is Morse code?"

Chanda smiled. "Morse is English translated into dots and dashes. It was one of the first things I tried. I didn't really expect it to work, and I doubt if it would on a human patient."

"Thanks, Chanda." Verd stood up and the Brain doctor sat down. "All I will have to say, group, is that we're going to take a bad loss this trip. The Brain is sure to need expensive repairs, and it looks to me like the Jumper will have to be almost completely torn out. It gave one awful discharge when the meteor hit, and most of the parts are fused—Lourdi, what's wrong? We can afford it."

Lourdi shook her head. Her delicate surgeon's fingers gripped hard at the arms of her chair.

"Why not?" Verd asked gently. "We land on Earth and take a vacation while the orbital repair companies do the worrying."

Lourdi Coursefinder gulped air before she could speak. "We'll have to do the worrying, dear," she said brightly. "I couldn't ask the Brain to do it, so I used the telescope myself. That's not Sol."

The others looked at her.

"It's not the Sun. It's a greenish-white dwarf, a dead star. I couldn't find the Sun."

II

Once it had its orders, the Brain was much faster with the telescope than Lourdi. It confirmed her description of the star which was where Sol should have been, and added that it was no star in the Brain's catalogue. Furthermore the Brain could not recognize the volume of space around it. It was still scanning stars, hoping to find its bearings.

They sat in the crew common room drinking droobleberry juice and vodka.

The two dozen passengers had been told nothing as yet, but they must have been getting restless. Interstellar law gave each passenger access at all times to the ship's Brain. Someone must know by now that the Brain was incommunicado.

Lourdi stopped making rings on the tabletop. "Chanda, will you translate for me?"

Chanda looked up hopefully. "Of course."

"Ask the Brain to find the planet in this system which most resembles Saturn."

"Saturn?" Chanda's homely face lost its hopeful expression. She turned to the Brain speaker and tapped next to it with a stylus.

Almost immediately a line of short and long white lines began moving left to right across the top of the Brain screen. The screen itself went white, cleared, showing what looked like a picture of Saturn. But there were too many gaps in the ring, and they were too well defined. Chanda said, "Fifth major planet from star. Six moons. Period, 29.46 years. Distance from Sun: 9.54 a. u. Diameter: 72,000 miles. Type gas giant. So?"

Lourdi nodded to herself. Verd and Parliss were watching her. "Ask it to show us the second and third planets."

The second planet was in its quarter phase. The Brain screen showed it looking like a large Moon, but less badly pocked, and with one major difference: an intensely bright area across the middle. Chanda translated the marching dots: "Distance 1.18 a. u. Period 401.4. Diameter 7918 miles. No moon. No air."

The third planet—"That's Mars!" said Lourdi.

It was.

And the second planet was Earth.

"I believe I now know what has happened," said Verd, speaking very loudly. Twenty-seven faces looked back at him across the dining room. He was addressing crew and passengers, and he had to address them in person, for the Brain could no longer repeat his words over the speakers in the rooms. Verd discovered that he did not like public speaking.

"You know that a Jumper creates an overspace in which the speed of light becomes infinite in a neighborhood of the ship. When—"

"Almost infinite," said a passenger.

"That's a popular misconception," Verd snapped. With an effort he resumed his speaking voice. "The speed of light goes all the way to infinity. If it weren't for the braking spines, which keep our speed finite by projecting almost into normal space, we'd wind up by going simultaneous—being everywhere at once. The braking spines are those things that point out from the girdle of the ship.

"Well, there was a rock in our way, inside the range of the meteor gun, when the Jumper went off. It went through the Jumper and into the Brain.

"The damage it did to our Brain is secondary. Something happened to the Jumper while the rock was in there.

Maybe some metal vaporized and caused a short circuit. Anyway the *Goat* jumped back into overspace in the other direction. The speed of light went to zero.

"The braking spines stuck out, or we wouldn't have come out until the bitter end of time. Well, then. In a region around the ship, the speed of light was zero. Our mass was infinite, our clocks and hearts stopped, the ship became an infinitesimally thin disc. This state lasted for no time—in ship's time. But when it ended several billion years had passed."

A universal gasp, and then pandemonium.

"Billion?" "Kdapt stomp it—" "Oh, my God!" "Practical joke, Marna. I must say—" "Shut up and let him finish."

The shouting died away. A last voice shouted, "But if our mass—"

"Only in a region around the ship!" Verd recognized the man; it was Strac Astrophysics.

"Oh," said Strac, apparently shrugging off a picture of suns and galaxies snatched brutally down upon his cringing head by the *Goat*'s infinite gravity.

"The zero effect has been used before," Verd continued. "For suspended animation, for very long range time capsules, et cetera. But it has never happened to a spacecraft, to my knowledge. Our position is very bad. The Sun has become a greenish-white dwarf. The Earth has lost all its air and has become a one-face world. Like Mercury, it no longer rotates. Mercury isn't there any more. Neither is the Moon.

"You can forget the idea of going home, and say good-by to anyone you knew outside this ship. This is the universe, ourselves and nobody else, and our only duty is to survive. We will keep you informed of developments. Anyone who wishes his passage money refunded is welcome to it."

In a crackle of weak, graveyard laughter, Verd bobbed his head in dismissal.

The passengers weren't taking the hint. Hearing the captain in person was as strange to them as it was to Verd.

They sat looking at each other, and a few got up, changed thier minds and sat down again. One called, "What will you do next?"

"Ask the Brain for suggestions," said Verd. "Out, now!"

"We'd like to stay and listen," said the same man. He was short and broad and big-footed, probably from one of the heaviest planets, and he had the rough-edged compactness of a land tank. "We've the right to consult the Brain at any time. If it takes a translator we should have a translator."

Verd nodded. "That's true." Without further comment he turned to Chanda and said. "Ask the Brain what actions will maximize our chance of survival for maximal time."

Chanda tapped her stylus rhythmically next to the Brain speaker.

The dining room seemed raucous with the sound of breathing and the stealthy shuffling of feet. Everyone seemed to be leaning forward.

The Brain answered in swiftly moving dots of light. Chanda said. "Immediately replace—Eve of Kdapt!" Chanda looked very startled, then grinned around at Verd. "Sorry, Captain. 'Immediately replace Verd Spacercaptain with Strac Astrophysics in supreme authority over ship.' "

In the confusion that followed, Verd's voice was easily the loudest. "Everybody out! Everybody but Strac Astrophysics."

Miraculously, they obeyed.

III

Strac was a long, tall oldster, old in habits and manners and mode of dress; a streak of black-enameled steel wool emphasized his chocolate scalp, and his ears spread like wings. Verd wondered why he didn't have them fixed, and then wondered no longer. Strac obviously made a fetish of keeping what he was born with. His hairline didn't start until the top of his forehead. His fingernails had not been removed. They must have required constant trimming. It was a wonder he didn't have a mustache!

"I believe you've traveled on my ship before," Verd told him. "Have you ever said or done anything to give the Brain, or any passenger, the idea that you want to command my ship?"

"Certainly not!" Strac seemed as ruffled by the Brain's suggestion as Verd himself. "The Brain must be insane," he muttered venomously. Then he looked up uneasily. "*Could* the Brain be insane?"

"No," Chanda answered. "Mechanical Brains can be damaged, they can be destroyed, but if they come up with an answer it's the right one. If there's even the slightest doubt you'll get an 'insufficient data'."

"Then why would it try to take my command?"

"I don't know. Captain, there's something you should know right now."

"What?"

"The Brain has stopped answering questions. It stopped right after the passengers left. It obeys orders if they're given in Morse, but it won't answer back."

"Oh, Kdapt take the Brain!" Verd rubbed his temples with his fingertips. "Parliss, what did the Brain know about Strac?"

"Same as any other passenger. Name, profession, medical state and history, mass, world of origin. That's all."

"Hmph. Strac, where were you born?"

"The Canyon."

"Oh? Kind of lonely, wasn't it?"

"In a way, yes. Three hundred thousand is a tiny population for a solar system, and there's no room for more. There's no air above the Canyon rim, of course. I got out as soon as I could. Haven't been back in almost a century."

"I see."

"No, Captain, I don't think you can. In the Canyon, it's the culture that's lonely. The people are constantly surrounded by others, and everybody thinks just like everybody else. You'd say there's no cultural cross-fertilization. The pressure to conform is brutal.''

"Interesting. Strac, do you have any bright ideas that the Brain might have latched onto somehow? Or do you perhaps have a reputation so large in scientific circles that the Brain might know of it?''

"No. I'm sure that's not the case.''

"Well, do you have any ideas at all? We need them badly.''

"I'm afraid not. Captain, just what *is* our position? It seems that the biggest emergency is that everyone is dead but us. How do we cope with an emergency like that?''

"We don't," said Verd. "Not without time travel, and that's impossible. Isn't it?''

"Of course.''

"Chanda, exactly what did you ask the Brain? How did you phrase it?''

"Maximize the probability of our surviving for maximum time. That's what you asked for. Excuse me, Captain, but the Brain almost certainly assumed that 'maximum time' meant 'forever'.''

"All right. Parliss, how long will the ship keep us going.''

Parliss was only thirty years old, and was burdened with youth's habitual unsureness; but he knew his profession well enough. "A long time, Captain. Decades, maybe centuries. There's some boosterspice seeds in our consignment for the Zoo Of Earth; if we could grow boosterspice aboard ship we could keep ourselves young. The air plant will work as long as there's sunlight or starlight. But the food converter—well, it can't *make* elements. Eventually they'll get lost somewhere in the circuit, and we'll start getting deficiency diseases, and—hmmm. I could probably keep us all alive for a century and a half. And if we institute cannibalism we could—''

"Never mind. Let's call that our limit if we stay in space. We've got other choices, Strac, none of them pleasant.

"We can get to any planet in the solar system, using the photon drive. There's enough solid core in the landing rockets to land us on any world smaller than Uranus, or to land and take off from a world the size of Venus or smaller, and we can take off from anywhere with the photon drive, leaving nothing but boiling rock behind. But nothing in the system is habitable."

"If I may interrupt," said Strac. "Why do we have a photon drive?"

"Excuse me?"

"Why does the *Hogan's Goat* need a photon drive? Why didn't she just use the Jumper to get from one planet to another, and the solids to get up and down?"

"Oh. It's like this. The math of Jumper travel postulates a figure for the mass of a very large neighborhood, one which takes in most of the local group of galaxies. That figure is almost twice the actual rest mass in the neighborhood. So we have to accelerate until the external universe is heavy enough for us to use the Jumper."

"I see."

"Even with total mass conversion we have to carry an awful lot of fuel. And without the artificial gravity to protect us it would take years to reach the right velocity. The drive gives us a good one hundred gee in uncluttered space." Verd grinned at Strac's awed expression. "We don't advertise that. Passengers might start wondering what would happen if the artificial gravity went off.

"Third choice. We can go on to other stars. It would take decades for each trip, but by refueling in each system we could get to a few nearby stars in the hundred and fifty years Parliss gives us. But every world we ever used must be dead by now, and the G type stars we can reach in the time we've got may have no useful worlds. It would be a gamble."

Strac shifted uneasily in his chair. "It would be worse than that. We don't necessarily need G type suns, we can settle under any sun that won't roast us with ultraviolet, but we do need a binary planet. They're extremely rare, you know. I would hate to gamble that we could reach one by accident. Can't you order the Brain to search out a habitable planet and go there?"

"No," said Lourdi, from across the room. "The telescope isn't that good, not when it has to peer out of one gravity well into another. The light gets all bent up."

"And finally," said Verd, "if we did land on an Earth-sized planet that looked habitable, and then found out it wasn't, we couldn't land anywhere else. Well what do you think?"

Strac appeared to consider. "I think I'll go have a drink. I think I'll have several. I wish you'd kept our little predicament secret a few centuries longer." He stood up with great dignity and turned to the door, then spoiled the exit by turning back. "By the way, Captain, have you ever been to a one-face world? Or have your travels been confined to the habitable worlds?"

"I've been to the Moon, but that's all. Why?"

"I'm not sure," said Strac, and left, looking thoughtful. Verd noticed that he turned right. The bar was aft of the dining room, to the left.

Gloom thickened in the nearly empty dining room. Verd fumbled in his belt pouch, brought out a white tube not much bigger than a cigarette. Eyes fixed morosely on a wall, he hung the tube between his lips, sucked through it, inhaled through the side of his mouth. He exhaled cool, thick orange smoke.

The muscles around his eyes lost a little of their tension.

Chanda spoke up. "Captain, I've been wondering why the Brain didn't answer me directly, why it didn't just give us a set of detailed instructions."

"Me too. Have you got an answer?"

"It must have computed just how much time it had before its motor aphasia became complete. So instead of trying to give a string of instructions it would never finish, it just named the person most likely to have the right answer."

"That sounds right, Chanda. But why Strac? Why not me, or one of you?"

"Good question," said Chanda wearily. She closed her

eyes and began to recite, "Name, profession, mass, world of origin, medical history. Strac Astrophysics, the Canyon . . ."

IV

In the next few days, each member of the crew was busy at his own specialty.

Lourdi spent most of her time at the telescope. It was a powerful instrument, and Chanda told the Brain to find planets of nearby suns and hold the telescope on them while Lourdi looked. But even the nearest were only circular dots.

She did manage to find the Moon—in a Trojan orbit, trailing sixty degrees behind the Earth in its path around the Sun.

Parliss spent his waking hours in the ship's library, looking up tomes on the medical aspects of privation. Gradually he was putting together a detailed program that would keep the passengers healthy for a good long time, and alive for a long time after that, with safety factors allowing for breakdown of the more delicate parts of the life-support system.

Later he intended to prepare a similar program using cannibalism to its best medical advantage . . . but that could wait. The problem was more complex than it seemed, involving subtle physiological effects from moral shock. It wouldn't give them more than another century anyway, since the air circulator wouldn't last longer than that.

Very slowly and painfully, with miniature extensible waldo machinery, Chanda searched out the tiny burns in the Brain's cortex and scraped away the charred semiconducting ash. "Probably won't do any good," she admitted grimly, "but the ash may be causing short circuits, and I certainly can't do any *harm* by getting it out. I wish I had some fine wire."

Once he was convinced that the Jumper was stone cold dead, Verd left it alone. That gave him little to do but worry.

He worried about the damage to the Brain, and wondered if Chanda was being overoptimistic. She was like a surgeon forced to operate on a friend; she refused even to consider that the Brain might get worse instead of better. Verd worried, and he very carefully checked the wiring in the manual override for the drives, moving along outside the hull in a vacuum suit.

He worried about the passengers, too. They would be better off if they were given the illusion that they were helping. The log had a list of passengers, and Chanda got the Brain to put it on the screen, but the only useful professions Verd could find were:

Strac Astrophysics

Jimm Farmer

Avran Zooman

The other professions were all useless here. Taxer, Carmaker, Adman—he was lucky to find anything at all. "All the same," he told Lourdi that night, "I'd have given anything to find a Jak FTLsystems."

"How 'bout a Harlan All-trades?"

"On this tub? Specializing nonspecialists ride the luxury liners." He twisted restlessly in the air between the sleeping plates. "Wanta buy an aircar? It was owned by a sniveling coward—"

Jimm Farmer was the heavy-planet man, with long, smooth muscles and big broad feet. He had a Jinx accent, Verd guessed, which meant he could probably kick holes in hullmetal.

"I've never worked without machinery," he said. "Farming takes an awful lot of machinery. Diggers, plowers, seeders, transplanters, aerators, you name it. Even if you gave me seeds and a world to grow them on I could do nothing by myself." He scratched his bushy eyebrows. For some reason he'd let them grow outward from the end of his hairline. "But if all the passengers and crew pitched in and followed directions, and if they didn't mind a little

back-breaking labor, I think we could raise something . . . if we had a planet with good dirt and some
seeds."

"At least we've got the seeds," said Verd. "Thanks,
Mr. Farmer."

Verd had first seen Avran Zooman walking through the
hall at the beginning of the trip. Zooman was a shocking
sight. His thin strip of hair was bleached-bone white and
started halfway back on his scalp. His skin had faint lines
in it, like the preliminary grooves made in tooled leather.
Verd remembered dodging into an empty stateroom to
regain his composure. Obviously this man was a member
of one of those strange, nearly extinct religious orders
which prohibit the taking of boosterspice.

But he didn't behave like a religious nut. Verd found
him friendly, alert, helpful and very likable. His thick We
Made It accent was heavy with esses.

"In this one respect we are lucky," Avran was saying.
"Or you are lucky. I should have been lucky enough to
miss my ship. I came to protect your cargo, which is a
selection of fertile plant seeds and frozen animal eggs for
the Zoo Of Earth Authority."

"Exactly what's in the consignment?"

"Nearly everything you could think of, Captain. The
Central Government wished to establish a zoo which
would show all the life that Earth has lost as a result of her
intense population compression. I suspect they wished to
encourage emigration. This is the first consignment, and it
contains a male and female of every variety of domestic
life on We Made It. There were to be other shipments from
other worlds, including some extremely expensive muta-
tions from Wonderland designed to imitate the long extinct 'big cats'. We do not have those, nor the useless
decorative plants such as orchids and cactus, but we do
have everything we need for farming. All we need is a
place to plant it."

"Not quite. Not unless you're carrying an all-purpose
incubator for the animals."

"Unfortunately I am not. Perhaps I could show how to
make one out of other machinery." Avran smiled humor-

ously. "But there is a problem. I am fatally allergic to boosterspice extract. This means that I will be dead in less than a century, which unfortunately limits the length of any journey of exploration that I can make."

Frantically Verd tried to sort his climbing emotions before they strangled him. There was admiration that Avran could live so casually with the knowledge of imminent death, wonder that he could have achieved such a state of emotional maturity in what could be no more than fifty years. There was shame, and horror; compounded horror at the knowledge that he was flushing, and Avran could see it.

Avran looked concerned. "Perhaps I should come back later."

"No! I'm all right." Verd had found his tobac stick without thinking. He pulled in a deep, cooling draft of orange smoke, and held it in his lungs for a long moment.

"A few more questions," he said briskly. "Does the Zoo consignment have grass seed? Is there any bacteria or algae?"

"Grass, yes. Forty-three different varieties. But no bacteria, I'm afraid."

"That's not good. It takes bacteria to turn rock dust into fertile soil."

"Yes." Avran considered. "We could start the process with sewage from the ship, and use transplants of intestinal flora. Mix in the rock dust a little at a time. We have earthworms fortunately. It might work."

"Good."

"Now I have a question, Captain. What is that?"

Verd following his pointing finger. "Never seen a tobac stick?"

Avran shook his head.

"There's a funny tranquilizer in tobacco that helps you concentrate, lets you block out distractions. People used to have to inhale the tobacco smoke to get it. That caused lung cancer. Now we do it better. Is there any tobacco in the hold?"

"I'm afraid not. Can you give up the habit?"

"If I have to. But I won't like it."

Verd sat for a moment after Avran had left, then got up and hunted down Parliss. "Avran claims to be allergic to boosterspice," he told him. "I want to know if it's true. Can you find out?"

"Sure, Captain. It'll be in the medical record."

"Good."

"Why would he lie, Captain?"

"He may have a religious ban on boosterspice. If so, he'd be afraid I'll shoot him full of it if I think I need him."

There was no point in interviewing Strac Astrophysics again. Parliss told him that Strac spent most of his time in his room, and that he had borrowed a pocket computer from Chanda.

"He must have something in mind," said Parliss.

The next day he came to the cabin. "I've gone through the medical histories," he said. "We're all in good shape, except Avran Zooman and Laspia Waitress. Avran has just what he said he had. Laspia has a pair of cultured arms, no telling how she lost the old ones, and both ulnae have machinery in them. One's a dooper, one's a multirange sonic. I wonder what that sweet girl is doing armed to the teeth like that."

"So do I. Did you manage to sabotage her?"

"I put a power gain in her room. If she tries to shoot anyone she'll find her batteries are dead."

The sixth day was the day of the mutiny.

V

Verd and Parliss were in the crew common room going over Parliss' hundred-and-fifty-year schedule for shipboard living, when the door opened and Chanda walked in. The first hint came from Chanda's taut, determined expression. Then Verd saw that someone was following her in.

He stood up to protest, then stood speechless as a line of

passengers trooped into the crew room, filling it nearly to bursting.

"I'm sorry, Captain," said Chanda, "but we've come to demand your resignation."

Verd, still standing, let his eyes run over them.

The pretty auburn-haired woman in front, the one who held her arms in an inconspicuously strained attitude while the others took care not to crowd her elbows—she must be Laspia Waitress. Jimm Farmer was also in the front rank. And Strac Astrophysics, looking acutely embarrassed, and many looked angry; Verd wasn't sure who they were angry at. He gave himself a few seconds to think. Let 'em wait it out . . .

"On what grounds?" he asked mildly.

"On the grounds that it's the best chance we have to stay alive," said Chanda.

"That's not sufficient grounds. You know that. You need some criminal charge to bring against me— dereliction of duty, sloppiness with the photon drive, murder, violation of religious tenets, drug addiciton. Do you wish to make such a charge?"

"Captain, you're talking about impeachment—legal grounds for mutiny. We don't have such grounds. We don't want to impeach you, regardless."

"Well, just what did you think this was, Chanda? An election?"

"We're inviting you to resign."

"Thank you, but I think not."

"We could impeach you, you know," said Jimm Farmer. He was neither embarrassed nor angry; he was a man doing a job. "We could charge you with addiction to tobac sticks, try you and convict you."

"Tobac sticks?"

"Sure, everyone knows they're not addictive. The point is that there aren't any higher courts to reverse our decision."

"I guess that's true. Very well, go ahead."

Parliss broke in, in a harsh whisper. "Chanda, what are

you doing?'' His face, scalp and ears were flushed sunset red.

"Quiet, Parl. I'm only doing what needs to be done.''

"You're out of your head with grief for that damn mechanical moron.''

Chanda flashed him a smoking glare. Parliss returned it. She turned away, aloofly ignoring him.

Strac spoke for the first time. "Don't make us use force, Captain.''

"Why not? Do you idiots realize what you're asking?'' Verd's self control was going. He'd been a young man when the *Hogan's Goat* was built. In nearly two centuries he'd flown her further than the total distance to Andromeda and back; nursed her and worried about her and lived his life in her lighted, rushing womb. What he felt must have showed in his face, for the girl with the auburn hair raised her left arm and held it innocently bent, pointed right at him. Probably the sonic; no doubt he would have been swathed in calming vibrations if her batteries had worked. But all he felt was nausea and a growing rage.

"I do,'' Strac said quietly. "We're asking you to make it possible for us to give you back the *Hogan's Goat* after we're through with it.''

Verd jumped at him. A cold corner of his mind was amazed at himself, but most of him only wanted to get his hands around Strac's bony throat.

He glimpsed Laspia Waitress staring in panic at her forearms, and then something clamped a steel hand around his ankle and jerked. Verd stopped suddenly in midair. It was Jimm Farmer. He had jumped across the room like a kangaroo. Verd looked back over his shoulder and carefully kicked him hard under the jaw. Jimm looked surprised and hurt. He squeezed!

"All right,'' said Verd. "All right. I'll resign.''

VI

The autodoc mended two cracked ankle bones, injected mysterious substances into the badly bruised lower terminal of his Achilles tendon, and ordered a week of bed rest.

Strac's plans were compatible. He had ordered the ship
to Earth. Since the *Goat* was still moving at nearly the
speed of light, and had gone well past the solar system, the
trip would take about two weeks.

Verd began to enjoy himself. It seemed the first time
since the last Jump that he had stopped worrying for more
than a few minutes at a time. He even persuaded Lourdi to
cooperate with Strac. At first she would have nothing to do
with the mutineers, but Verd convinced her that the passengers needed her professional help.

After a week on his back he started to move around the
ship, trying to get an idea of the state of the ship's morale.
He did little else. He was perversely determined not to
interfere with the new captain.

Laspia Waitress stopped him in the hall. "Captain, I've
got to take you into my confidence. I am an ARM, a
member of the Central Government Police. There's a
badly wanted man aboard this ship." And before Verd
could start to humor her she produced authentic-looking
credentials.

"He's involved in the Free Wonderland conspiracy,"
she went on. "Yes, it still exists. We had reason to think
he was aboard the *Hogan's Goat*, but I wasn't sure until he
found some way to disarming me. I still don't know just
who he is."

Verd saw she was frightened. "I did that. I didn't want
anyone wandering around my ship with concealed
weapons."

"You fool! How am I going to arrest him?"

"Why would you arrest him? Who would you turn him
over to if you did? What harm can he do now?"

"What *harm*? He's a revolutionary, a—a seditionist!"

"Sure. He's fanatically determined to free Wonderland
from the tyranny of the Central Government of Earth.
Only Wonderland and the Central Government are eons
dead, and we haven't a single Earthman on board. Unless
you're one, and if you are nobody knows it."

He left her sputtering.

• • •

Surprisingly, Strac had talked to no one, except to ask questions of the crew members. If he had plans they were all his. Perhaps he wanted one last look at Earth, ancient grandmother Earth, dead now of old age. Many passengers felt the same.

Verd did not. He and Lourdi had last seen Earth twelve years ago—subjective time—when the *Goat* was getting her lift support systems renovated. They had spent a wonderful two months in Rio de Janeiro, a teeming hive of multicolored human beings moving among buildings that reached like frustrated spacecraft toward the sky. Once they had even seen two Pierson's Puppeteers, natives from l'Elephant, shouldering their way unconcerned among the swarming humans, but shying like three-legged fawns at the sight of a swooping aircar.

Perhaps Puppeteers survived even now, somewhere in the smoky arms of this galaxy or another. Perhaps even human beings lived on, though they must be changed beyond recognition. But Verd did not want to look on the corpse face of Earth. He wanted his memories unspoiled.

He was not asked.

On the fifteenth ship's-morning the Earth was a wide, brilliant crescent, brightest where the seas had dried across the sunward face and left a vast, smooth bed of salt. The sun shone with eery greenish-white radiance beyond the polarized windows. Verd and Lourdi were finishing breakfast when Strac appeared outside the one-way transparent door. Lourdi let him in.

"I thought I'd better come personally," said Strac. "We'll be meeting in the crew common room in an hour. I'd appreciate it if you'd be there, Verd."

"I'd just as soon not," said Verd. "Thanks anyway. Have a roast dove?"

Strac politely declined and left. He did not repeat his invitation.

"He wasn't just being polite," said Lourdi. "He needs you."

"Let 'im suffer."

Lourdi took him gently by the ears and turned him to face her—a trick she had developed to get his undivided attention. "Friend, this is the wrong time to exercise your right to be inconsistent. You talked me into working for the usurper on grounds that the passengers need my help. Well, I'm telling you they need yours."

"Dammit, Lourdi, if they needed me I'd still be captain!"

"They need you as a crewman!"

Verd set his jaw and looked stubborn. Lourdi let go of his ears, patted them gently and stepped back. "That's my say. Think it through, Lord and Master."

Six people sat in a circle around the table. Verd was there, and Lourdi and Parliss and Chanda. Strac sat in the Captain's chair, under the Brain screen. The sixth man was Jimm Farmer.

"I know what we have to do now," said Strac. His natural dignity seemed to have deepened lately; his thin, dark face didn't smile, and his shoulders sagged as if ship's gee were too heavy for him. "But I want to consider alternatives first. To that end I want you all to hear the answers to questions I've been asking you individually. Lourdi, will you tell us about the Sun?"

Lourdi stood up. She seemed to know exactly what was wanted.

"It's very old," she said. "Terribly old and almost dead. The Sun followed the Main Sequence all the way. After our Jumper went funny it continued to get hotter and brighter and bigger and bluer as the region of fusing hydrogen burned its way up to the surface. It could have left the Main Sequence by going supernova or by suddenly expanding into a red giant, but if it had there wouldn't be any inner planets. So the Sun expanded to a white giant, absorbed Mercury, burnt up the last of its hydrogen and collapsed.

"It contracted to a white dwarf. There was unradiated heat working its way out, and heat of contraction, and there were still fusion reactions going on inside, because nuclear fusion gives heat all the way up to iron. So the Sun still gave off light, and still does, even though for all practical purposes there's no fuel left. Now it's a greenish dwarf, and still cooling. In millions of years it'll be a reddish dwarf, and in more millions, a black one.''

''Only millions?''

''Yes, Starc. Only millions.''

''How much radiation is being put out now?''

Lourdi considered. ''About the same as in our time, but it's bluer light. The Sun is much hotter than when we knew it, but all its light has to come through a smaller surface area.''

''Thanks, Lourdi. Jimm Farmer, could you grow food-stuffs under such a star?''

Peculiar question, thought Verd. He sat up straighter, fighting a horrible suspicion.

Jimm looked puzzled, but answered readily. ''If the air was right, and I had enough water, sure I could. Plants like ultraviolet. The animals might need protection from sunburn.''

''Lourdi, what's the state of the galaxy?''

''Lousy,'' she said promptly. ''Too many dead stars, and most of what's left are blue-white and white giants. Too hot. I'd bet that any planet that had the right tempera-ture for life would be a gas giant like Jupiter. The young stars are all in the tips of the galactic arms, and they've been scattered by the spinning of the Galaxy. There are still younger stars in the globular clusters. Do you want to hear about them?''

''We'd never reach them,'' said Verd. His suspicion was a certainty. He blew orange smoke and waited, silent-ly daring Strac to put his intention into words.

''Right,'' said Strac. ''Chanda, how is the Brain?''

''Very, very sick. It might stop working before the decade's end. It'll never last out the century, crippled as it is.'' Chanda wasn't looking so good herself. Her eyes were red, underlined with blue shadows. Verd thought she had lost weight. Her hair hadn't had its usual care. She continued, as if to herself, ''Twice I've given it ordinary commands and gotten the Insufficient Data sign. That's very bad. It means the Brain is starting to distrust its own memory banks."

"Thanks, Chanda." Strac was carrying it off pretty well, but beneath his commander's dignity he looked determined and—frightened. If Verd was right he had reason. "Now you know everything," he said. "Any comments?"

Parliss said, "If we're going star hunting we ought to stop on Pluto and pick up an air reserve. We could stay alive maybe three hundred years that way."

"Uh-huh. Anyone else?"

Nobody.

"Well, that's that." Strac drew a deep breath, let it out slowly. "Now you know everything. There's too much risk in searching the nearby stars. We'll have to go down. Chanda, please order the Brain to land us on the highest flat point in the noon-equator region."

Chanda didn't move. Nobody moved.

"I knew it," Verd said, very quietly. His voice echoed in the greater quiet. The crew common room was like a museum exhibit. Everyone seemed afraid to move. Everyone but Jimm Farmer, who in careful silence was getting to his feet.

"You're out of your mind." Verd paused and tried to make his voice persuasive. "Didn't you understand, Strac? The Brain put you in charge because you had more useful knowledge than the rest of us. You were supposed to find a new home for the human race."

They were all staring at Strac with varying degrees of horror. All but Jimm, who stood patiently waiting for the others to make up their minds.

"You were not supposed to give up and take us home to die!" Verd snapped. But Strac was ignoring him. Strac was glaring back at them all, with rage and contempt in his eyes.

Parliss, normally Nordic-pale, was white as moonlight. "Strac, it's dead! Leave it! We can find another world—"

"You mewling litter of blind idiots!"

Even Jimm Farmer looked shocked.

"Do you think I'd kill us all for a twinge of homesickness? Verd, you know better than that, even if nobody else does. They were on *your* back, twenty-seven people and all their potential children, all waiting for you to tell them how to die. Then suddenly there was a mutiny. You're free! They're all shifted to me!"

His eyes left Verd's and ranged over his shocked, silent crew. "Idiots blindly following the orders of a damaged mechanical brain. Accepting everything you're told. Lourdi!" he snapped. "What does 'one face' mean?"

Lourdi jumped. "It means the planet doesn't rotate with respect to its star."

"It doesn't mean the planet has only one face?"

"Wha-at?"

"The Earth has a back to it."

"Sure!"

"What's it look like?"

"I don't know." Lourdi thought a moment. "The Brain knows. You remember you asked Chanda to make the Brain use the radar to find out. Then she couldn't get it to show us the picture. We can't use the telescope because there's no light, not even infra-red. It must be terribly cold. Colder than Pluto."

"You don't know," said Strac. "Well, I do. We're going down, Chanda?"

"Tell us about it," said Jimm Farmer.

"No." Verd spoke with all the authority he could muster. The responsibility Strac carried showed in his bent shoulders and bleak expression, in his deep, painful breathing, in his previous attempts to pass the buck to someone else. Strac must know exactly what he was doing. He must! If he didn't he couldn't have moved at all!

"Tell us," Jimm repeated. His tone was flat with menace.

"No. Shut up, Jimm. Or we'll let you make all the decisions from now on."

Jimm thought it over, suddenly laughed and sat down. Chanda picked up her stylus and began tapping on the speaker.

VII

The *Hogan's Goat* lay at an odd angle, nearly in the center of a wide, ancient asteroid crater, under a small, fiercely bright sun set in a black sky.

There, marring the oversized girdle with its remaining spires, was the ragged, heat-stained hole where the meteor had struck. There, extending for two thirds of her length, was the gash a rack had made along her belly in the last seconds of the landing. And at the tail, aft of the girdles, that static explosion of curved metal strips was where the photon drive had been before Strac had ordered it cut free.

It had been a bad landing. Even at the start the Brain was a fraction of a second slow in adjusting the ship's gravity, so that the floor had bucked queasily under them as they dropped. Then, when the ship was already falling toward the crater, Strac had suddenly told Chanda that the photon drive had to be accessible after landing. Chanda had started tapping—and the ship had flipped at an angle.

The *Hogan's Goat* had never been built to land that way. Most of the passengers sported bruises. Avran Zooman had a broken arm. Without boosterspice the bone was slow to heal.

A week of hard, grinding labor was nearly over.

Only servomachinery now moved on the crater floor. Most of the activity centered around the huge silver tube which was aimed like a cannon at a point ten degrees above the horizon. The drive tube had been towed up against the crater wall, and a great mound of piled, heat-fused earth now buried its lower end. Cables and fuel pipes joined it higher up.

"Hi! Is that you, Captain?"

Verd winced. "I'm on top of the crater wall," he said,

because Strac couldn't locate him from the sound of his voice. The indeterminate voice had to be Strac. Only Strac would shout into a suit radio. "And I'm not the captain."

Strac floated down beside him. "I thought I'd see the sights."

"Good. Have a seat."

"I find it strange to have to call you Verd," said the astrophysicist. "It used to be just 'Captain'."

"Serves you right for staging a mutiny—Captain."

"Of course. I always knew my unquenchable thirst for power would get me in trouble."

"Don't give me that."

They watched as a tractor-mounted robot disconnected a fuel pipe from the drive, then rolled back.

A moment later a wash of smoky flame burst from the pipe. It changed color and intensity a dozen times within a few seconds, then died as abruptly as it had begun. The robot waited for the white heat to leave the pipe, then rolled forward to reconnect it.

Verd asked, "Why are you so calm all of a sudden?"

"My job's over," said Strac with a shrug in his voice. "Now it's in the lap of the gods."

"Aren't you taking an awful chance?"

"Oh? You've guessed what I'm trying to do?"

"Sure. You're using the photon drive to start the Earth spinning again."

"Why?" Strac baited him.

"You must be hoping there's air and water frozen on the dark side. But it seems like a thin chance. Why were you afraid to explain before?"

"You put it that way—and then ask why I didn't put it to a vote? Verd, would you have done what I did?"

"No. It's too risky."

"Suppose I tell you that I *know* the air and water is there. It has to be there. I can even tell you what it looks like, a great shallow ice dome, stratified according to freezing point, with water ice on the bottom, then carbon dioxide, and all the way up to a few shifting pools of helium II. Surely you don't expect a one-face world to have a gaseous atmosphere? It would all freeze out on the night side. It has to."

"It's there? There's air here? Your professional word?"

"My word as an astrophysicist."

Verd stretched like a great cat. He couldn't help himself. He could actually feel the muscles around his eyes and cheeks rippling as they relaxed, and a great grin crawled toward his ears. "You comedian!" he laughed. "Why didn't you say so?"

"Suppose I kept talking."

Verd turned to look at him.

"You'll have thought of some of these things yourself. Can we breathe the air? It had billions of years to change chemically before it froze. Is there enough of it? Or did too much boil off while the Sun was a blue-white giant? Maybe there's too much, generated by volcanic action after the Moon was too far away to skim it off. Lourdi said the sun is putting out about the right amount of heat, but just *how* close will it be to a livable temperature? Can Jimm Farmer make us topsoil? There'll be live soil on the nightside, but can we get there if we have to? The Earth must be frozen all the way to the center by now, there can't be any radioactivity left—but the drive could still cause serious earthquakes. Kdapt knows I've sweated over that one! Well, Captain, would you have taken all those risks?"

"She blows."

Traces of hydrogen, too thin to stop a meteor, glowed faintly in the destroying light of the drive. A beam like a spotlight reached out over the sharp horizon.

Anything that light touched would flame and blow away on the wings of the photon wind. The drive nosed a little deeper into its tomb of lava.

The ground trembled. Verd turned on his flying unit, and Strac rose after him. Together they hovered over the shaking ground.

In space the drive would have been generating one

hundred savage gravities. Here . . . almost none. Almost.

Little quick ripples came running from the horizon where the drive beam pointed. They ran in parallel lines of dancing dust across the crater floor, sent rocks tumbling from the crater wall, coming closer and closer together.

"Maybe I wouldn't have risked it," said Verd. "I don't know."

"That's the real reason the Brain put me in charge. Did you see the oxygen ice as we went by the nightside? Or was it too dark? To you this frozen air is purely imaginary, isn't it?"

"I'll take your professional word."

"But I don't have to. I take one less risk than you do," Strac said.

Dust danced over the shaking ground. But the ripples were less violent, and were coming less frequently now.

"The Brain was damaged," Verd said softly, musing aloud.

"Yes," said Strac, frowning down into the old crater. Suddenly he touched his controls and started swimming down. "Come on, Verd. In a few days we'll have air. We've got to get ready for wind and rain."

THE MAN WHO LOST THE SEA

Theodore Sturgeon

Long before it was fashionable to allow any sort of emotional intensity in a science-fiction story, a few writers—Bradbury, Leiber, Kornbluth, Sturgeon, mainly—were trying to explore the interior of the soul as well as the intricacies of a spaceship's plumbing. Especially Sturgeon. This one was published first in 1959. Somewhere along the way from there to here, humanity has misplaced the drive that was carrying it into space, but this story has lost none of its impact for that, perhaps even has gained some.

Say you're a kid, and one dark night you're running along the cold sand with this helicopter in your hand, saying very fast *witchy-witchy-witchy*. You pass the sick man and he wants you to shove off with that thing. Maybe he thinks you're too old to play with toys. So you squat next to him in the sand and tell him it isn't a toy, it's a model. You tell him look here, here's something most people don't know about helicopters. You take a blade of the rotor in your fingers and show him how it can move in the hub, up and down a little, back and forth a little, and twist a little, to change pitch. You start to tell him how this flexibility does away with the gyroscopic effect, but he won't listen. He doesn't want to think about flying, about helicopters, or about you, and he most especially does not want explanations about anything by anybody. Not now. Now, he wants to think about the sea. So you go away.

The sick man is buried in the cold sand with only his head and his left arm showing. He is dressed in a pressure suit and looks like a man from Mars. Built into his left sleeve is a combination timepiece and pressure gauge, the gauge with a luminous blue indicator which makes no sense, the clock-hands luminous red. He can hear the pounding of surf and the soft swift pulse of his pumps. One time long ago when he was swimming he went too deep and stayed down too long and came up too fast, and when he came to it was like this: they said, "Don't move, boy. You've got the bends. Don't even *try* to move." He had tried anyway. It hurt. So now, this time, he lies in the sand without moving, without trying.

His head isn't working right. But he knows clearly that it isn't working right, which is a strange thing that happens to people in shock sometimes. Say you were that kid, you could say how it was, because once you woke up lying in the gym office in high school and asked what had happened. They explained how you tried something on the parallel bars and fell on your head. You understood exactly, though you couldn't remember falling. Then a minute later you asked again what had happened and they told you. You understood it. And a minute later . . . forty-one times they told you, and you understood. It was just that no matter how many times they pushed it into your head, it wouldn't stick there; but all the while you *knew* that your head would start working again in time. And in time it did. . . . Of course, if you were that kid, always explaining things to people and to yourself, you wouldn't want to bother the sick man with it now.

Look what you've done already, making him send you away with that angry shrug of the mind (which, with the eyes, are the only things which will move just now). The motionless effort costs him a wave of nausea. He has felt seasick before but he has never *been* seasick, and the

formula for that is to keep your eyes on the horizon and
stay busy. Now! Then he'd better get busy—now; for
there's one place especially not to be seasick in, and that's
locked up in a pressure suit. Now!

So he busies himself as best he can, with the seascape,
landscape, sky. He lies on high ground, his head propped
on a vertical wall of black rock. There is another such
outcrop before him, whip-topped with white sand and with
smooth flat sand. Beyond and down is valley, salt-flat,
estuary; he cannot yet be sure. He is sure of the line of
footprints, which begin behind him, pass to his left, disap-
pear in the outcrop shadows, and reappear beyond to
vanish at last into the shadows of the valley.

Stretched across the sky is old mourning cloth, with
starlight burning holes in it, and between the holes the
black is absolute—wintertime, mountaintop sky-black.

(Far off on the horizon within himself, he sees the swell
and crest of approaching nausea; he counters with an
undertow of weakness, which meets and rounds and settles the wave before it can break. Get busier. *Now*.)

Burst in on him, then, with the X-15 model. That'll get
him. Hey, how about this for a gimmick? Get too high for
the thin air to give you any control, you have these little
jets in the wingtips, see? and on the sides of the *empen-
nage*: bank, roll, yaw, whatever, with squirts of compressed air.

But the sick man curls his sick lip: oh, git, kid, git, will
you?—that has nothing to do with the sea. So you git.

Out and out the sick man forces his view, etching all he
sees with a meticulous intensity, as if it might be his
charge, one day, to duplicate all this. To his left is only
starlit sea, windless. In front of him across the valley,
rounded hills with dim white epaulettes of light. To his
right, the jutting corner of the black wall against which his
helmet rests. (He thinks the distant moundings of nausea
becalmed, but he will not look yet. So he scans the sky,
black and bright, calling Sirius, calling Pleiades, Polaris,
Ursa Minor, calling that . . . that . . . Why, it *moves*.

Watch it: yes, it moves! It is a fleck of light, seeming to be wrinkled, fissured rather like a chip of boiled cauliflower in the sky. (Of course, he knows better than to trust his own eyes just now.) But that movement .

As a child he had stood on cold sand in a frosty Cape Cod evening, watching Sputnik's steady spark rise out of the haze (madly, dawning a little north of west); and after that he had sleeplessly wound special coils for his receiver, risked his life restringing high antennas, all for the brief capture of an unreadable *tweetle-eep-tweetle* in his earphones from Vanguard, Explorer, Lunik, Discoverer, Mercury. He knew them all (well, some people collect match covers, stamps) and he knew especially that unmistakable steady sliding in the sky.

This moving fleck was a satellite, and in a moment, motionless, uninstrumented but for his chronometer and his part-brain, he will know which one. (He is grateful beyond expression—without that sliding chip of light, there were only those footprints, those wandering footprints, to tell a man he was not alone in the world.)

Say you were a kid, eager and challengeable and more than a little bright, you might in a day or so work out a way to measure the period of a satellite with nothing but a timepiece and a brain; you might eventually see that the shadow in the rocks ahead had been there from the first only because of the light from the rising satellite. Now if you check the time exactly at the moment when the shadow on the sand is equal to the height of the outcrop, and time it again when the light is at the zenith and the shadow gone, you will multiply this number of minutes by 8—think why, now: horizon to zenith is one-fourth of the orbit, give or take a little, and halfway up the sky is half that quarter—and you will then know this satellite's period. You know all the periods—ninety minutes, two, two-and-a-half hours; with that and the appearance of this bird, you'll find out which one it is.

But if you were that kid, eager or resourceful or whatever, you wouldn't jabber about it to the sick man, for not only does he not want to be bothered with you, he's thought of all that long since and is even now watching the shadows for that triangular split second of measurement. *Now!* His eyes drop to the face of his chronometer: 0400, near as makes no never mind.

He has minutes to wait now—ten? . . . thirty? . . . twenty-three?—while this baby moon eats up its slice of shadowpie; and that's too bad, the waiting, for though the inner sea is calm there are currents below, shadows that shift and swim. Be busy. Be busy. He must not swim near that great invisible amoeba whatever happens: its first cold pseudopod is even now reaching for the vitals.

Being a knowledgeable young fellow, not quite a kid any more, wanting to help the sick man too, you want to tell him everything you know about that cold-in-the-gut, that reaching invisible surrounding implacable amoeba. You know all about it—listen, you want to yell at him, don't let that touch of cold bother you. Just know what it is, that's all. Know what it is that is touching your gut. You want to tell him, listen:

Listen, this is how you met the monster and dissected it. Listen, you were skin-diving in the Grenadines, a hundred tropical shoalwater islands; you had a new blue snorkel mask, the kind with face plate and breathing tube all in one, and new blue flippers on your feet, and a new blue spear gun—all this new because you'd only begun, you see; you were a beginner, aghast with pleasure at your easy intrusion into this underwater otherworld. You'd been out in a boat, you were coming back, you'd just reached the mouth of the little bay, you'd taken the notion to swim the rest of the way. You'd said as much to the boys and slipped into the warm silky water. You brought your gun.

Not far to go at all, but then beginners find wet distances deceiving. For the first five minutes or so it was only delightful, the sun hot on your back and the water so warm it seemed not to have any temperature at all and you were flying. With your face under the water, your mask was not so much attached as part of you, your wide blue flippers trod away yards, your gun rode all but weightless in your hand, the taut rubber sling making an occasional hum as your passage plucked it in the sunlit green. In your ears crooned the breathy monotone of the snorkel tube, and through the invisible disk of plate glass you saw wonders. The bay was shallow—ten, twelve feet or so—and sandy, with great growths of brain-, bone-, and fire-coral, intricate waving sea fans, and fish—such fish! Scarlet and green and aching azure, gold and rose and slate-color studded with sparks of enamel blue, pink and peach and silver. And that *thing* got into you, that . . . monster.

There were enemies in this otherworld: the sand-colored spotted sea snake with his big ugly head and turned-down mouth, who would not retreat but lay watching the intruder pass; and the mottled moray with jaws like bolt cutters; and somewhere around, certainly, the barracuda with his undershot face and teeth turned inward so that he must take away whatever he might strike. There were urchins—the plump white sea egg with its thick fur of sharp quills and the black ones with the long slender spines that would break off in unwary flesh and fester there for weeks; and filefish and stonefish with their poisoned barbs and lethal meat; and the stingaree who could drive his spike through a leg bone. Yet these were not *monsters*, and could not matter to you, the invader churning along above them all. For you were above them in so many ways—armed, rational, comforted by the close shore (ahead the beach, the rocks on each side) and by the presence of the boat not too far behind. Yet you were . . . attacked.

At first it was uneasiness, not pressing, but pervasive, a contact quite as intimate as that of the sea; you were sheathed in it. And also there was the touch—the cold inward contact. Aware of it at last, you laughed: for Pete's sake, what's there to be scared of?

The monster, the amoeba.

You raised your head and looked back in air. The boat had edged in to the cliff at the right; someone was giving a last poke around for lobster. You waved at the boat; it was your gun you waved, and emerging from the water it gained its latent ounces so that you sank a bit, and as if you had no snorkel on, you tipped your head back to get a breath. But tipping your head back plunged the end of the tube under water; the valve closed; you drew in a hard lungful of nothing at all. You dropped your face under; up came the tube; you got your air, and along with it a bullet of seawater which struck you somewhere inside the throat. You coughed it out and floundered, sobbing as you sucked in air, inflating your chest until it hurt, and the air you got seemed no good, no good at all, a worthless devitalized inert gas.

You clenched your teeth and headed for the beach, kicking strongly and knowing it was the right thing to do; and then below and to the right you saw a great bulk mounding up out of the sand floor of the sea. You knew it was only the reef, rocks and coral and weed, but the sight of it made you scream; you didn't care what you knew. You turned hard left to avoid it, fought by as if it would reach for you, and you couldn't get air, couldn't get air, for all the unobstructed hooting of your snorkel tube. You couldn't bear the mask, suddenly, not for another second, so you shoved it upward clear of your mouth and rolled over, floating on your back and opening your mouth to the sky and breathing with a sort of quacking noise.

It was then and there that the monster well and truly engulfed you, mantling you round and about within itself —formless, borderless, the illimitible amoeba. The beach, mere yards away, and the rocky arms of the bay, and the not too distant boat—these you could identify but no longer distinguish, for they were all one and the same thing . . . the thing called unreachable.

You fought that way for a time, on your back, dangling the gun under and behind you and straining to get enough warm sunstained air into your chest. And in time some particles of sanity began to swirl in the roil of your mind, and to dissolve and tint it. The air pumping in and out of your square grinned frightened mouth began to be meaningful at last, and the monster relaxed away from you.

You took stock, saw surf, beach, a leaning tree. You felt the new scend of your body as the rollers humped to become breakers. Only a dozen firm kicks brought you to where you could roll over and double up; your shin struck coral with a lovely agony and you stood in foam and waded ashore. You gained the wet sand, hard sand, and ultimately with two more paces powered by bravado, you crossed high-water mark and lay in the dry sand, unable to move.

You lay in the sand, and before you were able to move or to think, you were able to feel a triumph—a triumph because you were alive and knew that much without thinking at all.

When you *were* able to think, your first thought was of the gun, and the first move you were able to make was to let go at last of the thing. You had nearly died because you had not let it go before; without it you would not have been burdened and you would not have panicked. You had (you began to understand) kept it because someone else would have had to retrieve it—easily enough—and you could not have stood the laughter. You had almost died because They might laugh at you.

This was the beginning of the dissection, analysis, study of the monster. It began then; it had never finished. Some of what you had learned from it was merely important; some of the rest—vital.

You had learned, for example, never to swim farther with a snorkel than you could swim back without one. You learned never to burden yourself with the unnecessary in an emergency; even a hand or a foot might be as expendable as a gun; pride was expendable, dignity was. You learned never to dive alone, even if they laugh at you, even if you have to shoot a fish yourself and say afterwards "we" shot it. Most of all, you learned that fear has many fingers, and one of them—a simple one, made of too great a concentration of carbon dioxide in your blood, as from too rapid breathing in and out of the same tube—is not really fear at all but feels like fear, and can turn into panic and kill you.

Listen, you want to say, listen, there isn't anything wrong with such an experience or with all the study it leads to, because a man who can learn enough from it could become fit enough, cautious enough, foresighted, unafraid, modest, teachable enough to be chosen, to be qualified for—

You lose the thought, or turn it away, because the sick man feels that cold touch deep inside, feels it right now, feels it beyond ignoring, above and beyond anything that you, with all your experience and certainty, could explain to him even if he would listen, which he won't. Make him, then; tell him the cold touch is some simple explainable thing like anoxemia, alike gladness even: some triumph that he will be able to appreciate when his head is working right again.

Triumph? Here he's alive after . . . whatever it is, and that doesn't seem to be triumph enough, though it was in the Grenadines, and that other time, when he got the bends, saved his own life, saved two other lives. Now, somehow, it's not the same: there seems to be a reason why just being alive afterwards isn't a triumph.

Why not triumph? Because not twelve, not twenty, not even thirty minutes is it taking the satellite to complete its eighth-of-an-orbit: fifty minutes are gone, and still there's a slice of shadow yonder. It is this, *this* which is placing the cold finger upon his heart, and he doesn't know why, he doesn't know why, he *will* not know why; he is afraid he shall when his head is working again . . .

Oh, where's the kid? Where is any way to busy the mind, apply it to something, anything else but the watch hand which outruns the moon? Here, kid: come over here—what you got there?

If you were the kid, then you'd forgive everything and

hunker down with your new model, not a toy, not a helicopter or a rocket-plane, but the big one, the one that looks like an overgrown cartridge. It's so big even as a model that even an angry sick man wouldn't call it a toy. A giant cartridge, but watch: the lower four-fifths is Alpha—all muscle—over a million pounds thrust. (Snap it off, throw it away.) Half the rest is Beta—all brains—it puts you on your way. (Snap it off, throw it away.) And now look at the polished fraction which is left. Touch a control somewhere and see—see? it has wings—wide triangular wings. This is Gamma, the one with wings, and on its back is a small sausage; it is a moth with a sausage on its back. The sausage (click! it comes free) is Delta. Delta is the last, the smallest: Delta is the way home.

What will they think of next? Quite a toy. Quite a boy. Beat it, kid. The satellite is almost overhead, the sliver of shadow going—going—almost gone and . . . gone.

Check: 0459. Fifty-nine minutes?, give or take a few Time eight . . . 472 . . . is, uh, 7 hours 52 minutes.

Seven hours fifty-two minutes? Why there isn't a satellite round earth with a period like that. In all the solar system there's only . . .

The cold finger turns fierce, implacable.

The east is paling and the sick man turns to it, wanting the light, the sun, an end to questions whose answers couldn't be looked upon. The sea stretches endlessly out to the growing light, and endlessly, somewhere out of sight, the surf roars. The paling east bleaches the sandy hilltops and throws the line of footprints into aching relief. That would be the buddy, the sick man knows, gone for help. He can not at the moment recall who the buddy is, but in time he will, and meanwhile the footprints make him less alone.

The sun's upper rim thrusts itself above the horizon with a flash of green, instantly gone. There is no dawn, just the green flash and then a clear white blast of unequivocal sunup. The sea could not be whiter, more still, if it were frozen and snow-blanketed. In the west, stars still blaze, and overhead the crinkled satellite is scarcely

abashed by the growing light. A formless jumble in the
valley below begins to resolve itself into a sort of tent-city,
or installation of some kind, with tube-like and sail-like
buildings. This would have meaning for the sick man if his
head was working right. Soon, it would. Will.
(Oh . . .)

The sea, out on the horizon just under the rising sun, is
behaving strangely, for in that place where properly be-
longs a pool of unbearable brightness, there is instead a
notch of brown. It is as if the white fire of the sun is
drinking dry the sea—for look, look! the notch becomes a
bow and the bow a crescent, racing ahead of the sunlight,
white sea ahead of it and behind it a cocoa-dry stain
spreading across and down toward where he watches.

Beside the finger of fear which lies on him, another
finger places itself, and another, making ready for that
clutch, that grip, that ultimate insane squeeze of panic.
Yet beyond that again, past that squeeze when it comes, to
be savored if the squeeze is only fear and not panic, lies
triumph—triumph, and a glory. It is perhaps this which
constitutes his whole battle: to fit himself, prepare himself
to bear the utmost that fear could do, for if he can do that,
there is a triumph on the other side. But . . . not yet.
Please, not yet awhile.

Something flies (or flew, or will fly—he is a little
confused on this point) toward him, from the far right
where the stars still shine. It is not a bird and it is unlike
any aircraft on earth, for the aerodynamics are wrong.
Wings so wide and so fragile would be useless, would melt
and tear away in any of earth's atmosphere but the outer
fringes. He sees then (because he prefers to see it so) that it
is the kid's model, or part of it, and for a toy, it does very
well indeed.

It is the part called Gamma, and it glides in, balancing,
parallels the sand and holds away, holds away slowing,
then settles, all in slow motion, throwing up graceful sheet
fountains of fine sand from its skids. And it runs along the
ground for an impossible distance, letting down its weight
by the ounce and stingily the ounce, until *look out* until a

skid *look out* fits itself into a bridged crevasse *look out, look out!* and still moving on, it settles down to the struts. Gamma then, tired, digs her wide left wingtip carefully into the racing sand, digs it in hard; and as the wing breaks off, Gamma slews, sidles, slides slowly, pointing her other triangular tentlike wing at the sky, and broadside crushes into the rocks at the valley's end.

As she rolls smashing over, there breaks from her broad back the sausage, the little Delta, which somersaults away to break its back upon the rocks, and through the broken hull, spill smashed shards of graphite from the moderator of her power pile. *Look out! Look out!* and at the same instant from the finally checked mass of Gamma there explodes a doll, which slides and tumbles into the sand, into the rocks and smashed hot graphite from the wreck of Delta.

The sick man numbly watches this toy destroy itself: what will they think of next?—and with a gelid horror prays at the doll lying in the raging rubble of the atomic pile: *don't stay there, man—get away! get away! that's hot, you know?* But it seems like a night and a day and half another night before the doll staggers to its feet and, clumsy in its pressure-suit, runs away up the valleyside, climbs a sand-topped outcrop, slips, falls, lies under a slow cascade of cold ancient sand until, but for an arm and the helmet, it is buried.

The sun is high now, high enough to show the sea is not a sea, but brown plain with the frost burned off it, as now it burns away from the hills, diffusing in air and blurring the edges of the sun's disk, so that in a very few minutes there is no sun at all, but only a glare in the east. Then the valley below loses its shadows, and like an arrangement in a diorama, reveals the form and nature of the wreckage below: no tent-city this, no installation, but the true real ruin of Gamma and the eviscerated hulk of Delta. (Alpha was the muscle, Beta the brain; Gamma was a bird, but Delta, Delta was the way home.)

And from it stretches the line of footprints, to and by the

sick man, above to the bluff, and gone with the sandslide which had buried him there. Whose footprints?

He knows whose, whether or not he knows that he knows, or wants to or not. He knows what satellite has (give or take a bit) a period like that (want it exactly?—it's 7.66 hours). He knows what world has such a night, and such a frosty glare by day. He knows these things as he knows how spilled radio-actives will pour the crash and mutter of surf into a man's earphones.

Say you were that kid: say, instead, at last, that you are the sick man, for they are the same; surely then you can understand why of all things, even while shattered, shocked, sick with radiation calculated (leaving) radiation computed (arriving) and radiation past all bearing (lying in the wreckage of Delta) you would want to think of the sea. For no farmer who fingers the soil with love and knowledge, no poet who sings of it, artist, contractor, engineer, even child bursting into tears at the inexpressible beauty of a field of daffodils—none of these is as intimate with Earth as those who live on, live with, breathe and drift in its seas. So of these things you must think; with these you must dwell until you are less sick and more ready to face the truth.

The truth, then, is that the satellite fading here is Phobos, that those footprints are your own, that there is no sea here, that you have crashed and are killed and will in a moment be dead. The cold hand ready to squeeze and still your heart is not anoxia or even fear, it is death. Now, if there is something more important than this, now is the time for it to show itself.

The sick man looks at the line of his own footprints, which testify that he is alone, and at the wreckage below, which states that there is no way back, and at the white east and the mottled west and the paling bleak-like satellite above. Surf sounds in his ears. He hears his pumps. He hears what is left of his breathing. The cold clamps down and folds him round past measuring, past all limits.

Then he speaks, cries out: then with joy he takes his

triumph at the other side of death, as one takes a great fish, as one completes a skilled and mighty task, rebalances at the end of some great daring leap; and as he used to say "we shot a fish" he uses no "I":

"God," he cries, dying on Mars, "God, we made it!"

THE HAPPIEST CREATURE

Jack Williamson

When "The Happiest Creature" was first published, in 1953 in Frederik Pohl's remarkable *Star Science Fiction* anthology series, Jack Williamson was already one of the revered old masters of the science-fiction field. His first story, after all, had appeared in 1928, and *The Legion of Space*, his classic novel, had been serialized in 1934—when Messrs. Sheckley, Dick, Anderson, and Budrys were struggling to master the ABC and Messrs. Niven, Brunner, Silverberg, and Zelazny were yet unborn. Now "The Happiest Creature" itself is 25 years old; and what are we to make of the fact that the revered old master of 1953, Jack Williamson, is still very much in our midst, a hearty, healthy, good-humored, well-beloved man, teaching and writing critical essays on science fiction and active as a writer of s-f even now? (As I write this, he and Frederik Pohl have just embarked on a trilogy of collaborative novels.) Of course, Williamson did begin his career, like so many of us, before he turned twenty; but to continue to write for fifty years, and to grow and change and improve constantly over so long a span, is a remarkable achievement. The man is a phenomenon.

The collector puffed angrily into the commandant's office in the quarantine station, on the moon of Earth. He was a heavy hairless man with shrewd little ice-green eyes sunk deep in fat yellow flesh. He had a genial smile when he was getting what he wanted. Just now he wasn't.

"Here we've come a good hundred light-years, and you can see who I am." He riffled his psionic identification films under the commandant's nose. "I intend to collect at least one of those queer anthropoids, in spite of all your silly red tape."

The shimmering films attested his distinguished scientific attainments. He was authorized to gather specimens for the greatest zoo in the inhabited galaxy, and the quarantine service had been officially requested to expedite his search.

"I see." The commandant nodded respectfully, trying to conceal a weary frown. The delicate business of safeguarding Earth's embryonic culture had taught him to deal cautiously with such unexpected threats. "Your credentials are certainly impressive, and we'll give you whatever help we can. Won't you sit down?"

The collector wouldn't sit down. He was thoroughly annoyed with the commandant. He doubted loudly that the quarantine regulations had ever been intended to apply to such a backward planet as Earth, and he proposed to take his specimen without any further fiddle-faddle.

The commandant, who came from a civilization which valued courtesy and reserve, gasped in spite of himself at the terms that came through his psionic translator, but he attempted to restrain his mounting impatience.

"Actually, these creatures are human," he answered firmly. "And we are stationed here to protect them."

"Human?" The collector snorted. "When they've never got even this far off their stinking little planet!"

"A pretty degenerate lot," the commandant agreed regretfully. "But their human origins have been well established, and you'll have to leave them alone."

The collector studied the commandant's stern-lipped face and modified his voice.

"All we need is a single specimen, and we won't injure that." He recovered his jovial smile. "On the contrary, the creature we pick up will be the luckiest one on the planet. I've been in this game a good many centuries, and I know what I'm talking about. Wild animals in their native environments are invariably diseased. They are in constant physical danger, generally undernourished, and always more or less frustrated sexually. But the beast we take will receive the most expert attention in every way."

A hearty chuckle shook his oily yellow jowls.

"Why, if you allowed us to advertise for a specimen, half the population would volunteer."

"You can't advertise," the commandant said flatly. "Our first duty here is to guard this young culture from any outside influence that might cripple its natural development."

"Don't upset yourself." The fat man shrugged. "We're undercover experts. Our specimen will never know that it has been collected, if that's the way you want it."

"It isn't." The commandant rose abruptly. "I will give your party every legitimate assistance, but if I discover that you have tried to abduct one of these people I'll confiscate your ship."

"Keep your precious pets," the collector grunted ungraciously. "We'll just go ahead with our field studies. Live specimens aren't really essential, anyhow. Our technicians have prepared very authentic displays, with only animated replicas."

"Very well." The commandant managed a somewhat sour smile. "With that understanding, you may land."

He assigned two inspectors to assist the collector and make certain that the quarantine regulations were respected. Undercover experts, they went on to Earth ahead of the expedition, and met the interstellar ship a few weeks later at a rendezvous on the night side of the planet.

The ship returned to the moon, while the outsiders spent several months traveling on the planet, making psionic records and collecting specimens from the unprotected species. The inspector reported no effort to violate the Covenants, and everything went smoothly until the night when the ship came back to pick up the expedition.

Every avoidable hazard had been painstakingly avoided. The collector and his party brought their captured specimens to the pickup point in native vehicles, traveling as Barstow Brothers' Wild Animal Shows. The ship dropped to meet them at midnight, on an uninhabited desert plateau. A thousand such pickups had been made without an incident, but that night things went wrong.

A native anthropoid had just escaped from a place of confinement. Though his angered tribesmen pursued, he had outrun them in a series of stolen vehicles. They blocked the roads, but he got away across the desert. When his last vehicle stalled, he crossed a range of dry hills on foot in the dark. An unforeseen danger, he blundered too near the waiting interstellar ship.

His pursuers discovered his abandoned car, and halted the disguised outsiders to search their trucks and warn them that a dangerous convict was loose. To keep the natives away from the ship, the inspectors invented a tale of a frightened man on a horse, riding wildly in the opposite direction.

They guided the native officers back to where they said they had seen the imaginary horseman, and kept them occupied until dawn. By that time, the expedition was on the ship, native trucks and all, and safely back in space.

The natives never recaptured their prisoner. Through that chance-in-a-million that can never be eliminated by even the most competent undercover work, he had got aboard the interstellar ship.

The fugitive anthropoid was a young male. Physically, he appeared human enough, even almost handsome. Lean from the prison regimen, he carried himself defiantly erect. Some old injury had left an ugly scar across his cheek and his thin lips had a snarling twist, but he had a poised alertness and a kind of wary grace.

He was even sufficiently human to possess clothing and a name. His filthy garments were made of twisted animal and vegetable fibers and the skins of butchered animals. His name was Casey James.

He was armed like some jungle carnivore, however,

with a sharpened steel blade. His body, like his whole planet, was contaminated with parasitic organisms. He was quivering with fear and exhaustion, like any hunted animal, the night he blundered upon the ship. The pangs of his hunger had passed, but a bullet wound in his left arm was nagging him with unalleviated pain.

In the darkness, he didn't even see the ship. The trucks were stopped on the road, and the driver of the last had left it while he went ahead to help adjust the loading ramp. The anthropoid climbed on the unattended truck and hid himself under a tarpaulin before it was driven aboard.

Though he must have been puzzled and alarmed to find that the ship was no native conveyance, he kept hidden in the cargo hold for several days. With his animal craftiness, he milked one of the specimen animals for food, and slept in the cab of an empty truck. Malignant organisms were multiplying in his wounded arm, however, and pain finally drove him out of hiding.

He approached the attendants who were feeding the animals, threatened them with his knife, and demanded medical care. They disarmed him without difficulty and took him to the veterinary ward. The collector found him there, already scrubbed and disinfected, sitting up in his bed.

"Where're we headed for?" he wanted to know.

He nodded without apparent surprise when the collector told him the mission and the destination of the ship.

"Your undercover work ain't quite so hot as you seem to think," he said. "I've seen your flying saucers myself."

"Flying saucers!" The collector sniffed disdainfully, "They aren't anything of ours. Most of them are nothing but refracted images of surface lights, produced by atmospheric inversions. The quarantine people are getting out a book to explain that to your fellow creatures."

"A good one for the cops!" The anthropoid grinned. "I bet they're still scratching their dumb skulls, over how I dodged 'em." He paused to finger his bandaged arm, in evident appreciation of the civilized care he had received.

"And when do we get to this wonderful zoo of yours?"

"You don't," the collector told him. "I did want exactly such a specimen as you are, but those stuffy bureaucrats wouldn't let me take one."

"So you gotta get rid of me?"

The psionic translator revealed the beast's dangerous desperation, even before his hard body stiffened.

"Wait!" The collector retreated hastily. "Don't alarm yourself. We won't hurt you. We couldn't destroy you, even to escape detection. No civilized man can destroy a human life."

"Nothing to it," the creature grunted. "But if you ain't gonna toss me out in space, then what?"

"You've put us in an awkward situation." The yellow man scowled with annoyance. "If the quarantine people caught us with you aboard, they'd cancel our permits and seize everything we've got. Somehow, we'll have to put you back."

"But I can't go back." The anthropoid licked his lips nervously. "I just gut-knifed a guard. If they run me down this time, it's the chair for sure."

The translator made it clear that the chair was an elaborate torture machine in which convicted killers were put to a ceremonial death, according to a primitive tribal code of blood revenge.

"So you gotta take me wherever you're going." The creature's dark, frightened eyes studied the collector cunningly. "If you put me back, you'll be killing me."

"On the contrary." The collector's thick upper lip twitched slightly, and a slow smile oozed across his wide putty face, warming everything except his frosty little eyes. "Human life is sacred. We can arrange to make you the safest creature of your kind—and also the happiest—so long as you are willing to observe two necessary conditions."

"Huh?" The anthropoid squinted. "Whatcha mean?"

"You understand that we violated the quarantine in allowing you to get aboard," the collector explained patiently. "We, and not you, would be held responsible in case of detection, but we need your help to conceal the violation. We are prepared to do everything for you, if you will make and keep two simple promises.''

''Such as?''

''First, promise you won't talk about us.''

''Easy enough.'' The beast grinned. ''Nobody'd believe me, anyhow.''

''The quarantine people would.'' The collector's cold eyes narrowed. ''Their undercover agents are alert for rumors of any violation.''

''Okay, I'll keep my mouth shut.'' The creature shrugged. ''What else?''

''Second, you must promise not to kill again.''

The anthropoid stiffened. ''What's it to you?''

''We can't allow you to destroy any more of your fellow beings. Since you are now in our hands, the guilt would fall on us.'' The collector scowled at him. ''Promise?''

The anthropoid chewed thoughtfully on his thin lower lip. His hostile eyes looked away at nothing. The collector caught a faint reflection of his thoughts, through the translator, and stepped back uneasily.

''The cops are hot behind me,'' he muttered. ''I gotta take care of myself.''

''Don't worry.'' The collector snapped his fat fingers. ''We can get you a pardon. Just say you won't kill again.''

''No.'' Lean muscles tightened in the anthropoid's jaws. ''There's one certain man I gotta knock off. That's the main reason I busted outa the pen.''

''Who is this enemy?'' The collector frowned. ''Why is he so dangerous?''

''But he ain't so dangerous,'' the beast grunted. ''I just hate his guts.''

''I don't understand.''

''I always wanted to kick his face in.'' The creature's thin lips snarled. ''Ever since we was kids together, back in Las Verdades.''

''Yet you have never received any corrective treatment, for such a monstrous obsession?'' The collector shook his head incredulously, but the anthropoid ignored him.

"His name is Gabriel Meléndez," the creature muttered. "Just a dirty greaser, but he makes out he's just as good as me. I had money from my rich aunt and he was hungry half the time, but he'd never stay in his place. Even when he was just a snotty-nosed kid, and knew I could beat him because I was bigger, he was always trying to fight me." The beast bared his decaying teeth. "I aim to kill him, before I'm through."

"Killing is never necessary," the collector protested uneasily. "Not for civilized men."

"But I ain't so civilized." The anthropoid grinned bleakly. "I aim to gut-knife Gabe Meléndez, just like I did that dumb guard."

"An incredible obsession!" The collector recoiled from the grim-lipped beast and the idea of such raw violence. "What has this creature done to you?"

"He took the girl I wanted." The beast caught a rasping breath. "And he put the cops on me. At least I think it was him, because I got caught not a month after I stuck up the filling station where he works. I think he recognized me, and I aim to get him."

"No——"

"But I will!" The anthropoid slipped out of bed and stood towering over the fat man defiantly, his free hand clenched and quivering. "You can't stop me, not with all your fancy gadgets."

The beast glared down into the collector's bright little eyes. They looked back without blinking, and their lack of brows or lashes made them seem coldly reptilian. Abruptly, the animal subsided.

"Okay, okay!" He spat deliberately on the spotless floor and grinned at the collector's involuntary start. "What's it worth, to let him live?"

The collector shook off his shocked expression.

"We're undercover experts and we know your planet." A persuasive smile crept across his gross face. "Our resources are quite adequate to take care of anything you can demand. Just give your word not to kill again, or talk about us, and tell me what you want."

The anthropoid rubbed his hairy jaw, as if attempting to think.

"First, I want the girl," he muttered huskily. "Carmen Quintana was her name, before she married Gabe. She may give you a little trouble, because she don't like me a bit. Nearly clawed my eyes out once, even back before I shot her old man at the filling station." His white teeth flashed in a wolfish grin. "Think you can make her go for me?"

"I think we can." The collector nodded blandly. "We can arrange nearly anything."

"You'd better arrange that." The anthropoid's thin brown hand knotted again. "And I'll make her sorry she ever looked at Gabe!"

"You don't intend to injure her?"

"That's my business." The beast laughed. "Just take me to Las Verdades. That's a little 'dobe town down close to the border."

The anthropoid listed the rest of his requirements, and crossed his heart in a ritual gesture of his tribe to solemnize his promises. He knew when the interstellar craft landed again, but he had to stay aboard a long time afterwards, living like a prisoner in a sterile little cell, while he waited for the outsiders to complete their underground arrangements for his return. He was fuming with impatience, stalking around his windowless room like a caged carnivore, when the collector finally unlocked his door.

"You're driving me nuts," he growled at the hairless outsider. "What's the holdup?"

"The quarantine people." The collector shrugged. "We had to manufacture some new excuse for every move we made, but I don't think they ever suspected anything. And here you are!"

He dragged a heavy piece of primitive luggage into the room and straightened up beside it, puffing and mopping at his broad wet face.

"Open it up," he wheezed. "You'll see that we intend to keep our part of the bargain. Don't forget yours."

The anthropoid dropped on his knees to burrow eagerly through the garments and the simple paper documents in the bag. He looked up with a scowl.

"Where is it?" he snapped.

"You'll find everything," the fat man panted. "Your pardon papers. Ten thousand dollars in currency. Forty thousand in cashier's checks. The clothing you specified——"

"But where's the gun?"

"Everything has been arranged so that you will never need it." The collector shifted on his feet uncomfortably. "I've been hoping you might change your mind about——"

"I gotta protect myself."

"You'll never be attacked."

"You said you'd give me a gun."

"We did." The collector shrugged unhappily. "You may have it, if you insist, when you leave the ship. Better get into your new clothing now. We want to take off again in half an hour."

The yellow Cadillac convertible he had demanded was waiting in the dark at the bottom of the ramp, its chrome trim shimmering faintly. The collector walked with him down through the airlock to the car, and handed him a heavy little package.

"Now don't turn on the headlamps," the yellow man cautioned him. "Just wait here for daylight. You'll see the Albuquerque highway then, not a mile east. Turn right to Las Verdades. We have arranged everything to keep you very happy there, so long as you don't attempt to betray us."

"Don't worry." He grinned in the dark. "Don't worry a minute."

He slid into the car and clicked on the parking lights. The instrument panel lit up like a Christmas tree. He settled himself luxuriously at the wheel, appreciatively sniffing the expensive new-car scents of leather and rubber and enamel.

"Don't you worry, butter-guts," he muttered. "You'll never know."

The ramp was already lifting back into the interstellar ship when he looked up. The bald man waved at him and vanished. The airlock thudded softly shut. The great disk took off into the night, silently, like something falling upward.

The beast sat grinning in the car. Quite a deal, he was thinking. Everything he had thought to ask for, all for just a couple of silly promises they couldn't make him keep. He already had most of his pay, and old clabber-guts would soon be forty thousand miles away, or however far it was out to the stars.

Nobody had ever been so lucky.

They had fixed his teeth, and put him in a hundred-dollar suit, and stuffed his pockets with good cigars. He unwrapped one of the cigars, bit off the end, lit it with the automatic lighter, and inhaled luxuriously. He had everything.

Or did he?

A sudden uncertainty struck him, as dawn began to break. The first gray shapes that came out of the dark seemed utterly strange, and he was suddenly afraid the outsiders had double-crossed him. Maybe they hadn't really brought him back to Earth, after all. Maybe they had marooned him on some foreign planet, where he could never find Carmen and Gabe Meléndez.

With a gasp of alarm, he snapped on the headlights. The wide white beams washed away all that terrifying strangeness, and left only a few harmless clumps of yucca and mesquite. He slumped back against the cushions, laughing weakly.

Now he could see the familiar peaks of Dos Lobos jutting up like jagged teeth, black against the green glass sky. He switched off the headlights and started the motor and eased the swaying car across the brown hummocks toward the dawn. In a few minutes he found the highway.

JOSE'S OASIS, ONE STOP SERVICE, 8 MILES AHEAD

He grimaced at the sign, derisively. What if he had got his twenty years for sticking up the Oasis and shooting down old José. Who cared now if his mother and his aunt had spent their last grubby dimes, paying the lawyers to keep him out of the chair? And Carmen, what if she had spat in his face at the trial? The outsiders had taken care of everything.

Or what if they hadn't?

Cautiously, he slowed the long car and pulled off the pavement where it curved into the valley. The spring rains must have already come, because the rocky slopes were all splashed with wild flowers and tinted green with new grass. The huge old cottonwoods along the river were just coming into leaf, delicately green.

The valley looked as kind as his old mother's face, when she was still alive, and the little town beyond the river seemed clean and lovely as he remembered Carmen. Even the sky was shining like a blue glass bowl, as if the outsiders had somehow washed and sterilized it. Maybe they had. They could do anything, except kill a man.

He chuckled, thinking of the way old baldy had made him cross his heart. Maybe the tallow-gutted fool had really thought that would make him keep his promises. Or was there some kind of funny business about the package that was supposed to be a gun?

He ripped it open. There in the carton was the automatic he had demanded, a .45, with an extra cartridge clip and two boxes of ammunition. It looked all right, fiat and black and deadly in his hand. He loaded it and stepped out of the car to test it.

He was aiming at an empty whisky bottle beside the pavement when he heard a mockingbird singing in the nearest cottonwood. He shot at the bird instead, and grinned when it dissolved into a puff of brown feathers.

"That'll be Gabe." His hard lips curled sardonically. "Coming at me like a mad dog, if anybody ever wants to know, and I had to stop him to save my own hide."

He drove on across the river bridge into Las Verdades. The outsiders had been here, he knew, because the dirt streets were all swept clean, and the wooden parts of all the low adobe buildings were bright with new paint, and all he could smell was the fragrances of coffee and hot bread, when he passed the Esperanza Café.

Those good odors wet his dry mouth with saliva, but he didn't stop to eat. With the automatic lying ready beside him on the seat, he pulled into the Oasis. The place looked empty at first and he thought for a moment that everybody was hiding from him.

As he sat waiting watchfully, crouched down under the wheel, he had time to notice that all the shattered glass had been neatly replaced. Even the marks of his bullets on the walls had been covered with new plaster, and the whole station was shining with fresh paint, like everything else in town.

He reached for the gun when he saw the slight dark boy coming from the grease rack, wiping his hands on a rag. It was Carmen's brother Tony, smiling with an envious adoration at the yellow Cadillac. Tony had always been wild about cars.

"Yes, sir! Fill her up?" Tony recognized him then, and dropped the greasy rag. "Casey James!" He ran out across the driveway. "Carmen told us you'd be home!"

He was raising the gun to shoot when he saw that the boy only wanted to shake his hand. He hid the gun hastily; it wasn't Tony that he had come to kill.

"We read all about your pardon." Tony stood grinning at him, caressing the side of the shining car lovingly. "A shame the way you were framed, but we'll all try to make it up to you now." The boy's glowing eyes swept the long car. "Want me to fill her up?"

"No!" he muttered hoarsely. "Gabe Meléndez—don't he still work here?"

"Sure, Mr. James," Tony drew back quickly, as if the car had somehow burned his delicate brown hands. "Eight to five, but he isn't here yet. His home is that white stucco beyond the acequia madre——"

"I know."

He gunned the car. It lurched back into the street, roared

across the acequia bridge, skidded to a screaming stop in front of the white stucco. He dropped the gun into the side pocket of his coat and ran to the door, grinning expectantly.

Gabe would be taken by surprise. The outsiders had set it up for him very cleverly, with all their manufactured evidences that he had been innocent of any crime at all, and Gabe wasn't likely to be armed.

The door opened before he could touch the bell, but it was only Carmen. Carmen, pale without her makeup but beautiful anyhow, yawning sleepily in sheer pink pajamas that were half unbuttoned. She gasped when she saw him.

"Casey!" Strangely, she was smiling. "I knew you'd come!"

She swayed toward him eagerly, as if she expected him to take her in his arms, but he stood still, thinking of how she had watched him in the courtroom, all through his trial for killing her father, with pitiless hate in her dark eyes. He didn't understand it, but old puffy-guts had somehow changed her.

"Oh!" She turned pink and buttoned her pajamas hastily. "No wonder you were staring, but I'm so excited. I've been longing for you so. Come on in, darling. I'll get something on and make us some breakfast."

"Wait a minute!"

He shook his head, scowling at her, annoyed at the outsiders. They had somehow cheated him. He wanted Carmen, but not this way. He wanted to fight Gabe to take her. He wanted her to go on hating him, so that he would have to beat and frighten her. Old blubber-belly had been too clever and done too much.

"Where's Gabe?" He reached in his pocket to grip the cold gun. "I gotta see Gabe."

"Don't worry, darling." Her tawny shoulders shrugged becomingly. "Gabriel isn't here. He won't be here any more. You see, dear, the state cops talked to me a lot while they were here digging up the evidence to clear you. It came over me then that you had always been the one I loved. When I told Gabriel, he moved out. He's living down at the hotel now, and we're getting a divorce right away, so you don't have to worry about him."

"I gotta see him, anyhow."

"Don't be mean about it, darling." Her pajamas were coming open again, but she didn't seem to care. "Come on in, and let's forget about Gabriel. He has been so good about everything, and I know he won't make us any trouble."

"I'll make the trouble." He seized her bare arm. "Come along."

"Darling, don't!" She hung back, squirming. "You're hurting me!"

He made her shut up, and dragged her out of the house. She wanted to go back for a robe, but he threw her into the car and climbed over her to the wheel. He waited for her to try to get out, so that he could slap her down, but she only whimpered for a Kleenex and sat there sniffling.

Old balloon-belly had ruined everything.

He tried angrily to clash the gears, as he started off, as if that would damage the outsiders, but the Hydra-Matic transmission wouldn't clash, and anyhow the saucer ship was probably somewhere out beyond the moon by now.

"There's Gabriel," Carmen sobbed. "There crossing the street, going to work. Don't hurt him, please!"

He gunned the car and veered across the pavement to run him down, but Carmen screamed and twisted at the wheel. Gabriel managed to scramble out of the way. He stopped on the sidewalk, hatless and breathless but grinning stupidly.

"Sorry, mister. Guess I wasn't looking—" Then Gabriel saw who he was. "Why, Casey! We've been expecting you back. Seems you're the lucky one, after all." Gabriel had started toward the car, but he stopped when he saw the gun. His voice went shrill as a child's. "What are you doing?"

"Just gut-shooting another dirty greaser, that's all."

"Darling!" Carmen snatched at the gun. "Don't——"
He slapped her down.

"Don't strike her!" Gabriel stood gripping the door of

the car with both hands. He looked sick. His twitching face was bright with sweat, and he was gasping hoarsely for his breath. He was staring at the gun, his wide eyes dull with horror.

"Stop me!"

He smashed the flat of the gun into Carmen's face, and grinned at the way Gabriel flinched when she screamed. This was more the way he wanted everything to be.

"Just try and stop me!"

"I—I won't fight you," Gabriel croaked faintly. "After all, we're not animals. We're civilized humans. I know Carmen loves you. I'm stepping out of the way. But you can't make me fight——"

The gun stopped Gabriel.

Queerly, though, he didn't fall. He just stood there like some kind of rundown machine, with his stiffened hands clutching the side of the car.

"Die, damn you!"

Casey James shot again; he kept on shooting till the gun was empty. The bullets hammered into the body, but somehow it wouldn't fall. He leaned to look at the wounds, at the broken metal beneath the simulated flesh of the face and the hot yellow hydraulic fluid running out of the belly, and recoiled from what he saw, shaking his head, shuddering like any trapped and frightened beast.

"That—*thing*!"

With a wild burst of animal ferocity, he hurled the gun into what was left of its plastic face. It toppled stiffly backward then, and something jangled faintly inside when it struck the pavement.

"It—it ain't human!"

"But it was an excellent replica." The other thing, the one he had thought was Carmen, gathered itself up from the bottom of the car, speaking gently to him with what now seemed queerly like the voice of old barrel-belly. "We had taken a great deal of trouble to make you the happiest one of your breed." It looked at him sadly with Carmen's limpid dark eyes. "If you had only kept your word."

"Don't——" He cowered back from it, shivering. "Don't k-k-kill me!"

"We never kill," it murmured. "You need never be afraid of that."

While he sat trembling, it climbed out of the car and picked up the ruined thing that had looked like Gabe and carried it easily away toward the Oasis garage.

Now he knew that this place was only a copy of Los Verdades, somewhere not on Earth. When he looked up at the blue crystal sky, he knew that it was only some kind of screen. He felt the millions of strange eyes beyond it, watching him like some queer monster in a cage.

He tried to run away.

He gunned the Cadillac back across the acequia bridge and drove wildly back the way he had come in, on the Albuquerque highway. A dozen miles out, an imitation construction crewman tried to flag him down, pointing at a sign that said the road was closed for repairs. He whipped around the barriers and drove the pitching car on across the imitation desert until he crashed into the bars.

KLYSTERMAN'S SILENT VIOLIN

Michael Rogers

Of Michael Rogers I knew nothing at all when, a few months back, I happened upon this brilliant little story in a four-year-old issue of *Analog* that had somehow been misfiled unread all that time. So far as I've been able to discover, "Klysterman's Silent Violin" is still the only piece he's had published in a science-fiction magazine; but he's hardly been inactive as a writer. He is a regular contributor to *Rolling Stone*, has appeared frequently in *Esquire* since 1971, is the author of a novel, *Mindfogger*, published by Knopf, and in 1975 won the American Association for the Advancement of Science Award for a piece on a total eclipse of the sun. He is working now on a book covering current research in molecular genetics. A formidable record; and, though I feel abashed at having failed for so long to notice the byline of so capable a writer, he can be certain that he'll no longer be so neglected in these quarters.

September 17—
Klysterman is a fool. He is building a silent violin; taking up space in the laboratory, using unrequisitioned materials, interfering with more valuable projects, all to create a violin that will make no sound. He explained it to me this morning: the bow and strings are to be some piezoelectric substance, he claims, that in contacting itself

creates not audible vibrations but electrical ones which will be amplified and fed into headphones that the musician will wear. He insisted that he will sell millions of these silent violins, one to every parent whose child is forced to take up the instrument. I told him he was a fool and not to waste my time talking about it. Late this afternoon I saw him wiring a small integrated amplifier. It is difficult to make out what has motivated him to this project but if he is successful I will never hear the end of it.

September 19—

Ludmila W., a young woman who came to the Lab late in the summer, and who is apparently some acquaintance of Klysterman's, gave a short talk at breakfast this morning. She has developed an electrochemical device to create parrot-fever virus from nickel-cadmium cells and carbon tetrachloride. This is the strategic battlefield psittacosis synthesizer that has been predicted for several years. This Ludmila W., although undeniably brilliant, must, I am warned, be watched carefully. For several months she was involved with last year's psilocybin intensification project before it was shut down. She appears to be perfectly normal in every respect, to me at least.

September 20—

On the fourth floor there was another outbreak of the augmented wheat rust this morning. We have emphasized, repeatedly, the necessity of hermetically sealing the *puccinia graminis* spore containers after each working day but mistakes continue to occur. The fool Klysterman was in charge of the carbon dioxide unit that cornered and destroyed the ergot fungus beside the reactor pool. He will undoubtedly get a commendation, ignoring the fact that he released nearly five thousand cubic feet of the gas in fifteen minutes. A child could have done it with less. He is a cretin, Klysterman is, but he has such luck.

September 21—

A surprise this morning. Ludmila W. came to my office

a bit before noon asking advice. It was a minor problem but it seems significant that she chose me to visit. She was troubled by extreme thermal run-away in the sustenance modulation circuits of her viral synthesizer. I sketched for her the necessary thermistor modifications and then expressed my polite amazement that she would need help on such a basic and straight-forward matter. It turns out that she is not an electronician by education, but a neural paralysis biotist. At one time she worked for a year on the ganglion-destructor toxin at Delta laboratories. She made no mention of the psilocybin intensification project and I was hesitant to bring it up.

I am very much impressed: I had no idea that there was someone of this competence on our staff. She is, as well, an unusually attractive young lady who has not followed the shaven-scalp fashion so popular among the female lab assistants. The effect of hair is truly striking, and easily worth the slight risk of biological contamination. I suspect that she has some interest in me. Perhaps the two of us together can work toward minimizing the massive annoyance of Klysterman here in Beta laboratories. We will, I am certain, get to know one another better.

September 22—

Today Klysterman played his silent violin incessantly. He supports it on his body with thick canvas straps over his shoulders, and insists that it works perfectly but will allow no one else to wear the headphones. I am convinced, for one, that Klysterman is an insane fraud, and it is only a matter of time before he is found out.

At lunch today I sat with Ludmila W. I can detect slight signs, now that I have watched her carefully, of previous involvement with the ill-fated psilocybin intensification project. Several times I clearly noticed her listening to conversations taking place at least two hundred feet away from us, on the other side of the cafeteria. She also stares intently at blank walls, for reasons I have yet to fully understand. After dessert there was a short ceremony presenting Klysterman with a commendation for destroy-

ing the augmented wheat rust outbreak, just as I predicted.
He accepted it as the frivolous buffoon he has become,
grinning and smirking and waving grandly from the
podium to individuals in the audience. He waved particularly at Ludmila W., and she waved back, but this, I think,
was only politeness on her part.

September 23—
   This morning I was transferred up to temporarily super-
vise the augmented wheat rust project, which has encountered a remarkable turn of events. The wheat rust entered
its fourteenth generation today and is now entirely carnivorous. It shows no interest in grains or synthetic protein
substitutes. Naturally, we are all concerned. Although
there was some slight suspicion that the augmentation
might produce an omnivorous fungus, certainly no one
ever considered the possibility of a spore-reproducing
carnivore.
   I think the entire situation may be blamed on modern
education. I would wager that the biotechnicians who
originally modified the genetic structure of the wheat rust
were younger men, trained in method but with no sense of
craftsmanship. I shudder to imagine those eager over-
stuffed minds, tearing apart the RNA binders of the wheat
rust the way one disassembles the encoder of an infrared
spectrometer, with a screwdriver and long-nosed pliers.
And, of course, now that they have wreaked their damage
they have no idea as to how to set it straight again.
   We spent the day examining the genetic profiles for
each generation. There appears to be some unprecedented
spontaneous evolution taking place between sporings that
has no familiar textbook characteristics: a most notable
free-form mutation. Klysterman drifted in several times
today, with the headphones perched on his huge head,
playing his silent violin. It is not altogether silent, I can
report with some satisfaction. The piezoelectric materials
make a faint scraping noise which I find very annoying.
This afternoon Klysterman produced a further consideration to threaten my position when he disconnected

himself from his violin long enough to run a future-generational analysis of the wheat rust. The readouts indicate that by the twenty-second, or perhaps twenty-third, generation, the wheat rust may begin to produce activated gaseous lysergic acid derivatives in quantity.

Klysterman immediately suggested that we seal up all the spore cases and ship them to the counter-insurgency hallucinogenic toxin project at Epsilon labs, although he has promised not to make his findings official for several more days. I will not give up the administration of the wheat rust so easily: with sufficient care I think we can produce the strain of augmented ergot that was originally specified in the genetic contract. Klysterman simply wishes to discredit me.

Tonight I went to visit Ludmila W. at her dormitory but she was not in. This is the third evening in a row that she has been gone. Perhaps it is my natural dislike for the man but I cannot help but suspect Klysterman. The two of them associate far too much for Ludmila's best interests, in my view.

September 24—

At my suggestion, Ludmila W. has been temporarily assigned to the augmented wheat rust project. In order to meet the contract deadline someone must devote full time to developing the deployment devices for the new ergot strain.

At present we are considering sound-actuated capsules, perhaps two inches in length, faced with a sensitive audio-range disintegration diaphragm. These would be deployed from high-level aircraft, or upper atmosphere, MIRV targeted over the enemy agricultural center. The capsules would lie dormant in the fields until the slightest sound—the roar of a tractor starting, feet tramping the rows, even loud voices—fractures the diaphragm that holds the ergot spores in place. Once fractured, the oxygen in the atmosphere would react with the inner lining of the capsule and ultimately the entire assembly would decompose into the soil.

Ludmila W., although she is less excited about the deployment apparatus than I would like, will undoubtedly complete the assignment competently, giving me the necessary time to restructure the carnivorous wheat rust.

This afternoon the ergot entered its twentieth generation. It now lies in thick yellow-brown slabs in the bottom of the spore container, consuming nearly thirty pounds of raw beef a day. Klysterman suspects that we are starving it, at that; but here there are budgetary considerations to take into account. The most recent projections leave little doubt now that the ergot will begin to actively produce lysergic acid in several generations. Klysterman is threatening to make a full report on this matter tomorrow. This supra-paranoia on his part is not becoming of a scientist: his unwarranted caution, I think, is in reality a desire to see me fail.

September 25—

It is hard to know what to do with an annoyance like Klysterman. Today he came into the augumented wheat rust lab several times, I suspect, simply to make me nervous. He has also allowed Ludmila W. to listen to his silent violin. She wore the headphones for nearly half an hour today while he played. She says that he plays beautifully, and the tone that he produces from his massive sheet-aluminum violin is vastly superior to wooden varieties. I find all of this hard to believe. Although it is an unpleasant thought, I recall a memorandum issued last year warning specifically about the survivors of the psilocybin intensification experiments: they are "highly suggestible," the memorandum states, and "given to unusual, spontaneous, sympathetic flights of fancy of a highly irrational nature." Perhaps an unflattering thing to think of the marvelous Ludmila W., but a possibility we must keep firmly in mind.

The augmented wheat rust is doing very well, although I have yet to eliminate—or even isolate the origin of—its powerful carnivorous tendency. On the other hand, it occurred to me quite suddenly this morning that we should perhaps not be so hasty to stamp out this genetic miscalculation. Many of the greatest advances in science have come about through chance and error skillfully taken advantage of, and it seems to me that a spore-reproducing carnivore could have valuable tactical applications. Carnivorous wheat rust, I imagine, might well prove to be the ideal perimeter deterrent to guerilla warfare. I plan to keep my opinion carefully hidden from Klysterman, who still insists on the destruction of the augmented ergot. He would be certain to try to steal any credit due me

September 26—

Tragedy in the lab today—but tragedy of the most educational nature. A technician, in feeding the augmented wheat rust this morning, discovered unwittingly that the ergot has, as predicted, now developed the capacity to generate effective lysergic acid derivatives. What we did not suspect was that it would concurrently develop the instinct to use this hallucinogenic ability in a tactical, strategic manner. In bending over the spore case—which we now estimate contains nearly fifty pounds of the mutated *puccinia graminis*—the technician was suddenly and without any apparent warning sprayed with a gaseous hallucinogen. Stunned and disoriented by the surprise attack he allowed his ungloved hand to brush the surface of the carnivorous ergot. The damaged portion of his arm was amputated and vaporized and at this hour the wheat rust is apparently still confined to its spore case. The technician is under heavy sedation and being treated by competent prostheticians.

There is no question in my mind that the carnivorous ergot has happened upon a remarkable new offensive device; enough, I would say, to put the spitting cobra and even the sophisticated toxin of the lionfish to shame. A new confidence fills me at this moment: the ideal biological weapon may be within our grasp.

Ludmila has perfected the wheat rust deployment device. The slightest sound fractures the case and allows the contents to escape, and the material of the unit is entirely biodegradable. I joked with her a bit: a sound-actuated trigger, I told Ludmila, not much defense against a silent violin. She seemed remarkably subdued considering the unqualified success of her project.

Ludmila W. continues to show what I must consider an unhealthy and even perverse interest in Klysterman. I have learned lately that she has visited him in his dormitory room several times this week, presumably to hear his silent violin. I mean to discuss this matter seriously, at length. It is necessary that she understand the nature of his fraudulent appearance. This silent violin prank has gone on long enough.

September 27—

Klysterman is no longer so vocal in his threats that he will have the project taken out of my hands. He is building a second silent violin which I fear he may try to present to Ludmila W. The massive foolishness that this waste of man hours and materials represents is astounding to me. Klysterman is a perpetual annoyance; in and out of the lab constantly, with his silent violin and his plans for a new one. Ludmila W. talks to him with animation and enthusiasm. I cannot stand Klysterman. He would like to see me fail; his attitude and new frivolity are altogether beyond my understanding.

September 28—

As of this morning, my speculations on the strategic value of carnivorous ergot have become a matter of laboratory record. To say that my modest efforts were received with intense interest, even enthusiasm, would be only to understate the truth. The spore-bearing carnivore has already generated more excitement, I think, than any project since selective botulism. This is very gratifying to me.

Klysterman, however, remains an annoying puzzle. He has for the most part ceased to be antagonistic about my augmented ergot; no more talk about destruction of the fungus or shipping it away from my authority—in fact he now displays an almost proprietary interest in the welfare of the wheat rust, coming in four or five times a day to lean over the spore case, his huge nose pressed against the plexiglass, smearing the plastic by wiggling his fingers and tapping on the cover.

A brief and somewhat laudatory announcement was made at lunch today regarding the tactical ergot project, so I suspect that by now Klysterman has realized the magnitude of what I have isolated, and he hopes to curry favor through his solicitousness. Little good it will do him, I might add, though it is, at any rate, a pleasant turn in his unappealing character.

September 29—

While the augmented ergot project is easily a significant professional victory, I cannot help but feel that somehow I have failed personally with Ludmila W. I had hoped that we might develop some sort of relationship that would extend past the laboratory and into more intimate realms. She is with Klysterman continually now, except for the short time she is compelled to spend with the wheat rust project. He has begun to instruct her in the silent violin and I think this occupies more of her attention and interest than all of what we are doing experimentally. The Tchaikovsky Concerto in D, Ludmila tells me, the first movement alone as Klysterman plays it would say more to me about life than a full chart of the Crosby-James amino acid progressions. Her new mysticism is both distracting and disconcerting to me. I am soundly disappointed at her adolescent foolishness.

September 30—

My initial requisition for experimental animals arrived today; fully twice as many as I had ordered—some indication, perhaps, of the new priority of tactical ergot. The basement of the lab is now crowded with a generous complement of the smaller rodents, an excellent assortment of domestic barnyard animals, a full kennel of dogs and a neat, compact selection of the more notable tropical and subtropical vertebrates and lower primates: a total of

nearly four hundred subjects ready for our investigation of
the carnivorous ergot strain, and Ludmila W., the beautiful, inscrutable Ludmila W., shows no more interest, or
enthusiasm, at the prospect than do our thirty-five rhesus
monkeys freshly out of quarantine. She and Klysterman
are entirely beyond my understanding: there is such a gap
between us that we might as well not try to talk at all.

Klysterman, I think, does not as yet realize the jeopardy
that his light-hearted excesses here at Beta Lab have
placed him in. There is serious talk, I am told, about
relieving him of his technical responsibilities and repro-
cessing his work-status, due to the extreme and frivolous
nature of his current experimental diversions. No more
than two months ago Klysterman completed a magnificent, elegant central nervous system disrupter—massive,
noiseless, long-distance CNS disruption operating on the
most sophisticated of principles—and then he dropped it
almost overnight to pursue the idiocy of his silent violin.
Individuals who have examined the violin tell me that at
least half of it is based directly on devices pirated by
Klysterman from his discarded CNS disrupter. While a
great deal of eccentricity is tolerated here at Beta Lab, in
wise recognition of the part free inquiry plays in scientific
progress, prolonged pointless nonsense, such as Klysterman's violin, simply will not do, and I am certain that
Klysterman will soon feel a small amount of pressure on
him to return to productive pursuits.

October 1—

Although it is a distasteful idea, I cannot help but
wonder once again what influence the psilocybin intensification project had on my attractive colleague Ludmila W.
I have noticed certain aspects of her behavior that are odd:
odd, perhaps, past the delicate point of personal whimsy.
Ludmila W., I suspect, harbors unusual notions—how to
say this properly?—is a bearer of remarkable fancies that
make it nearly impossible for us to communicate at any
length. She has begun of late to bring small portions of
food wrapped up in a napkin back from lunch to feed the

ergot—"treats" she tells me, "treats for the fungus." I have explained to her the experimental necessity for a careful regimentation of the ergot's diet—no chicken salad, I admonish her, no meat balls, no gravy. Ludmila ignores me as if I do not exist. There are moments when I sense that, regardless of her prodigious technical abilities, she is not happy with the work done here at Beta Lab—and that, in fact, she bears me some malice for my own successful career here.

And I would in no way be surprised to learn that she is responsible for influencing Klysterman away from the promising professional future which he now seems intent upon destroying with foolishness.

Klysterman continues his ritual of visiting the ergot daily, waggling his fingers and moving his lips silently as he leans over the case, oblivious to the stares of my colleagues. I have begun to entertain disquieting feelings about smug Klysterman and the carnivorous ergot: is there something that Klysterman is aware of that has escaped me?

This evening, however, I am elated: today we ran the first series of tests with the lower primates—remarkable in every respect. The ergot is quick, efficient, silent, hardy—certainly all that one would want a fungus to be.

October 2—

This morning I noticed that Klysterman has logged a great deal of computer time in the last two days. It is not difficult to tell from the records that he has been running extended analyses of the ergot's future generational profiles. Yet he has said nothing of this to me and has even removed the duplicate readouts of his computations from Central Reference. This is most suspicious, and, in fact, upsetting to me. There is some significance here, I am certain.

October 3—

Today I stopped Klysterman when he first came in to moon vacantly over the ergot. I demanded that he tell me what work he had been doing with the generational profiles on the wheat rust and why I had not been informed. Klysterman is slippery—Klysterman is a sly individual, there is no doubt about that—and he simply smiled in his distracted fashion and said little. Nothing had come of it, he told me, far too much genetic distortion had taken place to allow accurate predictions and it was pointless to try anymore. Perhaps he was telling the truth: he is the expert and I am inclined to believe him, for the time, at least.

The hallucinogen generated by the carnivorous ergot is becoming increasingly sophisticated with each new sporing. While initially it appeared to effectively produce instantaneous disorientation, our most recent results with the primates strongly suggest that it now has some positive attractant factor. The youngest of the ergot simply waits placidly in one corner of the test cell and the subjects go to it. The lower primates, in truth, seem to be distinctly cheerful throughout the entire procedure, as nearly as we can tell: all of this is very strange and exciting to me, and only furthers my conviction that augmented wheat rust will presently give us some interesting and significant turns.

October 4—

I have come to wonder: just what is Klysterman doing? He and Ludmila W. have taken to almost constant association with each other and a reticence—should I say almost a fanatic secrecy?—that inspires the worst sort of suspicion in me. There is some pattern in all of this, I am certain, some small key that Klysterman is deliberately concealing from me. He continues to log computer time for his generational analyses, clumsily disguising his efforts by using misleading programs and inputs—but the nature of his activity is transparently clear to me.

I stop Klysterman in the halls now when I see him and demand as strongly as I am able that he inform me of what he is doing. He smiles—that wondering, beatific smile—and shrugs; "no more is possible" he tells me. Too much genetic distortion he insists, nothing else can be done. This is untrue; Klysterman has developed techniques, he and Ludmila W. together have created projection procedures that are unavailable to me. The two of them have become a significant distraction and a source of no little concern.

The augmented wheat rust continues a magnificent evolution—unquestionably we here at the lab are the first to witness living matter achieve such sophistication in so few generations. I predict a general leveling-off of the mutation process within three or four generations: it seems to me that there is little left to improve on in this magnificent fungus. Production has already begun to tool up for the deployment devices—slightly modified now, with somewhat more of the antipersonnel flavor about them—and the final series of trials will be run this week with South African vertebrates. Within the month I will be sent East for a program of briefings. I feel more than slight pride with each generation that develops, thick and yellow-brown on the spore case. Klysterman is, in perspective, only a minor annoyance against this achievement in strategic biology.

October 5—

I will not allow Ludmila W. and Klysterman to distract me. All I can conclude is that they are in the grip of some contagious insanity and that their odd behavior is symptomatic of mutual mental disturbance. I will have to take steps unless Klysterman excludes himself from the premises of the tactical ergot project and Ludmila W. returns to her normal duties. There is only so much which I can tolerate.

October 6—

Klysterman in and out many times today, his silent violin strapped to his shoulders, checking on the ergot. There seems to be no way to keep him out. More computer time registered under his name this afternoon. Ludmila W.

leaves the lab early today claiming illness. All this very suspicious.

October 7—
What is Klysterman trying to do to me?

October 8—
Symbiosis: I could never have foreseen it—there is no way I might have guessed. Klysterman and Ludmila must have had techniques, derivations, extrapolations, syntheses: they must have had insight, pure burning insight, to see in the tracings of sugars and phosphates, in the bondings of adenines and cytosines and guanines and thymines —to perceive even most dimly the conditions that signal symbiosis. And I fear that they perceived far better than dimly.

This morning I unlock the door of the ergot project and find Klysterman already inside, Ludmila W. standing behind him, the plexiglass cover and sides of the ergot case smashed almost completely. "Best not touch me," Klysterman says and sweet Ludmila nods her head. When I come closer the change in their appearance is obvious; Klysterman is completely covered with a thick layer of the ergot—only his hair and eyes and fingernails are as they were. Ludmila W. is the same, a fine yellow brown velvety covering spreads over her features like stage makeup, adhering as tightly as skin. "A step forward," Klysterman tells me. "A logical extension of your fine work. Evolution in its purest state."

The spore case is empty: as neatly cleaned as if by ultrasonics. Klysterman babbles on about evolution, but I cease to listen to him. Ludmila's arm is a chalky brown, thicker now, and nonreflectant as dried mud. When she smiles her teeth are intensely white.

"The most marvelous of symbiotic relationships," Klysterman insists. "A genetic contract signed and sealed for eternity."

This afternoon Klysterman went out on the street to find someone to perform a marriage ceremony for him and

Ludmila. No one was certain just how to stop him. For the moment it seems wiser to give Klysterman his way: the ergot is apparently neutralized only so far as its symbiote is concerned. God knows what reality is for Klysterman now, wrapped up in lysergic ergot like a lungfish in mud.

While Klysterman is gone, Ludmila W. perches on my desk, headphones over her thick brown ears, sawing away on her silent violin as if all were normal. To be polite I attempt to make conversation. We discuss her impending marriage. She would like children, she says, and I ask her how many. Maybe ten, she tells me, or twenty, or forty, or fifty. She laughs: maybe more.

Ludmila hasn't heard of overpopulation?, I wonder aloud.

She looks puzzled: What overpopulation? Two of us, she tells me, are not even enough for a string quartet.

THE NEW REALITY

Charles L. Harness

Charles L. Harness is a Texas-born patent attorney who startled science fiction readers of the 1948-53 period with eight or ten intricate, provocative, intellectually challenging short stories and a baffling but fascinating novel, *Flight Into Yesterday*. His fiction, tough-minded but with strong metaphysical overtones, attracted a passionately devoted following, and one short novel, "The Rose," became virtually an object of cult adoration in England after its publication there in 1953. (It remained unpublished in the United States for sixteen years thereafter.) Harness's first burst of fiction was followed by a decade of silence, after which he reappeared in the late 1960s with a clutch of short stories and a new novel, *The Ring of Ritornel* (1968). Since then, his published output has consisted of a single story published in 1974, but who knows what surprises he has in store? "The New Reality" is one of Harness's first stories, altogether characteristic of his work. I hope to bring you more.

Prentiss crawled into the car, drew the extension connector from his concealed throat mike from its clip in his right sleeve, and plugged it into the ignition key socket.

After a moment he said, "Get me the Censor."

The seconds passed as he heard the click of forming circuits. Then: "E speaking."

"Prentiss, honey."

"Call me 'E,' Prentiss. What news?"

"I've met five classes under Professor Luce. He has a private lab. Doesn't confide in his graduate students. Evidently conducting secret experiments in comparative psychology. Rats and such. Nothing overtly censorable."

"I see. What are your plans?"

"I'll have his lab searched tonight. If nothing turns up, I'll recommend a drop."

"I'd prefer that you search the lab yourself."

A. Prentiss Rogers concealed his surprise and annoyance. "Very well."

His ear button clicked a dismissal.

With puzzled irritation he snapped the plug from the dash socket, started the car, and eased it down the drive into the boulevard bordering the university.

Didn't she realize that he was a busy Field Director with a couple of hundred men under him fully capable of making a routine night search? Undoubtedly she knew just that, but nevertheless was requiring that he do it himself. Why?

And why had she assigned Professor Luce to him personally, squandering so many of his precious hours, when half a dozen of his bright young physical philosophers could have handled it? Nevertheless E, from behind the august anonymity of her solitary initial, had been adamant.

A mile away he turned into a garage on a deserted side street and drew up alongside a Cadillac.

Crush sprang out of the big car and silently held the rear door open for him.

Prentiss got in. "We have a job tonight."

His aide hesitated a fraction of a second before slamming the door behind him. Prentiss knew that the squat, asthmatic little man was surprised and delighted.

As for Crush, he'd never got it through his head that the control of human knowledge was a grim and hateful business, not a kind of cruel lark.

"Very good, sir," wheezed Crush, climbing in behind

the wheel. "Shall I reserve a sleeping room at the Bureau for the evening?"

"Can't afford to sleep," grumbled Prentiss. "Desk so high now I can't see over it. Take a nap yourself, if you want to."

"Yes, sir. If I feel the need of it, sir."

The ontologist shot a bitter glance at the back of the man's head. No, Crush wouldn't sleep, but not because worry would keep him awake. A holdover from the days when all a Censor man had was a sleepless curiosity and a pocket Geiger, Crush was serenely untroubled by the dangerous and unfathomable implications of philosophical nucleonics. For Crush, "ontology" was just another definition in the dictionary: "The science of reality."

The little aide could never grasp the idea that unless a sane world-wide pattern of nucleonic investigation were followed, some one in Australia—or next door—might one day throw a switch and alter the shape of that reality. That's what made Crush so valuable; he just didn't know enough to be afraid.

Prentiss had clipped the hairs from his nostrils and so far had breathed in complete silence. But now, as that cavernous face was turned toward where he lay stomach-to-earth in the sheltering darkness, his lungs convulsed in an audible gasp.

The mild, polite, somewhat abstracted academic features of Professor Luce were transformed. The face beyond the lab window was now flushed, the lips were drawn back in soundless amusement, the sunken black eyes were dancing with red pinpoints of flame.

By brute will the ontologist forced his attention back to the rat.

Four times in the past few minutes he had watched the animal run down an inclined chute until it reached a fork, chose one fork, receive what must be a nerve-shattering electric shock, and then be replaced in the chute-beginning for the next run. No matter which alternative fork was chosen, the animal always had been shocked into convulsions.

On this fifth run the rat, despite needling blasts of compressed air from the chute walls, was slowing down. Just before it reached the fork it stopped completely.

The air jets struck at it again, and little cones of up-ended gray fur danced on its rump and flanks.

It gradually ceased to tremble; its respiration dropped to normal. It seemed to Prentiss that its eyes were shut.

The air jets lashed out again. It gave no notice, but just lay there, quiescent, in a near coma.

As he peered into the window, Prentiss saw the tall man walk languidly over to the little animal and run a long hooklike forefinger over its back. No reaction. The professor then said something, evidently in a soft slurred voice, for Prentiss had difficulty in reading his lips.

"—when both alternatives are wrong for you, but you *must* do something, you hesitate, don't you, little one? You slow down, and you are lost. You are no longer a rat. Do you know what the universe would be like if a *photon* should slow down? You don't? Have you ever taken a bite out of a balloon, little friend? Just the tiniest possible bite?"

Prentiss cursed. The professor had turned and was walking toward the cages with the animal, and although he was apparently still talking, his lips were no longer visible.

After relatching the cage-door the professor walked toward the lab entrance, glanced carefully around the room, and then, as he was reaching for the light switch, looked toward Prentiss's window.

For a moment the investigator was convinced that by some nameless power the professor was looking into the darkness, straight into his eyes.

He exhaled slowly. It was preposterous.

The room was plunged in darkness.

The investigator blinked and closed his eyes. He wouldn't really have to worry until he heard the lab door opening on the opposite side of the little building.

The door didn't open. Prentiss squinted into the darkness of the room.

Where the professor's head had been were now two mysterious tiny red flames, like candles.

Something must be reflecting from the professor's corneas. But the room was dark; there was no light to be reflected. The flame-eyes continued their illusion of studying him.

The hair was crawling on Prentiss's neck when the twin lights finally vanished and he heard the sound of the lab door opening.

As the slow heavy tread died away down the flagstones to the street, Prentiss gulped in a huge lungful of the chill night air and rubbed his sweating face against his sleeve.

What had got into him? He was acting like the greenest cub. He was glad that Crush had to man the televisor relay in the Cadillac and couldn't see him.

He got to his hands and knees and crept silently toward the darkened window. It was a simple sliding sash, and a few seconds sufficed to drill through the glass and insert a hook around the sash lock. The rats began a nervous squeaking as he lowered himself into the darkness of the basement room.

His ear-receptor sounded. "The prof is coming back!" wheezed Crush's tinny voice.

Prentiss said something under his breath, but did not pause in drawing his infra-red scanner from his pocket.

He touched his fingers to his throat mike. "Signal when he reaches the bend in the walk," he said. "And be sure you get this on the visor tape."

The apparatus got his first attention.

The investigator had memorized its position perfectly. Approaching as closely in the darkness as he dared, he 'panned' the scanner over some very interesting apparatus that he had noticed on the table.

Then he turned to the books on the desk, regretting that he wouldn't have time to record more than a few pages.

"He's at the bend," warned Crush.

"Okay," mumbled Prentiss, running sensitive fingers

over the book bindings. He selected one, opened it at random, and ran the scanner over the invisible pages. "Is this coming through?" he demanded.

"Chief, *he's at the door!*"

Prentiss had to push back the volume without scanning any more of it. He had just relocked the sash when the lab door swung open.

A couple of hours later the ontologist bid good-morning to his receptionist and secretaries and stepped into his private office. He dropped with tired thoughtfulness into his swivel chair and pulled out the infrared negatives that Crush had prepared in the Cadillac darkroom. The page from the old German diary was particularly intriguing. He laboriously translated it once more:

As I got deeper into the manuscript, my mouth grew dry, and my heart began to pound. This, I knew, was a contribution the like of which my family has not seen since Copernicus, Roger Bacon, or perhaps even Aristotle. It seemed incredible that this silent little man, who had never been outside of Koenigsberg, should hold the key to the universe— the *Critique of Pure Reason*, he calls it. And I doubt that even he realizes the ultimate portent of his teaching, for he says we cannot know the real shape or nature of anything, that is, the Thing-in-Itself, the Ding-an-Sich, or *noumenon*. He holds that this is the ultimate unknowable, reserved to the gods. He doesn't suspect that, century by century, mankind is nearing this final realization of the final things. Even this brilliant man would probably say that the earth was round in 600 B.C., even as it is today. But *I* know it was flat, then—as truly flat as it is truly round today. What has changed? Not the Thing-in-Itself we call the earth. No, it is the mind of man that has changed. But in his preposterous blindness, he mistakes what is really his own mental quickening

for a broadened application of science and more
precise methods of investigation—

Prentiss smiled.

Luce was undoubtedly a collector of philosophic in-
cunabula. Odd hobby, but that's all it could be—a hobby.
Obviously the earth had never been flat, and in fact hadn't
changed shape substantially in the last couple of billion
years. Certainly any notions as to the flatness of the earth
held by primitives of a few thousand years ago or even by
contemporaries of Kant were due to their ignorance rather
than to accurate observation, and a man of Luce's erudi-
tion could only be amused by them.

Again Prentiss found himself smiling with the tolerance
of a man standing on the shoulders of twenty centuries of
science. The primitives, of course, did the best they could.
They just didn't know. They worked with childish premises and infantile instruments.

His brows creased. To assume they had used childish
premises was begging the question. On the other hand,
was it really worth a second thought? All he could hope to
discover would be a few instances of how inferior apparatus coupled perhaps with unsophisticated deductions
had oversimplified the world of the ancients. Still, anything that interested the strange Dr. Luce automatically
interested him, Prentiss, until the case was closed.

He dictated into the scriptor:

"Memorandum to Geodetic Section. Rush a paragraph
history of ideas concerning shape of earth. Prentiss."

Duty done, he promptly forgot it and turned to the heavy
accumulation of reports on his desk.

A quarter of an hour later the scriptor rang and began
typing an incoming message.

> To the Director. Re your request for brief
> history of earth's shape. Chaldeans and Babylo-
> nians (per clay tablets from library of Assurban-
> ipal), Egyptians (per Ahmes papyrus, ca. 1700
> B.C.), Cretans (per inscriptions in royal library

at Knossos, ca. 1300 B.C.), Chinese (per Chou Kung ms. ca. 1100 B.C.), Phoenicians (per fragments at Tyre ca. 900 B.C.), Hebrews (per unknown Biblical historian ca. 850 B.C.), and early Greeks (per map of widely-traveled geographer Hecataeus, 517 B.C.) assumed earth to be flat disc. But from the 5th century B.C. forward earth's sphericity universally recognized. . . .

There were a few more lines, winding up with the work done on corrections for flattening at poles, but Prentiss had already lost interest. The report threw no light on Luce's hobby and was devoid of ontological implications.

He tossed the script into the waste basket and returned to the reports before him.

A few minutes later he twisted uneasily in his chair, eyed the scriptor in annoyance, then forced himself back to his work.

No use.

Deriding himself for an idiot, he growled at the machine:

"Memorandum to Geodetic. Re your memo history earth's shape. How do you account for change to belief in sphericity after Hecataeus? Rush. Prentiss."

The seconds ticked by.

He drummed on his desk impatiently, then got up and began pacing the floor.

When the scriptor rang, he bounded back and leaned over his desk, watching the words being typed out.

Late Greeks based spherical shape on observation that mast of approaching ship appeared first, then prow. Not known why similar observation not made by earlier seafaring peoples. . . .

Prentiss rubbed his cheek in perplexity. What was he fishing for?

He thrust the half-born conjecture that the earth really had once been flat back into his mental recesses.

Well, then how about the heavens? Surely there was no record of their having changed during man's brief lifetime.

He'd try one more shot and quit.

"Memo to Astronomy Division. Rush paragraph on early vs. modern sun size and distance."

A few minutes later he was reading the reply:

Skipping Plato, whose data are believed baseless (he measured sun's distance at only twice that of moon), we come to earliest recognized "authority." Ptolemy (Almagest, ca. 140 A.D. measured sun radius as 5.5 that of earth (as against 109 actual); measured sun distance at 1210 (23,000 actual). Fairly accurate measurements date only from 17th and 18th centuries. . . .

He'd read all that somewhere. The difference was easily explained by their primitive instruments. It was insane to keep this up.

But it was too late.

"Memo to Astronomy. Were erroneous Ptolemaic measurements due to lack of precision instruments?"

Soon he had his reply:

To Director: Source of Ptolemy's errors in solar measurement not clearly understood. Used astrolabe precise to 10 seconds and clepsydra water clock incorporating Hero's improvements. With same instruments, and using modern value of pi, Ptolemy measured moon radius (0.29 earth radius vs. 0.273 actual) and distance (59 earth radii vs. 60 1/3 actual). Hence instruments reasonably precise. And note that Copernicus, using quasi-modern instruments and technique, "confirmed" Ptolemaic figure of sun's distance at 12000 earth radii. No explanation known for glaring error.

Unless, suggested something within Prentiss's mind, the sun were closer and much different before the 17th century, when Newton was telling the world where and how big the sun *ought* to be. But *that* solution was too absurd for further consideration. He would sooner assume his complete insanity.

Puzzled, the ontologist gnawed his lower lip and stared at the message in the scriptor.

In his abstraction he found himself peering at the symbol "pi" in the scriptor message. *There*, at least, was something that had always been the same, and would endure for all time. He reached over to knock out his pipe in the big circular ash tray by the scriptor and paused in the middle of the second tap. From his desk he fished a tape measure and stretched it across the tray. Ten inches. And then around the circumference. Thirty-one and a half inches. Good enough, considering. It was a result any curious schoolboy could get.

He turned to the scriptor again.

"Memo to Math Section. Rush paragraph history on value of pi. Prentiss."

He didn't have to wait long.

To Director. Re history "pi." Babylonians used value of 3.00. Aristotle made fairly accurate physical and theoretical evaluations. Archimedes first to arrive at modern value, using theory of limits. . . .

There was more, but it was lost on Prentiss. It was inconceivable, of course, that pi had grown during the two millennia that separated the Babylonians from Archimedes. And yet, it was exasperating. Why hadn't they done any better than 3.00? Any child with a piece of string could have demonstrated their error. Countless generations of wise, careful Chaldean astronomers, measuring time and star positions with such incredible accuracy, all coming to grief with a piece of string and pi. It didn't make sense. And certainly pi hadn't grown, any more than the Babylonian 360-day year had grown into the modern 365-day year. It had always been the same, he told himself. The primitives hadn't measured accurately, that was all. That *had* to be the explanation.

He hoped.

He sat down at his desk again, stared a moment at his memo pad and wrote:

Check history of gravity—acceleration. Believe Aristotle unable detect acceleration. Galileo used same instruments, including same crude water clock, and found it. Why? . . . Any reported transits of Vulcan since 1914, when Einstein explained eccentricity of Mercury orbit by relativity instead of by hypothetical sunward planet? . . . How could Oliver Lodge detect an ether-drift and Michelson not? Conceivable that Lorentz contraction not a physical fact before Michelson experiment? . . . How many chemical elements were predicted before discovered?

He tapped absently on the pad a few times, then rang for a research assistant. He'd barely have time to explain what he wanted before he had to meet his class under Luce.

And he still wasn't sure where the rats fitted in.

Curtly Professor Luce brought his address to a close. "Well, gentlemen," he said, "I guess we'll have to continue this at our next lecture. We seem to have run over a little; class dismissed. Oh, Mr. Prentiss!"

The investigator looked up in genuine surprise. "Yes, sir?" The thin gun in his shoulder holster suddenly felt satisfyingly fat.

He realized that the crucial moment was near, that he would know before he left the campus whether this strange man was a harmless physicist, devoted to his life-work and his queer hobby, or whether he was an incarnate danger to mankind. The professor was acting out of turn, and it was an unexpected break.

"Mr. Prentiss," continued Luce from the lecture platform, "may I see you in my office a moment before you leave?"

Prentiss said, "Certainly." As the group broke up he followed the gaunt scientist through the door that led to Luce's little office behind the lecture room.

At the doorway he hesitated almost imperceptibly; Luce saw it and bowed sardonically. "After you, sir!"

Then the tall man indicated a chair near his desk. "Sit down, Mr. Prentiss."

For a long moment the seated men studied each other.

Finally the professor spoke. "About fifteen years ago a brilliant young man named Rogers wrote a doctoral dissertation at the University of Vienna on what he called . . . 'Involuntary Conformation of Incoming Sensoria to Apperception Mass.' "

Prentiss began fishing for his pipe. "Indeed?"

"One copy of the dissertation was sent to the Scholarship Society that was financing his studies. All others were seized by the International Bureau of the Censor, and accordingly a demand was made on the Scholarship Society for its copy. But it couldn't be found."

Prentiss was concentrating on lighting his pipe. He wondered if the faint trembling of the match flame was visible.

The professor turned to his desk, opened the top drawer, and pulled out a slim brochure bound in black leather.

The investigator coughed out a cloud of smoke.

The professor did not seem to notice, but opened the front cover and began reading: " '—a dissertation in partial fulfillment of the requirements for the degree of Doctor of Philosophy at the University of Vienna. A. P. Rogers, Vienna, 1957.' " The man closed the book and studied it thoughtfully. "Adrian Prentiss Rogers—the owner of a brain whose like is seen not once in a century. He exposed the gods—then vanished."

Prentiss suppressed a shiver as he met those sunken, implacable eye-caverns.

The cat-and-mouse was over. In a way, he was relieved.

"Why did you vanish then, Mr. Prentiss-Rogers?" demanded Luce. "And why do you now reappear?"

The investigator blew a cloud of smoke toward the low ceiling. "To prevent people like you from introducing sensoria that *can't* be conformed to our present apperception mass. To keep reality as is. That answers both questions, I think."

The other man smiled. It was not a good thing to see. "Have you succeeded?"

"I don't know. So far, I suppose."

The gaunt man shrugged his shoulders. "You ignore tomorrow, then. I think you have failed, but I can't be sure, of course, until I actually perform the experiment that will create novel sensoria." He leaned forward. "I'll come to the point, Mr. Prentiss-Rogers. Next to yourself —and possibly excepting the Censor—I know more about the mathematical approach to reality than anyone else in the world. I may even know things about it that you don't. On other phases of it I'm weak—because I developed your results on the basis of mere logic rather than insight. And logic, we know, is applicable only within indeterminate limits. But in developing a practical device—an actual machine—for the wholesale alteration of incoming sensoria, I'm enormously ahead of you. You saw my apparatus last night, Mr. Prentiss-Rogers? Oh, come, don't be coy."

Prentiss drew deeply on his pipe.

"I saw it."

"Did you understand it?"

"No. It wasn't all there. At least, the apparatus on the table was incomplete. There's more to it than a Nicol prism and a goniometer."

"Ah, you are clever! Yes, I was wise in not permitting you to remain very long—no longer than necessary to whet your curiosity. Look, then! I offer you a partnership. Check my data and apparatus; in return you may be present when I run the experiment. We will attain enlightenment together. We will know all things. We will be gods!"

"And what about two billion other human beings?" said Prentiss, pressing softly at his shoulder holster.

The professor smiled faintly. "Their lunacy—assuming they continue to exist at all—may become slightly more pronounced, of course. But why worry about them?

"Don't expect me to believe this aura of altruism, Mr. Prentiss-Rogers. I think you're afraid to face what lies behind our so-called 'reality.' "

"At least I'm a coward in a good cause." He stood up. "Have you any more to say?"

He knew that he was just going through the motions. Luce must have realized he had lain himself open to arrest half a dozen times in as many minutes: The bare possession of the missing copy of the dissertation, the frank admission of plans to experiment with reality, and his attempted bribery of a high Censor official. And yet, the man's very bearing denied the possibility of being cut off in mid-career.

Luce's cheeks fluffed out in a brief sigh. "I'm sorry you can't be intelligent about this, Mr. Prentiss-Rogers. Yet, the time will come, you know, when you must make up your mind to go—*through*, shall we say? In fact, we may have to depend to a considerable degree on one another's companionship—*out there*. Even gods have to pass the time of day occasionally, and I have a suspicion that you and I are going to be quite chummy. So let us not part in enmity."

Prentiss' hand slid beneath his coat lapel and drew out the snub-nosed automatic. He had a grim foreboding that it was futile, and that the professor was laughing silently at him, but he had no choice.

"You are under arrest," he said unemotionally. "Come with me."

The other shrugged his shoulders, then something like a laugh, soundless in its mockery, surged up in his throat. "Certainly, Mr. Prentiss-Rogers."

He arose.

The room was plunged into instant blackness.

Prentiss fired three times, lighting up the gaunt chuckling form at each flash.

"Save your fire, Mr. Prentiss-Rogers. Lead doesn't get far in an intense diamagnetic screen. Study the magnetic damper on a lab balance the next time you're in the Censor Building!"

Somewhere a door slammed.

Several hours later Prentiss was eyeing his aide with ill-concealed distaste. Prentiss knew Crush had been summoned by E to confer on the implications of Luce's escape, and that Crush was secretly sympathizing with him. Prentiss couldn't endure sympathy. He'd prefer that the asthmatic little man tell him how stupid he'd been.

"What do you want?" he growled.

"Sir," gasped Crush apologetically, "I have a report on that gadget you scanned in Luce's lab."

Prentiss was instantly mollified, but suppressed any show of interest. "What about it?"

"In essence, sir," wheezed Crush, "it's just a Nicol prism mounted on a goniometer. According to a routine check it was ground by an obscure optician who was nine years on the job, and he spent nearly all of that time on just one face of the prism. What do you make of that, sir?"

"Nothing, yet. What took him so long?"

"Grinding an absolutely flat edge, sir, so he says."

"Odd. That would mean a boundary composed exclusively of molecules of the same crystal layer, something that hasn't been attempted since the Palomar reflector."

"Yes, sir. And then there's the goniometer mount with just one number on the dial—forty-five degrees."

"Obviously," said Prentiss, "the Nicol is to be used only at a forty-five degree angle to the incoming light. Hence it's probably extremely important—why, I don't know—that the angle be *precisely* forty-five degrees. That would require a perfectly flat surface, too, of course. I suppose you're going to tell me that the goniometric gearing is set up very accurately."

Suddenly Prentiss realized that Crush was looking at him in mingled suspicion and admiration.

"Well?" demanded the ontologist irritably. "Just what

is the adjusting mechanism? Surely not geometrical? Too crude. Optical, perhaps?''

Crush gasped into his handkerchief. ''Yes, sir. The prism is rotated very slowly into a tiny beam of light. Part of the beam is reflected and part refracted. At exactly forty-five degrees it seems, by Jordan's law, that exactly half is reflected and half refracted. The two beams are picked up in a photocell relay that stops the rotating mechanism as soon as the luminosities of the beams are exactly equal.''

Prentiss tugged nervously at his ear. It was puzzling. Just what was Luce going to do with such an exquisitely-ground Nicol? At this moment he would have given ten years of his life for an inkling to the supplementary apparatus that went along with the Nicol. It would be something optical, certainly, tied in somehow with neurotic rats. What was it Luce had said the other night in the lab? Something about slowing down a photon. And then what was supposed to happen to the universe? Something like taking a tiny bite out of a balloon, Luce had said.

And how did it all interlock with certain impossible, though syllogistically necessary conclusions that flowed from his recent research into the history of human knowledge?

He wasn't sure. But he *was* sure that Luce was on the verge of using this mysterious apparatus to change the perceptible universe, on a scale so vast that humanity was going to get lost in the shuffle. He'd have to convince E of that.

If he couldn't, he'd seek out Luce himself and kill him with his bare hands, and decide on reasons for it afterward.

He was guiding himself for the time being by pure insight, but he'd better be organized when he confronted E.

Crush was speaking. ''Shall we go, sir? Your secretary says the jet is waiting.''

● ● ●

The painting showed a man in a red hat and black robes
seated behind a high judge's bench. Five other men in red
hats were seated behind a lower bench to his right, and
four others to his left. At the base of the bench knelt a
figure in solitary abjection.

"We condemn you, Galileo Galilei, to the formal prison of this Holy Office for a period determinable at Our
pleasure; and by way of salutary penance, We order you,
during the next three years, to recite once a week the seven
Penitential Psalms."

Prentiss turned from the inscription to the less readable
face of E. The oval olive-hued face was smooth, unlined,
even around the eyes, and the black hair was parted off-
center and drawn over the woman's head into a bun at
the nape of her neck. She wore no make-up, and apparently needed none. She was clad in a black, loose-fitting
business suit, which accentuated her perfectly molded
body.

"Do you know," said Prentiss coolly, "I think you like
being Censor. It's in your blood."

"You're perfectly right. I *do* like being Censor. According to Speer, I effectively sublimate a guilt complex
as strange as it is baseless."

"Very interesting. Sort of expiation of an ancestral guilt
complex, eh?"

"What do you mean?"

"Woman started man on his acquisition of knowledge
and self-destruction, and ever since has tried futilely to
halt the avalanche. In you the feeling of responsibility and
guilt runs exceptionally strong, and I'll wager that some
nights you wake up in a cold sweat, thinking you've just
plucked a certain forbidden fruit."

E stared icily up at the investigator's twitching mouth.
"The only pertinent question," she said crisply, "is
whether Luce is engaged in ontologic experiments, and if
so, are they of a dangerous nature."

Prentiss sighed. "He's in it up to his neck. But just
what, and how dangerous, I can only guess."

"Then guess."

"Luce thinks he's developed apparatus for the practical, predictable alteration of sensoria. He hopes to do something with his device that will blow physical laws straight to smithereens. The resulting reality would probably be unrecognizable even to a professional ontologist, let alone the mass of humanity."

"You seem convinced he can do this."

"The probabilities are high."

"Good enough. We can deal only in probabilities. The safest thing, of course, would be to locate Luce and kill him on sight. On the other hand, the faintest breath of scandal would result in Congressional hamstringing of the Bureau, so we must proceed cautiously."

"If Luce is really able to do what he claims," said Prentiss grimly, "and we let him do it, there won't be any Bureau at all—nor any Congress either."

"I know. Rest assured that if I decide that Luce is dangerous and should die, I shall let neither the lives nor careers of anyone in the Bureau stand in the way, including myself."

Prentiss nodded, wondering if she really meant it.

The woman continued. "We are faced for the first time with a probable violation of our directive forbidding ontologic experiments. We are inclined to prevent this threatened violation by taking a man's life. I think we should settle once and for all whether such harsh measures are indicated, and it is for this that I have invited you to attend a staff conference. We intend to reopen the entire question of ontologic experiments and their implications."

Prentiss groaned inwardly. In matters so important the staff decided by vote. He had a brief vision of attempting to convince E's hard-headed scientists that mankind was changing "reality" from century to century—that not too long ago the earth had been "flat." Yes, by now he was beginning to believe it himself!

"Come this way, please," said E.

• • •

Sitting at E's right was an elderly man, Speer, the famous psychologist. On her left was Goring, staff adviser on nucleonics; next to him was Burchard, brilliant chemist and Director of the Western Field, then Prentiss, and then Dobbs, the renowned metallurgist and Director of the Central Field.

Prentiss didn't like Dobbs, who had voted against his promotion to the directorship of Eastern.

E announced: "We may as well start this inquiry with an examaination of fundamentals. Mr. Prentiss, just what is reality?"

The ontologist winced. He had needed two hundred pages to outline the theory of reality in his doctoral thesis, and even so, had always suspected his examiners had passed it only because it was incomprehensible—hence a work of genius.

"Well," he began wryly, "I must confess that I don't know what *real* reality is. What most of us call reality is simply an integrated synthesis of incoming sensoria. As such it is nothing more than a working hypothesis in the mind of each of us, forever in a process of revision. In the past that process has been slow and safe. But we have now to consider the consequences of an instantaneous and total revision—a revision so far-reaching that it may thrust humanity face-to-face with the true reality, the world of Things-in-Themselves—Kant's *noumena*. This, I think, would be as disastrous as dumping a group of children in the middle of a forest. They'd have to relearn the simplest things—what to eat, how to protect themselves from ele- mental forces, and even a new language to deal with their new problems. There'd be few survivors.

"That is what we want to avoid, and we can do it if we prevent any sudden sweeping alteration of sensoria in our present reality."

He looked dubiously at the faces about him. It was a poor start. Speer's wrinkled features were drawn up in a serene smile, and the psychologist seemed to be contem- plating the air over Prentiss's head. Goring was regarding him with grave, expressionless eyes. E nodded slightly as

Prentiss's gaze traveled past her to a puzzled Burchard, thence to Dobbs, who was frankly contemptuous.

Speer and Goring were going to be the most susceptible. Speer because of his lack of a firm scientific background, Goring because nucleonics was in such a state of flux that nuclear experts were expressing the gravest doubts as to the validity of the laws worshipped by Burchard and Dobbs. Burchard was only a faint possibility. And Dobbs?

Dobbs said: "I don't know what the dickens you're talking about." The implication was plain that he wanted to add: "And I don't think you do, either."

And Prentiss wasn't so sure that he did know. Ontology was an elusive thing at best.

"I object to the term 'real reality,'" continued Dobbs. "A thing is real or it isn't. No fancy philosophical system can change *that*. And if it's real, it gives off predictable, reproducible sensory stimuli not subject to alteration except in the minds of lunatics."

Prentiss breathed more easily. His course was clear. He'd concentrate on Dobbs, with a little side-play on Burchard. Speer and Goring would never suspect his arguments were really directed at them. He pulled a gold coin from his vest pocket and slid it across the table to Dobbs, being careful not to let it clatter. "You're a metallurgist. Please tell us what this is."

Dobbs picked up the coin and examined it suspiciously. "It's quite obviously a five-dollar gold piece, minted at Fort Worth in nineteen sixty-two. I can even give you the analysis, if you want it."

"I doubt that you could," said Prentiss coolly. "For you see, you are holding a counterfeit coin minted only last week in my own laboratories especially for this conference. As a matter of fact, if you'll forgive my saying so, I had you in mind when I ordered the coin struck. It contains no gold whatever—drop it on the table."

The coin fell from the fingers of the astounded metallurgist and clattered on the oaken table top.

"Hear the false ring?" demanded Prentiss.

Pink-faced, Dobbs cleared his throat and peered at the

coin more closely. "How was I to know that? It's no
disgrace, is it? Many clever counterfeits can be detected
only in the laboratory. I knew the color was a little on the
red side, but that could have been due to the lighting of the
room. And of course, I hadn't given it an auditory test
before I spoke. The ring is definitely dull. It's obviously a
copper-lead alloy, with possibly a little amount of silver to
help the ring. All right, I jumped to conclusions. So what?
What does that prove?"

"It proves that you have arrived at two separate, dis-
tinct, and mutually exclusive realities, starting with the
same sensory premises. It proves how easily reality is
revised. And that isn't all, as I shall soon—"

"All right," said Dobbs testily. "But on second
thought I admitted it was false, didn't I?"

"Which demonstrates a further weakness in our routine
acquisition and evaluation of predigested information.
When an unimpeachable authority tells us something as a
fact, we immediately, and without conscious thought,
modify our incoming stimuli to conform with that *fact*.
The coin suddenly acquires the red taint of copper, and
rings false to the ear."

"I would have caught the queer ring anyhow," said
Dobbs stubbornly, "with no help from 'an unimpeachable
authority.' The ring would have sounded the same, no
matter what you said."

From the corner of his eye Prentiss noticed that Speer
was grinning broadly. Had the old psychologist divined
his trick? He'd take a chance.

"Dr. Speer," he said, "I think you have something
interesting to tell our doubting friend."

Speer cackled dryly. "You've been a perfect guinea
pig, Dobbsie. The coin was genuine."

The metallurgist's jaw dropped as he looked blankly
from one face to another. Then his jowls slowly grew red.
He flung the coin to the table. "Maybe I am a guinea pig.
I'm a realist, too. I think this is a piece of metal. You might
fool me as to its color or assay, but in essence and sub-

stance, it's a piece of metal.'' He glared at Prentiss and Speer in turn. "Does anyone deny that?''

"Certainly not,'' said Prentiss. "Our mental pigeonholes are identical in that respect; they accept the same sensory definition of 'piece of metal,' or 'coin.' Whatever this object is, it emits stimuli that our minds are capable of registering and abstracting as a 'coin.' But note: we make a coin out of it. However, if I could shuffle my cortical pigeonholes, I might find it to be a chair, or a steamer trunk, possibly with Dr. Dobbs inside, or, if the shuffling were extreme, there might be no semantic pattern into which the incoming stimuli could be routed. There wouldn't be anything there at all!''

"Sure,'' sneered Dobbs. "You could walk right through it.''

"Why not?'' asked Prentiss gravely. "I think we may do it all the time. Matter is about the emptiest stuff imaginable. If you compressed that coin to eliminate the space between its component atoms and electrons, you couldn't see it in a microscope.''

Dobbs stared at the enigmatic goldpiece as though it might suddenly thrust out a pseudopod and swallow him up. Then he said flatly: "No. I don't believe it. It exists as a coin, and only as a coin—whether I know it or not.''

"Well,'' ventured Prentiss, "how about you, Dr. Goring? Is the coin real to you?''

The nucleist smiled and shrugged his shoulders. "If I don't think too much about it, it's real enough. And yet . . .''

Dobb's face clouded. "And yet what? Here it is. Can you doubt the evidence of your own eyes?''

"That's just the difficulty.'' Goring leaned forward. "My eyes tell me, here's a coin. Theory tells me, here's a mass of hypothetical disturbances in a hypothetical sub-ether in a hypothetical ether. The indeterminacy principle tells me that I can never know both the mass and position of these hypothetical disturbances. And as a physicist I know that the bare fact of observing something is sufficient to change that something from its preobserved state. Nevertheless, I compromise by letting my senses and practical experience stick a tag on this particular bit of the unknowable. X, after its impact on my mind (whatever *that* is!) equals coin. A single equation with two variables has no solution. The best I can say is, it's a coin, but probably not really—''

''Hah!'' declared Burchard. ''I can demonstrate the fallacy of *that* position very quickly. If our minds make this a coin, then our minds make this little object an ash-tray, that a window, the thing that holds us up, a chair. You might say we make the air we breathe, and perhaps even the stars and planets. Why, following Prentiss's idea to its logical end, the universe itself is the work of man—a conclusion I'm sure he doesn't intend.''

''Oh, but I do,'' said Prentiss.

Prentiss took a deep breath. The issue could be dodged no longer. He had to take a stand. ''And to make sure you understand me, whether you agree with me or not, I'll state categorically that I believe the apparent universe to be the work of man.''

Even E looked startled, but said nothing.

The ontologist continued rapidly. ''All of you doubt my sanity. A week ago I would have, too. But since then I've done a great deal of research in the history of science. And I repeat, *the universe is the work of man*. I believe that man began his existence in some incredibly simple world—the original and true *noumenon* of our present universe. And that over the centuries man expanded his little world into its present vastness and incomprehensible intricacy solely by dint of imagination.

''Consequently, I believe that what most of you call the 'real' world has been changing ever since our ancestors began to think.''

Dobbs smiled superciliously. ''Oh, come now, Prentiss. That's just a rhetorical description of scientific progress over the past centuries. In the same sense I might say that modern transportation and communications have shrunk the earth. But you'll certainly admit that the physical state of things has been substantially constant ever since the galaxies formed and the earth began to cool, and that the simple cosmologies of early man were simply the result of lack of means for obtaining accurate information?''

"I *won't* admit it," rejoined Prentiss bluntly. "I maintain that their information was substantially accurate. I maintain that at one time in our history the earth was flat—as flat as it is now round, and no one living before the time of Hecataeus, though he might have been equipped with the finest modern instruments, could have proved otherwise. His mind was *conditioned* to a two-dimensional world. Any of us present, if we were transplanted to the world of Hecataeus, could, of course, establish terrestrial sphericity in short order. Our minds have been conditioned to a three-dimensional world. The day may come a few millennia hence when a four-dimensional Terra will be commonplace even to schoolchildren; they will have been intuitively conditioned in relativistic concepts." He added slyly: "And the less intelligent of them may attempt to blame our naive three-dimensional planet on our grossly inaccurate instruments, because it will be as plain as day to them that their planet has four dimensions!''

Dobbs snorted at this amazing idea. The other scientists stared at Prentiss with an awe which was mixed with incredulity.

Goring said cautiously: "I follow up to a certain point, I can see that a primitive society might start out with a limited number of facts. They would offer theories to harmonize and integrate those facts, and then those first theories would require that new, additional facts exist, and in their search for those secondary facts, extraneous data would turn up inconsistent with the first theories. Secondary theories would then be required, from which hitherto unguessed facts should follow, the confirmation of which would discover more inconsistencies. So the pattern of fact to theory to fact to theory, and so on, finally brings us into our present state of knowledge. Does that follow from your argument?''

Prentiss nodded.

"But won't you admit that the facts were there all the time, and merely awaited discovery?''

"The simple, unelaborated *noumenon* was there all the time, yes. But the new fact—man's new interpretation of the *noumenon*, was generally pure invention—a mental creation, if you like. This will be clearer if you consider how rarely a new fact arises before a theory exists for its explanation. In the ordinary scientific investigation, theory comes first, followed in short order by the 'discovery' of various facts deducible from it.''

Goring still looked skeptical. "But that wouldn't mean the fact wasn't there all the time.''

"Wouldn't it? Look at the evidence. Has it never struck you as odd in how many instances very obvious facts were 'overlooked' until a theory was propounded that required their existence? Take your nuclear building blocks. Protons and electrons were detected physically only after Rutherford had showed they had to exist. And then when Rutherford found that protons and electrons were not enough to build all the atoms of the periodic table, he postulated the neutron, which of course was duly 'discovered' in the Wilson cloud chamber.''

Goring pursed his lips. "But the Wilson cloud chamber would have shown all that prior to the theory, if anyone had only thought to use it.

"The mere fact that Wilson didn't invent his cloud chamber until nineteen-twelve and Geiger didn't invent his counter until nineteen-thirteen, would not keep subatomic particles from existing before that time.''

"You don't get the point," said Prentiss. "The primitive, ungeneralized noumenon that we today observe as subatomic particles existed prior to nineteen-twelve, true, *but not subatomic particles*.''

"Well, I don't know. . . ." Goring scratched his chin. "How about fundamental forces? Surely electricity existed before Galvani? Even the Greeks knew how to build up electrostatic charges on amber.''

"Greek electricity was nothing more than electrostatic charges. Nothing more could be created until Galvani introduced the concept of the electric current.''

"Do you mean the electric current didn't exist at all before Galvani?'' demanded Burchard. "Not even when lightning struck a conductor?''

"Not even then. We don't know much about pre-Galvanic lightning. While it probably packed a wallop, its destructive potential couldn't have been due to its delivery of an electric current. The Chinese flew kites for centuries before Franklin theorized that lightning was the same as galvanic electricity, but there's no recorded shock from a kite string until our learned statesman drew forth one in seventeen-sixty-five. *Now*, only an idiot flies a kite in a storm. It's all according to pattern: theory first, then we alter 'reality' to fit.''

Burchard persisted. "Then I suppose you'd say all the elements are figments of our imagination.''

"Correct,'' agreed Prentiss. "I believe that in the beginning there were only four *noumenal* elements. Man simply elaborated these according to the needs of his growing science. Man made them what they are today—and on occasion, *unmade* them. You remember the havoc Mendelyeev created with his periodic law. He declared that the elements had to follow valence sequences of increasing atomic weight, and when they didn't, he insisted his law was right and that the atomic weights were wrong. He must have had Stas and Berzelius whirling in their graves, because they had worked out the 'erroneous' atomic weights with marvelous precision. The odd thing was, when the weights were rechecked, they fitted the Mendelyeev table. But that wasn't all. The old rascal pointed out vacant spots in his table and maintained that there were more elements yet to be discovered. He even predicted what properties they'd have. He was too modest. I state that Nilson, Winkler, and De Boisbaudran merely *discovered* scandium, germanium, and gallium;

Mendelyeev *created* them, out of the original quadrelemental stuff.''

E leaned forward. ''That's a bit strong. Tell me, if man has changed the elements and the cosmos to suit his convenience, what was the cosmos like before man came on the scene?''

''There wasn't any,'' answered Prentiss. ''Remember, by definition, 'cosmos' or 'reality' is simply man's version of the ultimate *noumenal* universe. The 'cosmos' arrives and departs with the mind of man. Consequently, the earth—as such—didn't even exist before the advent of man.''

''But the evidence of the rocks . . .'' protested E. ''Pressures applied over millions, even billions of years, were needed to form them, unless you postulate an omnipotent God who called them into existence as of yesterday.''

''I postulate only the omnipotent human mind,'' said Prentiss. ''In the seventeenth century, Hooke, Ray, Woodward, to name a few, studied chalk, gravel, marble, and even coal, without finding anything inconsistent with results to be expected from the Noachian Flood. But now that we've made up our minds that the earth is older, the rocks *seem* older, too.''

''But how about evolution?'' demanded Burchard. ''Surely that wasn't a matter of a few centuries?''

''Really?'' replied Prentiss. ''Again, why assume that the facts are any more recent than the theory? The evidence is all the other way. Aristotle was a magnificent experimental biologist, and he was convinced that life could be created spontaneously. Before the time of Darwin there was no need for the various species to evolve, because they sprang into being from inanimate matter. As late as the eighteenth century, Needham, using a microscope, reported that he saw microbe life arise spontaneously out of sterile culture media. These abiogeneticists were, of course, discredited and their work found to be irreproducible, but only *after* it became evident that the then abiogenetic facts were going to run inconsistent with later 'facts' flowing from advancing biologic theory.''

"Then," said Goring, "assuming purely for the sake of argument, that man has altered the original *noumena* into our present reality, just what danger do you think Luce represents to that reality? How could he do anything about it, even if he wanted to? Just what is he up to?''

"Broadly stated," said Prentiss, "Luce intends to destroy the Einsteinian universe.''

Burchard frowned and shook his head. "Not so fast. In the first place, how can anyone presume to destroy this planet, much less the whole universe? And why do you say the 'Einsteinian' universe? The universe by any other name is still the universe, isn't it?''

"What Dr. Prentiss means," explained E, "is that Luce wants to revise completely and finally our present comprehension of the universe, which presently happens to be the Einsteinian version, in the expectation that the final version would be the true one—and comprehensible only to Luce and perhaps a few other ontologic experts.''

"I don't see it," said Dobbs irritably. "Apparently this Luce contemplates nothing more than publication of a new scientific theory. How can that be bad? A mere theory can't hurt anybody—especially if only two or three people understand it.''

"You—and two billion others," said Prentiss softly, "think that 'reality' cannot be affected by any theory that seems to change it—that it is optional with you to accept or reject the theory. In the past that was true. If the Ptolemaics wanted a geocentric universe, they ignored Copernicus. If the four-dimensional continuum of Einstein and Minkowsky seemed incomprehensible to the Newtonian school they dismissed it, and the planets continued to revolve substantially as Newton predicted. But this is different.

"For the first time we are faced with the probability that the promulgation of a theory is going to *force* an ungraspable reality upon our minds. It will not be optional.''

"Well," said Burchard, "if by 'promulgation of a theory' you mean something like the application of the quantum theory and relativity to the production of atomic energy, which of course has changed the shape of civilization in the past generation, whether the individual liked it or not, then I can understand you. But if you mean that Luce is going to make one little experiment that may confirm some new theory or other, and *ipso facto* and instantaneously reality is going to turn topsy turvy, why I say it's nonsense."

"Would anyone," said Prentiss quietly, "care to guess what would happen if Luce were able to destroy a photon?"

Goring laughed shortly. "The question doesn't make sense. The mass-energy entity whose three-dimensional profile we call a photon is indestructible."

"But if you *could* destroy it?" insisted Prentiss. "What would the universe be like afterward?"

"What difference would it make?" demanded Dobbs. "One photon more or less?"

"Plenty," said Goring. "According to the Einstein theory, every particle of matter—energy has a gravitational potential, lambda, and it can be calculated that the total lambdas are precisely sufficient to keep our four-dimensional continuum from closing back on itself. Take one lambda away—God! The universe would split wide open!"

"Exactly," said Prentiss. "Instead of a continuum, our 'reality' would become a disconnected melange of three-dimensional objects. Time, if it existed, wouldn't bear any relation to spatial things. Only an ontologic expert might be able to synthesize any sense out of such a 'reality.'"

"Well," said Dobbs, "I wouldn't worry too much. I don't think anybody's ever going to destroy a photon." He snickered. "You have to catch one first!"

"Luce can catch one," said Prentiss calmly. "And he can destroy it. At this moment some unimaginable post-Einsteinian universe lies in the palm of his hand. Final, true reality, perhaps. But we aren't ready for it. Kant, perhaps, or *Homo superior*, but not the general run of *H.*

sapiens. We wouldn't be able to escape our conditioning. We'd be stopped cold.''

He stopped. Without looking at Goring, he knew he had convinced the man. Prentiss sagged with visible relief. It was time for a vote. He must strike before Speer and Goring could change their minds.

''Madame''—he shot a questioning glance at the woman—''at any moment my men are going to report that they've located Luce. I must be ready to issue the order for his execution, if in fact the staff believes such disposition proper. I call for a vote of officers!''

''Granted,'' said E instantly. ''Will those in favor of destroying Luce on sight raise their right hands?''

Prentiss and Goring made the required signal.

Speer was silent.

Prentiss felt his heart sinking. Had he made a gross error of judgment?

''I vote against this murder,'' declared Dobbs. ''That's what it is, pure murder.''

''I agree with Dobbs,'' said Burchard shortly.

All eyes were on the psychologist. ''I presume you'll join us, Dr. Speer?'' demanded Dobbs sternly.

''Count me out, gentlemen. I'd never interfere with anything so inevitable as the destiny of man. All of you are overlooking a fundamental facet of human nature—man's insatiable hunger for change, novelty—for anything different from what he already has. Prentiss himself states that whenever man grows discontented with his present reality, he starts elaborating it, and the devil take the hindmost. Luce but symbolizes the evil genius of our race—and I mean both our species and the race toward intertwined godhood and destruction. Once born, however, symbols are immortal. It's far too late now to start killing Luces. It was too late when the first man tasted the first apple.

''Furthermore, I think Prentiss greatly overestimates the scope of Luce's pending victory over the rest of mankind. Suppose Luce is actually successful in clearing

space and time and suspending the world in the temporal
stasis of its present irreality. Suppose he and a few ontologic experts pass on into the ultimate, true reality. How
long do you think they can resist the temptation to alter it?
If Prentiss is right, eventually they or their descendants
will be living in a cosmos as intricate and unpleasant as the
one they left, while we, for all practical purposes, will be
pleasantly dead.

"No, gentlemen, I won't vote either way."

"Then it is my privilege to break the tie," said E coolly.
"I vote for death. Save your remonstrances, Dr. Dobbs.
It's after midnight. This meeting is adjourned." She stood
up in abrupt dismissal, and the men were soon filing from
the room.

E left the table and walked toward the windows on the
far side of the room. Prentiss hesitated a moment, but
made no effort to leave.

E called over her shoulder, "You, too, Prentiss."

The door closed behind Speer, the last of the group,
save Prentiss.

Prentiss walked up behind E.

She gave no sign of awareness.

Six feet away, the man stopped and studied her.

Sitting, walking, standing, she was lovely. Mentally he
compared her to Velasquez' Venus. There was the same
slender exquisite proportion of thigh, hip, and bust. And
he knew she was completely aware of her own beauty, and
further, must be aware of his present appreciative
scrutiny.

Then her shoulders sagged suddenly, and her voice
seemed very tired when she spoke. "So you're still here,
Prentiss. Do you believe in intuition?"

"Not often."

"Speer was right. He's always right. Luce will succeed." She dropped her arms to her sides and turned.

"Then may I reiterate, my dear, marry me and let's
forget the control of knowledge for a few months."

"Competely out of the question, Prentiss. Our natures
are incompatible. You're incorrigibly curious, and I'm

incorrigibly, even neurotically, conservative. Besides, how can you even think about such things when we've got to stop Luce?''

His reply was interrupted by the shrilling of the intercom: "Calling Mr. Prentiss. Crush calling Mr. Prentiss. Luce located. Crush calling."

With his pencil Crush pointed to a shaded area of the map. "This is Luce's Snake-Eyes estate, the famous game preserve and zoo. Somewhere in the center—about here, I think—is a stone cottage. A moving van unloaded some lab equipment there this morning."

"Mr. Prentiss," said E, "how long do you think it will take him to install what he needs for that one experiment?"

The ontologist answered from across the map table. "I can't be sure. I still have no idea of what he's going to try, except that I'm reasonably certain it must be done in absolute darkness. Checking his instruments will require but a few minutes at most."

The woman began pacing the floor nervously. "I knew it. We can't stop him. We have no time."

"Oh, I don't know," said Prentiss. "How about that stone cottage, Crush? Is it pretty old?"

"Dates from the eighteenth century, sir."

"There's your answer," said Prentiss. "It's probably full of holes where the mortar's fallen out. For total darkness he'll have to wait until moonset."

"That's three thirty-four A.M., sir," said Crush.

"We've time for an arrest," said E.

Crush looked dubious. "It's more complicated than that, Madame. Snake-Eyes is fortified to withstand a small army. Luce could hold off any force the Bureau could muster for at least twenty-four hours."

"One atom egg, well done," suggested Prentiss.

"That's the best answer, of course," agreed E. "But you know as well as I what the reaction of Congress would be to such extreme measures. There would be an investigation. The Bureau would be abolished, and all persons responsible for such an action would face life imprisonment, perhaps death." She was silent for a moment, then sighed and said: "So be it. If there is no alternative, I shall order the bomb dropped."

"There may be another way," said Prentiss.

"Indeed?"

"Granted an army couldn't get through. One man might. And if he made it, you could call off your bomb."

E exhaled a slow cloud of smoke and studied the glowing tip of her cigarette. Finally she turned and looked into the eyes of the ontologist for the first time since the beginning of the conference. "*You* can't go."

"Who, then?"

Her eyes dropped. "You're right, of course. But the bomb still falls if you don't get through. It's got to be that way. Do you understand that?"

Prentiss laughed. "I understand."

He addressed his aide. "Crush, I'll leave the details up to you, bomb and all. We'll rendezvous at these coordinates"—he pointed to the map—"at three sharp. It's after one now. You'd better get started."

"Yes, sir," wheezed Crush, and scurried out of the room.

As the door closed, Prentiss turned to E. "Beginning tomorrow afternoon—or rather, *this* afternoon, after I finish with Luce, I want six months off."

"Granted," murmured E.

"I want you to come with me. I want to find out just what this thing is between us. Just the two of us. It may take a little time."

E smiled crookedly. "If we're both still alive at three thirty-five, and such a thing as a month exists, and you still want me to spend six of them with you, I'll do it. And in return you can do something for me."

"What?"

"You, even above Luce, stand the best chance of adjusting to final reality if Luce is successful in destroying a photon. I'm a border-line case. I'm going to need all the help you can give me, if and when the times comes. Will you remember that?"

"I'll remember," Prentiss said.

At 3 A.M. he joined Crush.

"There are at least seven infra-red scanners in the grounds, sir," said Crush, "not to mention an intricate network of photo relays. And then the wire fence around the lab, with the big cats inside. He must have turned the whole zoo loose." The little man reluctantly helped Prentiss into his infra-red absorbing coveralls. "You weren't meant for tiger fodder, sir. Better call it off."

Prentiss zipped up his visor and grimaced out into the moonlit dimness of the apple orchard. "You'll take care of the photocell network?"

"Certainly, sir. He's using u.v.-sensitive cells. We'll blanket the area with the u.v.-spot at three-ten."

Prentiss strained his ears, but couldn't hear the 'copter that would carry the u.v.-searchlight—and the bomb.

"It'll be here, sir," Crush assured him. "It won't make any noise, anyhow. What you ought to be worrying about are those wild beasts."

The investigator sniffed at the night air. "Darn little breeze."

"Yeah," gasped Crush. "And variable at that, sir. You can't count on going in up-wind. You want us to create a diversion at one end of the grounds to attract the animals?"

"We don't dare. If necessary, I'll open the aerosol capsule of formaldehyde." He held out his hand. "Good-by, Crush."

His asthmatic assistant shook the extended hand with vigorous sincerity. "Good luck, sir. And don't forget the bomb. We'll have to drop it at three thirty-four sharp."

But Prentiss had vanished into the leafy darkness.

A little later he was studying the luminous figures on his watch. The u.v.-blanket was presumably on. All he had to be careful about in the next forty seconds was a direct collision with a photocell post.

But Crush's survey party had mapped well. He reached

the barbed fencing uneventfully, with seconds to spare. He listened a moment, and then in practised silence eased his lithe body high up and over.

The breeze, which a moment before had been in his face, now died away, and the night air hung about him in dark lifeless curtains.

From the stone building a scant two hundred yards ahead, a chink of light peeped out.

Prentiss drew his silenced pistol and began moving forward with swift caution, taking care to place his heel to ground before the toe, and feeling out the character of the ground with the thin soles of his sneakers before each step. A snapping twig might hurl a slavering wild beast at his throat.

He stopped motionless in midstride.

From the thicket several yards to his right came an ominous sniffing, followed by a low snarl.

His mouth went suddenly dry as he strained his ears and turned his head slowly toward the sound.

And then there came the reverberations of something heavy, hurtling toward him.

He whipped his weapon around and waited in a tense crouch, not daring to send a wild, singing bullet across the sward.

The great cat was almost upon him before he fired, and then the faint cough of the stumbling, stricken animal seemed louder than his muffled shot.

Breathing hard, Prentiss stepped away from the dying beast, evidently a panther, and listened for a long time before resuming his march on the cottage. Luce's extraordinary measures to exclude intruders but confirmed his suspicions: Tonight was the last night that the professor could be stopped. He blinked the stinging sweat from his eyes and glanced at his watch. It was 3:15.

Apparently the other animals had not heard him. He stood up to resume his advance, and to his utter relief found that the wind had shifted almost directly into his face and was blowing steadily.

In another three minutes he was standing at the massive

door of the building running practised fingers over the great iron hinges and lock. Undoubtedly the thing was going to squeak; there was no time to apply oil and wait for it to soak in. The lock could be easily picked.

And the squeaking of a rusty hinge was probably immaterial. A cunning operator like Luce would undoubtedly have wired an alarm into it. He just couldn't believe Crush's report to the contrary.

But he couldn't stand here.

There was only one way to get inside quickly, and alive.

Chuckling at his own madness, Prentiss began to pound on the door.

He could visualize the blinking out of the slit of light above his head, and knew that, somewhere within the building, two flame-lit eyes were studying him in an infra-red scanner.

Prentiss tried simultaneously to listen to the muffled squeaking of the rats beyond the great door and to the swift, padding approach of something big behind him.

"Luce!" he cried. "It's Prentiss! Let me in!"

A latch slid somewhere; the door eased inward. The investigator threw his gun rearward at a pair of bounding eyes, laced his fingers over his head, and stumbled into more darkness.

Despite the protection of his hands, the terrific blow of the blackjack on his temple almost knocked him out.

He closed his eyes, crumpled carefully to the floor, and noted with satisfaction that his wrists were being tied behind his back. As he had anticipated, it was a clumsy job, even without his imperceptible "assistance." Long fingers ran over his body in a search for more weapons.

Then he felt the sting of a hypodermic needle in his biceps.

The lights came on.

He struggled feebly, emitted a plausible groan, and tried to sit up.

From far above, the strange face of Dr. Luce looked down at him, illuminated, it seemed to Prentiss, by some unhallowed inner fire.

"What time is it?" asked Prentiss.

"Approximately three-twenty."

"*Hm*. Your kittens gave me quite a reception, my dear professor."

"As befits an uncooperative meddler."

"Well, what are you going to do with me?"

"Kill you."

Luce pulled a pistol from his coat pocket.

Prentiss wet his lips. During his ten years with the Bureau, he had never had to deal with anyone quite like Luce. The gaunt man personified megalomania on a scale beyond anything the investigator had previously encountered—or imagined possible.

And, he realized with a shiver, Luce was very probably justified in his prospects (not delusions!) of grandeur.

With growing alarm he watched Luce snap off the safety lock of the pistol.

There were two possible chances of surviving more than a few seconds.

Luce's index finger began to tense around the trigger.

One of those chances was to appeal to Luce's megalomania, treating him as a human being. Tell him, "I know you won't kill me until you've had a chance to gloat over me—to tell me, the inventor of ontologic synthesis, how you found a practical application of it."

No good. Too obvious to one of Luce's intelligence.

The approach must be to a demigod, in humility. Oddly enough his curiosity *was* tinged with respect. Luce *did* have something.

Prentiss licked his lips again and said hurriedly: "I must die, then. But could you show me—is it asking too much to show me, just how you propose to go through?"

The gun lowered a fraction of an inch. Luce eyed the doomed man suspiciously.

"Would you, please?" continued Prentiss. His voice was dry, cracking. "Ever since I discovered that new realities could be synthesized, I've wondered whether *Homo sapiens* was capable of finding a practical device for uncovering the true reality. And all who've worked on it have insisted that only a brain but little below the angels was capable of such an achievement.'' He coughed apologetically. ''It is difficult to believe that a mere mortal has really accomplished what you claim—and yet, there's something about you . . .'' His voice trailed off, and he laughed deprecatingly.

Luce bit; he thrust the gun back into his coat pocket. ''So you know when you're licked,'' he said. ''Well, I'll let you live a moment longer.''

He stepped back and pulled aside a black screen. ''Has the inimitable ontologist the wit to understand this?''

Within a few seconds of his introduction to the instrument everything was painfully clear. Prentiss now abandoned any remote hope that either Luce's method or apparatus would prove faulty. Both the vacuum-glassed machinery and the idea behind it were perfect.

Basically, the supplementary unit, which he now saw for the first time, consisted of a sodium-vapor light bulb, blacked out except for one tiny transparent spot. Ahead of the little window was a series of what must be hundreds of black discs mounted on a common axis. Each disc bore a slender radial slot. And though he could not trace all the gearing, Prentiss knew that the discs were geared to permit one and only one fleeting photon of yellow light to emerge at the end of the disc series, where it would pass through a Kerr electro-optic field and be polarized.

That photon would then travel one centimeter to that fabulous Nicol prism, one surface of which had been machined flat to a molecule's thickness. That surface was turned by means of an equally marvelous goniometer to meet the oncoming photon at an angle of exactly 45 degrees. And then would come chaos.

The cool voice of E sounded in his ear receptor. ''Prentiss, it's three-thirty. If you understand the apparatus, and find it dangerous, will you so signify? If possible, describe it for the tapes.''

''I understand your apparatus perfectly,'' said Prentiss.

Luce grunted, half irritated, half curious.

Prentiss continued hurriedly. "Shall I tell you how you decided upon this specific apparatus?"

"If you think you can."

"You have undoubtedly seen the sun reflect from the surface of the sea."

Luce nodded.

"But the fish beneath the surface see the sun, too," continued Prentiss. "Some of the photons are reflected and reach you, and some are refracted and reach the fish. But, for a given wave length, the photons are identical. Why should one be absorbed and another reflected?"

"You're on the right track," admitted Luce, "but couldn't you account for their behavior by Jordan's law?"

"Statistically, yes. Individually, no. In nineteen-thirty-four Jordan showed that a beam of polarized light splits up when it hits a Nicol prism. He proved that when the prism forms an angle, alpha, with the plane of polarization of the prism, a fraction of the light equal to cos²alpha passes through the prism, and the remainder, sin²alpha, is reflected. For example, if alpha is 60 degrees, three-fourths of the photons are reflected and one-fourth are refracted. But note that Jordan's law applied only to streams of photons, and you're dealing with a single photon, to which you're presenting an angle of exactly 45°. And how does a single photon make up its mind—or the photonic equivalent of a mind—when the probability of reflecting is exactly equal to the probability of refracting? Of course, if our photon is but one little mote along with billions of others, the whole comprising a light beam, we can visualize orders left for him by a sort of statistical traffic keeper stationed somewhere in the beam. A member of a beam, it may be presumed, has a pretty good idea of how many of his brothers have already reflected, and how many refracted, and hence knows which he must do."

"But suppose our single photon isn't in a beam at all?" said Luce.

"Your apparatus," said Prentiss, "is going to provide just such a photon. And I think it will be a highly confused little photon, just as your experimental rat was, that night not so long ago. I think it was Schroedinger who said that these physical particles were startlingly human in many of their aspects. Yes, your photon will be given a choice of equal probability. Shall he reflect? Shall he refract? The chances are 50 percent for either choice. He will have no reason for selecting one in preference to the other. There will have been no swarm of preceding photons to set up a traffic guide for him. He'll be puzzled; and trying to meet a situation for which he has no proper response, he'll slow down. And when he does, he'll cease to be a photon, which must travel at the speed of light or cease to exist. Like your rat, like many human beings, he solves the unsolvable by disintegrating.''

Luce said: ''And when it disintegrates, there disappears one of the lambdas that hold together the Einstein space-time continuum. And when *that* goes, what's left can be only final reality untainted by theory or imagination. Do you see any flaw in my plan?''

Tugging with subtle quickness on the cords that bound him, Prentiss knew there was no flaw in the man's reasoning, and that every human being on earth was now living on borrowed time.

He could think of no way to stop him; there remained only the bare threat of the bomb.

He said tersely: ''If you don't submit to peaceable arrest within a few seconds, an atom bomb is going to be dropped on this area.''

Sweat was getting into his eyes again, and he winked rapidly.

Luce's dark features convulsed, hung limp, then coalesced into a harsh grin. ''She'll be too late,'' he said with grim good humor. ''Her ancestors tried for centuries to thwart mine. But we were successful—always. Tonight I succeed again, and for all time.''

Prentiss had one hand free.

In seconds he would be at the man's throat. He worked with quiet fury at the loops around his bound wrist.

Again E's voice in his ear receptor. "I had to do it!" The tones were strangely sad, self-accusing, remorseful.

Had to do *what*?

And his dazed mind was trying to digest the fact that E had just destroyed him.

She was continuing. "The bomb was dropped ten seconds ago." She was almost pleading, and her words were running together. "You were helpless; you couldn't kill him. I had a sudden premonition of what the world would be like—afterward—even for those who go through. Forgive me."

Almost mechanically he resumed his fumbling with the cord.

Luce looked up. "What's that?"

"What?" asked Prentiss dully. "I don't hear anything."

"Of course you do! Listen!"

The wrist came free.

Several things happened.

That faraway shriek in the skies grew into a howling crescendo of destruction.

As one man Prentiss and Luce leaped toward the activator switches. Luce got there first—an infinitesimal fraction of time before the walls were completely disintegrated.

There was a brief, soundless interval of utter blackness.

And then it seemed to Prentiss that a titanic stone wall crashed into his brain, and held him, mute, immobile.

But he was not dead.

For the name of this armored, stunning wall was not the bomb, but Time itself.

He knew in a brief flash of insight, that for sentient, thinking beings, Time had suddenly become a barricade rather than an endless road.

The exploding bomb—the caving cottage walls—were hanging, somewhere, frozen fast in an immutable, eternal stasis.

Luce had separated this fleeting unseen dimension from the creatures and things that had flowed along it. There is

no existence without change along a temporal continuum.
And now the continuum had been shattered.

Was this, then the fate of all tangible things—of all
humanity?

Were none of them—not even the two or three who
understood advanced ontology, to—get through?

There was nothing but a black, eerie silence all around.

His senses were useless.

He even doubted he had any senses.

So far as he could tell he was nothing but an intelligence, floating in space. But he couldn't even be sure of
that. Intelligence—space—they weren't necessarily the
same now as before.

All that he knew for sure was that he doubted. He
doubted everything except the fact of doubting.

Shades of Descartes!

To doubt is to think!

Ergo sum!

I exist.

Instantly he was wary. He existed, but not necessarily
as Adrian Prentiss Rogers. For the *noumenon* of Adrian
Prentiss Rogers might be—whom?

But he was safe. He was going to get through.

Relax, be resilient, he urged his whirling brain. You're
on the verge of something marvelous.

It seemed that he could almost hear himself talk, and he
was glad. A voiceless final reality would have been
unbearable.

He essayed a tentative whisper:

"E!"

From somewhere far away a woman whimpered.

He cried eagerly into the blackness. "Is that you?"

Something unintelligible and strangely frightening answered him.

"Don't try to hold on to yourself," he cried. "Just let
yourself go! Remember, you won't be E any more, but the
noumenon, the essence of E. Unless you change enough to
permit your *noumenon* to take over your old identity,
you'll have to stay behind."

There was a groan. "But I'm *me!*"

"But you *aren't*—not really," he pleaded quickly. "You're just an aspect of a larger, symbolical *you*—the *noumenon* of E. It's yours for the asking. You have only to hold out your hand to grasp the shape of final reality. And you *must*, or cease to exist!"

A wail: "But what will happen to my body?"

The ontologist almost laughed. "I wouldn't know; but if it changes, I'll be sorrier than you!"

There was a silence.

"E!" he called.

No answer.

"E! Did you get through? *E!*"

The empty echoes skirled between the confines of his narrow blackness.

Had the woman lost even her struggling interstitial existence? Whenever, whatever, or wherever she now was, he could no longer detect.

Somehow, if it had ever come to this, he had counted on her being with him—just the two of them.

In stunned uneasy wonder he considered what his existence was going to be like from now on.

And what about Luce?

Had the demonic professor possessed sufficient mental elasticity to slip through?

And if so, just what was the professorial *noumenon*—the real Luce—like?

He'd soon know.

The ontologist relaxed again, and began floating through a dreamy patch of light and darkness. A pale glow began gradually to form about his eyes, and shadowy things began to form, dissolve, and reform.

He felt a great rush of gratitude. At least the shape of final reality was to be visible.

And then, at about the spot where Luce had stood, he saw the Eyes—two tiny red flames, transfixing him with unfathomable fury.

The same eyes that had burned into his that night of his first search!

Luce had got through—but wait!

An unholy aura was playing about the sinuous shadow that contained the jeweled flames. Those eyes were brilliant, horrid facets of hate in the head of a huge, coiling serpent-thing! Snake-Eyes!

In mounting awe and fear the ontologist understood that Luce had not got through—as Luce. That the *noumenon*, the essence, of Luce—was nothing human. That Luce, the bearer of light, aspirant to godhood, was not just Luce!

By the faint light he began shrinking away from the coiled horror, and in the act saw that *he*, at least, still had a human body. He knew this, because he was completely nude.

He was still human, and the snake-creature wasn't—and therefore never had been.

Then he noticed that the stone cottage was gone, and that a pink glow was coming from the east.

He crashed into a tree before he had gone a dozen steps.

Yesterday there had been no trees within three hundred yards of the cottage.

But that made sense, for there was no cottage any more, and no yesterday. Crush ought to be waiting somewhere out here—except that Crush hadn't got through, and hence didn't really exist.

He went around the tree. It obscured his view of the snake-creature for a moment, and when he tried to find it again, it was gone.

He was glad for the momentary relief, and began looking about him in the half-light. He took a deep breath.

The animals, if they still existed, had vanished with the coming of dawn. The grassy, flower-dotted swards scintillated like emeralds in the early morning haze. From somewhere came the babble of running water.

Meta-universe, by whatever name you called it, was beautiful, like a gorgeous garden. What a pity he must live and die here alone, with nothing but a lot of animals for company. He'd willingly give an arm, or at least a rib, if—

"Adrian Prentiss! Adrian!"

He whirled and stared toward the orchard in elated disbelief.

"E! *E!*"

She'd got through!

The whole world, and just the two of them!

His heart was pounding ecstatically as he began to run lithely upwind.

And they'd keep it this way, simple and sweet, forever, and their children after them. To hell with science and progress! (Well, within practical limits, of course.)

As he ran, there rippled about his quivering nostrils the seductive scent of apple blossoms.

**WATCH FOR THE MAJOR ROBERT SILVERBERG
PUBLISHING PROGRAM FROM
BERKLEY IN 1978**

ALPHA 6   (03048-2—$1.50)

ALPHA 7   (03530-1—$1.50)

NEW SCIENCE FICTION TITLES
FROM BERKLEY